# FINDING APRIL HOLLOW

*the tree in the window*

*in search of april hollow*

*For Denise Luenow*

**Jody M. Lewis and Laura Ziggle**

*a.ka. Marilyn O. Brown*

*for Nancy Y. Brown*
*and all who in their diverse ways*
*became a part of Mrs. Burch—*
*healers and healed,*
*human and spirit,*
*known and unknown*


*and with special thanks to Diana Landau,*
*friend with the excellent eyes,*
*for her many contributions to this book*

ISBN 0-9772115-1-7

Printed in the United States by Independent Publishing Corporation
St. Louis, Missouri 63011

# The Tree in the Window

*Laura*

I was lucky enough to grow up knowing what I wanted to do, and I do it: I write short stories and sometimes novels. I have known that writing was my calling since I first learned about letters when I was three. Also, I was fortunate to attend a school with people who made a great impact on me and to have had teachers who had an even greater impact. A lot of very strong students, strong individuals, emerged from Humphrey Catterson Bell Elementary School. I know the most important year I ever had, bar none, was my fifth grade year there. The events of that entire year have been with me every moment; but do not ask me which event was the most remarkable or the most significant, because all of them were immense. I did not know it at the time, but all that happened that year would depend on all of us. Our whole class was in it together; and we drew close and became, most of us, friends for life– even Jody, maybe especially Jody, who keeps in touch with us all and serves as our link when we go too far away. This story is of and for and about all of us, but Jody remains the main link; and I have agreed to write with her our story, as I have asked Julieanne to send me what she remembers, and add it to whatever else I have managed to find and write. Still, I know that it is mostly Jody's right to tell you as much of the story as she wishes.

This is our first adult collaboration and a departure for me from short stories. It will be my job to give you some of the setting and to fill in the details I was able to learn, although I have a feeling that roles may shift about before this story is finished. I thank many of our mothers who remembered some of what happened and were happy to talk to me about their memories of one day in particular. I thank my husband, Alvin, for handing over to me his childhood journals; I thank William Filamon for allowing me to invade his retirement and for corroborating, however reluctantly at first, some of the strange and important facts that took place in what was his best and worst year as a principal more than forty-five years ago. There is another whose contribution has been essential and whom I will want to thank, but she entered the picture later.

• • •

In spite of Bell's outer appearance of a modern school, inside it was substandard. Ceilings leaked and stayed water-stained; walls needed their peeling paint scraped off and could definitely profit from a change of color; offices were cramped, with all furniture serving at least two purposes; there was no air conditioning despite the steamy

Mays and Junes we endured; the heat failed frequently; the halls were dim to save on electric bills. Bell was not a beautiful school, nor was it interested in being one. It was, however, an established one. To us it seemed as though it had stood there on Prairie Road forever. So, for that matter, had the teachers, blowing their whistles and lining us up after years and years of accumulated history. They were institutions, fixtures, occasionally requiring substitutes, as we occasionally required medicine or inoculations; but always they were back quickly, for how else could they exist? They were teachers first, people maybe. Mr. Filamon, we thought, had been the principal long before any of us had been born and would remain principal, we assumed, forever. The only new thing that I ever remember at Bell in my seven years there was the fifth grade patio and its birch tree, but most of us paid little attention to either until The Day. Substitute teachers I do not count as new, but there was one who made all the difference, who made this story happen, and you will meet her right away.

We began that year with Mrs. Autray, a kind of fidgety woman who always ran her fingers through her fading reddish hair and seemed frequently on the edge of tears. It was not that she was at all unhappy; she just seemed intensely emotional about everything. She had tears of joy when we first came into the classroom and tears of sadness when we left that first day. She felt all things deeply, as she was fond of telling us.

Another of the first things we learned about Mrs. Autray was that she had a rivalry with Mr. Rynne, the other fifth grade teacher. The two of them would compete in games, assignments, anything, whether it was having the quietest class walking to the library or the best scores on some standardized test or other or the first to have ten students sign up for a pet project.

We did not have a particularly competitive class. Most of us did not care whether we were first to the water fountain or last in line. Mrs. Autray was disappointed immediately, and she let us know. When she announced the first Event– how many more of Us could get into the Good Writers' Club, we all looked at each other and shrugged. Only Sallee and Charlene made efforts to improve in writing. When she eagerly brought up the first of her planned food drives, we each brought in a couple of cans and one or two boxes of cereal; but Mr. Rynne gloated as his class brought in tons of cans and boxes. We were indifferent. We didn't object to doing things, but we did not want to compete in everything. Most of the class was happy enough with competing on the soccer field or in spelling bees. In this, we were given to understand, we were unusual, even a tad unkind. Possibly, she hinted, we were almost unpatriotic. There were tears, but of course they were not ours; they rolled down Mrs. Autray's round red cheeks that were used to them. Her makeup had little riverbeds etched in. Sadly she offered us one more chance: we were to design decorations for the birch tree to be put on it by October first, in time for a fall festival. The class that came up with the best designs would get to decorate the tree; she knew we would not let her down on this one. I ordinarily liked projects, but this one did seem stupid. No one else had any enthusiasm for it either, and that was too much for Mrs. Autray. Her eyes teared up and then she broke down. She bitterly portrayed us as unnatural children. Why would we not make use of the scraps of brocade and the yards of rickrack she had bought and donated for this very purpose? What was missing in us that we did not, as other children would, enjoy the creative spirit and the great artistic pleasure to be derived from decorating the birch tree? She had so been looking forward to our year, and was it to begin so unhappily? We looked away from her, out the window or at the floor.

"Maybe at Christmas," Amy suggested. Mrs. Autray was not consoled.

"It is just that it seems like a gross idea," Peter Walker whispered. Mrs. Autray was offended.

"If the rickrack didn't look like seaweed, maybe," Janice said sadly. Our teacher was deeply pained.

"Algae has many uses," Alvin announced irrelevantly.

"I want to do it," said Sallee in a kind of whiny voice. Mrs. Autray clutched Sallee to herself and kissed her on the forehead. The rest of us were disgusted.

"I am an Improver," Mrs. Autray announced to us, quietly straightening Sallee's hair ribbons. "It is true that Nature is a thing of beauty and a joy forever, as you will read someday, but nothing is perfect. Everything can be improved upon, and there are those of us who are creative spirits who know a thing or two about improving and who bear a genuine responsibility to do so." She gave Sallee a little squeeze and gently maneuvered her back into her desk.

"Boring," Hal whispered to Alvin, a little too loudly. Alvin smiled absently. Even Bobby thought the idea was dumb, and we were all kind enough not to make any comment on that score.

I think it was Amy Patterson who suggested that we could just decorate one of the plants on the window sill or, better still, bring in more plants and each of us decorate our own. Thomas, who was perfectly named, doubting everything, doubted that the school would be willing to provide plants for everyone. A small group discussion broke out on decorating Christmas trees, which Thomas also doubted would occur this year– too expensive, he assured us. Mrs. Autray was beside herself but moving in the direction of fury. "We are NOT speaking of Christmas trees," she coldly informed us. A large spider at that very moment chose to crawl up her leg, but our guiding creative spirit was oblivious until Alvin pounced on her leg and she shrieked.

"What a specimen!" Alvin said in awe, cradling the little beast tenderly in his palms.

"Get to your desks and take out your workbooks right now—immediately!" Mrs. Autray commanded, standing up rumpled and angry and humiliated. Her hands raked through her hair over and over, and I am sure that she regretted not having simply appointed a small committee of us to design autumn decorations and thus avoided the much chummier approach that had worked so well in her past. I also feel sure that she would not have assigned us fifteen pages in the tedious workbook had we cooperated with her, but on the whole we preferred the workbook to competing with Mr. Rynne's class. I don't know if we anticipated losing and wished to avoid that outcome or perhaps, as seems more possible now, we were already a precocious crew who knew within ourselves that there were things suitable for competition and things that occupied a separate sacred realm beyond such doings. Yet I think I would really give only Jody credit for that perspective back then. The rest of us who came to it did so at different rates, but she was born with it.

Mrs. Autray was absent the next day and the next. I believe we all were stunned. Sallee cried and whined all day about how we had hurt our teacher's feelings, and Bernardo asked each and every one of us what the big deal was. Why was it not okay to decorate the birch tree? but I don't remember if anyone gave him any real answer. Susan, I think, said something about rickrack not looking right on any tree. Julieanne and Holly and I all wished Jody would speak for us, but no one put anything into words. At recess a kind of vote was taken; tree decorating lost.

Back in class, the sub was making an assignment: twenty new spelling words, each to be used in a declarative sentence of at least eight but not more than twelve words. We were not used to such specific restrictions on our spelling sentences. Robert wrote one six-word question, which Ms Skimme read out loud and used as a launch pad for describing how she would not tolerate children who refused to follow directions. Robert then wrote a two-word phrase, which he whispered to Hal and Brett. Robert was marched to the door and asked if he could follow the even simpler direction of sitting on the hall floor for ten minutes. We were not prepared for this kind of teacher, and a few murmurs began to be heard about maybe tree decorating was not such a terrible thing.

Meanwhile Charlene wrote a sentence with an exclamation point, which Ms Skimme pounced on and reported to us all. I myself, as I always did, made my sentences form a story and was required to rewrite them, putting each on its own clearly numbered line. I think I was beginning to be willing to paint the birch tree purple if that would fetch Mrs. Autray from her gloomy sickbed. I happened to notice that Jody's eyes were large and frightened-looking, but I don't think she was the only one looking worried and intimidated. We wanted our own teacher back; we wanted this woman gone.

On her third day, she gave us a surprise test on a math unit we had not yet had. When we all protested, she informed us that according to the plan book, we had indeed had the unit a week earlier. "We didn't," we all assured her. (I believe we had been bogged down in the tree discussion instead.)

"I think I know whom to believe," she said icily. Hal did the best with 47%; most of the class got zeros. Sallee had to go to the nurse's office to recover from the shock; Holly and Julieanne were almost as upset. Janice, the most logical person I have ever known, got 33% and went home with a headache. I think it was about that time that Jody, always quiet, began her nearly constant staring out the window. Bobby, used to poor grades, was almost the happiest person in class, for he was doing no worse than ever and had not fallen in his limited self-esteem. Alvin, who was usually a very good student, allowed his mind to drop out. He spent hours counting dots in the acoustic tiles, looking for patterns in the spattered linoleum, and sneaking more and more moments of reading his library book on ancient civilizations. The only other person who was reasonably content was Peter, but he had the supreme bliss of knowing that he was moving in a week. Nothing fazed him. We grew terribly jealous of him, though not permanently.

At afternoon recess, Holly fell and scraped her knee and went for a bandaid. She was gone a long time but finally reappeared, breathing hard and red-eyed. I guessed she had been swabbed with iodine, but no. We crowded around her and she gave us the awful news that she had overheard while in the nurse's office, which was on the other side of the thin wall behind the principal's desk: Mrs. Autray was NOT sick; she was moving to Arizona, and Ms Skimme was taking her place for the whole year! All of us cried then, and I feel quite sure that we would have done anything to make those words untrue. What is the sanctity of a tree when one's soul is about to shrivel? some of us might have asked. But I believe that Jody would have been able to answer that question in a way to leave no doubt that our souls would have shriveled in equal ways had we desecrated that tree.

*Alvin, from his journals*

A whole lot happened at school today. I got a great new arachnid for my collection. I need to draw it better, but it is pretty squashed so it's hard. I hope Father won't be angry when he learns why this is not absolutely right.

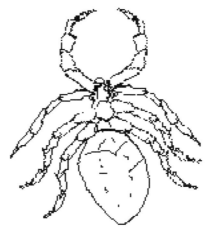

Date......■■■■■■■■■................
Location....Bell School, Room 5B, adult human leg
Condition....alive until Robert stepped on it.
Scientific data......to be filled in after dinner if I don't have to do the dishes

Credit: I used the encyclopedia to help me draw it better.


*"Julieanne"*

Dear Laura,

I was so happy to hear from you but also was concerned to learn of your plan to write about that strange year. Perhaps it will surprise you to know that I don't ever want to think of it, let alone to set myself to the task of consciously recalling it and writing my memories. They remain such a mix of pain and joy, and life has not made such mixes any easier to take. I am mailing you my diary from that year with permission to extract from it anything relevant. Well, you can extract anything you want, relevant or not. I have no intention of reading it again. Perhaps Jody is the one with the most willingness to recount and explain, but she never brings the subject up with me anymore and I am grateful.

I don't know if you are simply writing the story for a limited audience or if you plan to have it published. If the latter, please change our names– mine, for sure.

On another topic, I wonder if you know that Janice was just made President of Periwinkle University. I see her list of honors just keeps growing. I wonder if she would have time to contribute to your project. Also, I heard recently from Susan, who is doing research at one of the Eastern think tanks, but at the moment I don't remember the exact topic. She sent regards from Hal as well. Holly, of course, is fine; we correspond regularly. She is a doting grandmother of three! I think she would be willing to send you her own reminiscences if you need more.

I happened to bump into Sallee at the grocery store recently. She keeps in touch with Charlene, who is a freelance commercial artist with BW Productions. Did you know that the series of note cards with eyepatch masks is hers? Sallee, you will be pleased to know, is still her old self. She heads up the Mothers' Club at her son's college, and she runs a tight ship at her Book Club meetings. (I am surprised that I used that expression.) Life is funny, isn't it?

I guess I have led an ordinary life myself. I hope you can understand that extraordinary events still scare me, but I stopped feeling guilty about them. I hope it will be no great disappointment to you to learn that I decorate our Christmas tree every year, though never with sequins or rickrack.

### Jody

If you say *childhood* to me, I instinctively think first of the terrors, only later of the joys; but two places will be before my eyes: my room at home and my fifth grade classroom. Other sites will gradually develop, as if the chemicals that bring them from my memory out onto paper were just a few shades too weak or too diluted or perhaps were not allowed enough time to make the clearest of impressions. My room at home was ugly: chartreuse roses on gray paper; and unlike the knaves in the Red Queen's garden, I spent many hours with a ballpoint pen trying to turn the roses blue; but the room was larger than my ink supply and the cause was essentially hopeless. Still, that room was my refuge from outside terrors and my exulting place in moments of great happiness. Acidic yellowy-green, gray, and squarish, it nevertheless was usually safe, except for the nightmare episodes; and it was my own.

Bell Elementary School, to my secret delight, was built on a hexagonal plan. Five of its six off-white brick walls looked out to the fields and spotty woods, while the front façade was a dark chocolate cedar with that soft off-white trim. It looked out on Prairie Road, a place that seemed ordinary to me then, though I know better now; but except for that picture-book setting and the then-exotic shape, I guess it was a typical school. Being in a small town, it had the luxury of small classes– we never had more than twenty in our room, and in fifth grade we had fewer than that. We had two classes of each grade so that there could be interclass spelling bees and games.

Every school morning the first bell would ring at eight-thirty; and from the woods and the playgrounds and from the four yellow buses that bounced and jostled into the front driveway, we all would come running– or straggling– and noisily file in. Mr. Filamon would greet us with smiles and nods, and in most of my earlier memories all of the teachers were kind. Like lassos, the bell and Bell School itself reached out to catch us and gently to pull us, variously coated little dogies, to its hexagonal trough. There we would feed on my favorite foods, pictures and words, and with my favorite utensils, crayons and pencils. Bell School kept my home fears in suspension, as my room kept my neighborhood fears at bay.

Sometime before fourth grade, perhaps in the summer after third, though I don't remember precisely, things began to happen that changed my view of safety. Once I had loved people warmly, openly, immediately, and had trusted and run to them with open heart; then the world turned scary and I often found myself crying in my room, afraid to come out. There were good reasons for my fears and my sudden distrust of adults and children alike, and there was no one to tell. It became easier to stop talking, because then it was more possible not to cry. It was easier to concentrate on my assignments and my drawings and my little poems. At first it was hard to see the strange looks from the other kids, but it was better than having to explain what was happening. Dark things were happening, and I did not know why.

When I say there was no one to tell, I realize now that I mean there was no one I felt I could trust. I just did my work and mostly remained silent. This was going to change, and I was going to change; but at the grim beginning of fourth grade that is how it was– scary, silent. My room with the chartreuse roses became a more mixed source of security and additional gloom. I began to seek other refuges and found two: one in the upper limbs of an apple tree at the back of our yard and one on the little secluded patio just outside the fifth grade classrooms.

The patio had been a gift from the PTA the previous year as a result of the fifth grade bringing in the most money to the school by selling boxes of homemade popcorn. I mention this so that you can understand why the patio was a refuge: just a rectangular concrete slab with a bench, it was new and away from the popular playgrounds; and no one else had gotten used to it yet.

As the year wore on, a few more kids began to discover it; but at the beginning I could be quite alone there. I spent most recesses, all of my lunch times, and quite a bit of the weekends there. I usually took paper and pencil and crayons with me and would write my poems and make my drawings and would bury them at the base of the trunk of the beautiful paper birch tree that was planted after the patio was finished. I loved the tree. I offered it my small works and left them there for a day or two before digging them up and taking them home to burn. I never wanted anyone to find them, and I made sure that they were destroyed. In that way, I found a confidante of sorts in the tree and so was able to tell someTHING what was menacing me when I was not at school, as well as what was menacing me when I was at school. I always felt the tree understood, because its branches would sigh in the breeze and the soft yellow wands that autumn would caress my hair and whisper words that I could almost distinguish. From my spot beneath the tree, I could look across the mud fields where the soccer game would be underway and see also the battered slide and the chinning bars and the rusty climbing dome. From where I sat, the kids there looked like fat resting birds– upright sparrows and a few upside-down chickadees. Sometimes I could see Holly and Julieanne looking up toward the patio, and I would wonder if they were discussing me. We had been good friends in second grade, but I became a little bit afraid even of them. We were all in Mrs. Pingleigh's class, and Julieanne was the star pupil. Holly always tried to imitate her, but she just did not have the knack of it. I will say, though, that Julieanne never took advantage of that situation, which as I think of it now seems to me to be a kind of miracle. But then miracles come to my mind when I think of the patio and the tree, though really that comes later. In fourth grade life was gray and scary and mostly lonely. It had no miracle feeling at all.

In June, on the day when we learned who our teacher would be the next year, I was relieved to know that I was assigned to Mrs. Autray's class. She was not as good a teacher of math or science as Mr. Rynne, but she was kinder; and I felt that she would not add to my fear. It was quite all right with me that Holly and Julieanne were also assigned to her class. I was less pleased that bossy Sallee was there too, but mostly I was pretty happy with the class list. Susan and Laura (another writer) and Janice were in the class; and of the boys, Alvin and

Hal and Bernardo and Brett were all pretty nice. Bobby was going to have trouble– he still could not really read. Of course, Bernardo couldn't either, but that was because he still didn't know much English. I realized much later that he had some other learning problem too. I was surprised that all three Amys were put in one class, but they were.

As I look back, that was really the nicest class any of us could have made up for ourselves. Except for Sallee, as I have mentioned, no one was mean– not even Robert, although he did like to tease. He mainly teased the other boys, though, so I did not worry about him. You might think that having such good classmates would have made it easier for me to talk, but things were still happening. I did not want to cry at school, so I did not talk even with people I liked. All summer I was relatively happy, knowing that I was going to be in a great class with nice kids and a cheerful and kind teacher. I visited the patio daily, riding there the long way around on my bike, and wrote little poems about cozy nests in trees. The green wands of the birch tree swept low in the soft summer breeze, and often that summer I felt fairly safe and often smiled, though I did not speak.

But the year began very badly. All that silliness about a class competition to decorate the birch tree led to very strained feelings. I knew that for more than one reason I couldn't ask to be moved to the other classroom. I was disappointed with Mrs. Autray, but I was afraid of Mr. Rynne. He had a mean way of punishing kids who did not meet his demands by blowing his whistle a little too close to their ears. "Just getting your attention," he would say. I hated when he was on duty at recess, but at the patio I was never near him.

I remember being very surprised at how many of the kids refused to decorate the tree. At the time it seemed unlike most of them; but I think something special was rooted there that had a mind and will of its own and influenced all of our decisions, whether we were dimly conscious of it or not. I did not think that then, but later I did.

At any rate, I had been prepared for fifth grade to be better than fourth. Mrs. Autray had loomed pleasantly. And then it all turned sour and even for some nightmarish. We may picture monsters as large horned beasts or scar-faced wrecks with twisted souls, but some of our nightmares manifest as the people just next door. Sometimes their public ordinariness masks the real selves they show to their victims. Our classroom became the theater for the private view of Ms Skimme, as the path from my house to the school gave me a private view of a different monster.

## "Julieanne" ~ *from her diary*

. . . most of our class will be staying together another year and that is great!!! I am excited that Holly is also going to be in our class– her mother had thought about requesting a switch but decided not to. Everyone says Mrs. Autray is not the best teacher, but they like her. I don't think I'd like Mr. Rynne. This will be the year we get to have extra-special field trips. I wonder where we will go. And it's always a tradition that the fifth and sixth grades get to do the biggest part of the Christmas pageant. Fifth grade is just a great year!!! I love it!!!!

Diary, am I going to like any of the boys this year? Or will they still act stupid? I have to admit that the nicest boys in our grade are in our class, but I haven't "liked" any of them much. I wonder how it feels to have a best friend who is a boy? Or a twin? That must be weird. Susan doesn't seem to mind too much.

I am leaving now, Diary, to go get new school clothes. Holly is going with us. It is just going to be such a great year.

p.s. Daddy brought home a tiny female puppy! Could this year get any better?????

. . . .

I didn't write the first week of school, Diary, because I was really busy. I think I will love this year, though. Talk to you later.

. . . .

I can't believe it, Diary. Mrs. Autray left. The new teacher is horrible. The puppy has thrown up all over my carpet, and the room stinks. I don't think I can write about it right now or else I will just feel even sicker than I do. This year is going to be terrible. Just terrible. And I think I am going bald!!!

p.s. (Later) The hair was from the puppy, not me. Nothing else has changed.

p.s. again. I think I might like Brett!

## *Jody*

On the tiny calendar in my room I marked in black the day of Ms Skimme's arrival, and I counted it ever after as one of the five worst days of my life, although in truth the very bad times at school were still in a relatively safe stage. I have said that we were a good class; perhaps I should be more specific. We had an astonishing number of classmates who already showed signs of their strong talents. Laura wrote incredibly complex stories and had even had some of them published in children's magazines. Brett was an amazing pianist and had begun composing. His mother drove a hundred miles three times a week to take him to study with professional composer Alex Bogler, who was already impressed by Brett's work. Alvin was already busily demonstrating the patience and observation and brilliance that would later mark his wide-ranging scientific researches. Janice would receive her doctorate in logic structures, and she would do so before she was twenty-two. Bernardo, who could barely read his native Spanish, let alone his adopted language, could make anything you might want out of wood or metal; but he was happiest making things requiring saws or electricity, and he had already created several new appliances and was working out in his mind how he might fashion a computer. (You must keep in mind that when we were in fifth grade, computers were massive and exotic mysteries, not commonplace at all, and not used by children at all. Really, they were still like science fiction.)

Not everyone in our class was a genius, but it was a most remarkable group. We knew each other well, or at least most of us did, and we respected each other. I still leave out Sallee, who could not catch on that we were not to be bossed. I think she was a lot like Mrs. Autray, built to be a controlling self-styled improver. The chief problem was that she set out to improve things that were just fine.

That day that Ms Skimme set foot in our classroom, she set foot on all our hearts. One of her first assignments for us was to create a brief farewell card to Mrs. Autray– "using two crayons of different colors and not being maudlin, if you know what that word means, and not exceeding four lines." We looked around at each other, rolled our eyes, and got out our crayon boxes. She handed out white paper, cautioning us not to waste it. I watched as Sallee began writing and sobbing immediately. Ms Skimme was instantly escorting her to the tissue box and demanding that she get "hold" of herself. Laura looked disgusted, not with Sallee. I saw Holly and Julieanne exchange looks and get to work. Bernardo looked very glum as he sat there with a red and a blue crayon and the blank paper that would always make him nervous. Bobby doodled all over the white paper and signed his name in his first-grade style of printing.

I took a black crayon, just a black one, and in the tiniest letters I could make with the blunt crayon I wrote these lines that I still remember:

> *Dark little owls are hooting gray;*
> *like feathers their hoots float through the air.*
> *the trees are swaying; they're dark and bare:*
> *no leaves to feather the night, the day.*
> > *Good-bye.*

And then when Ms Skimme was looking straight at me, I tore the white paper into the tiniest scraps and swept them carefully into a kleenex and delicately put them into my pocket to bury them later beneath the birch tree. I sat and stared hard at Ms Skimme, and I did not care what she thought. When she half-dragged me to the wastebasket to deposit the tissue of scraps, I stood there mute and resisting. She took the little packet and dropped it hard into the basket and pushed me out into the hall. I took off at a run and never stopped until I got home and into my room, but of course I had to return the next day. Laura smiled at me, and I have never forgotten that. Of course I did not apologize, despite the angry demands. I was grateful to Mr. Filamon for intervening when he happened to walk past and hear her. When she explained to him her objective, he sent us all to recess and there was no further attempt to force me to speak.

That memory is unpleasant, but I did not have the worst of it from Ms Skimme. The one I felt sorriest for most often was Brett. Since second grade, Brett had been given the honor and pleasure of getting to accompany us during music time. He had not asked to do so, but all of the teachers recognized his ability and had been delighted to let him play, especially those who did not have any ability in that way themselves. They had been thrilled to let Brett play! So it was only natural that on the first music day of Ms Skimme's time with us, Brett walked to the piano and sat down.

"Young man, just how much conceit do you possess? Who gave you the authority to declare yourself the designated accompanist for this class? I cannot get over the gall of so many of you!" Brett had hurried back to hide himself among the other boys, red-faced, terribly humiliated, and near tears.

"Brett always plays for us," Janice said.

"Children should be seen and not heard," Ms Skimme bitingly announced. I smiled a tiny smile to myself, and Laura and Julieanne smiled at me too. But best of all, when Ms Skimme sat down to play the piano, no one sang.

"But children should be seen and not heard," Robert fearlessly declared; and all the boys roared, except Brett, who had quietly left the room and was crying out in the hall. Ms Skimme was in a rage, and we knew things were more than out of hand. We all trembled at the thought of the rest of the year, but at least we had had this moment.

Robert was assured of a place of honor in our hearts, even if he had a place of dishonor in the principal's office that day; and Brett we all wished to avenge. If I could have had the words and could have brought myself to say anything to anyone, it would have been that day to Brett. I would have wanted to tell him how it is in this life, that there are those who have power to hurt us, though none of us will ever know why they must use it. There are those who delight in tormenting, but surely they are punishing themselves, too. Stand strong, Brett, and all of us as well, even though it may seem for the moment that we are dying from coldness and lack of love. But I was in fifth grade and silent, so I wrote slightly more childlike words on a scrap of blue paper and buried them under the tree.

A few days later, after another morning and afternoon of those increasingly familiar atrocities against virtually all of our strained, unhappy classmates, I rode my bike to the patio and deposited a little prayer:

> *Who knows I am me but the tree?*
> *No one, no one at all.*
> *Tree, I wish you could talk;*
> *tree, I wish you could walk*
> *with us, with me.*

But on the following Monday I saw Julieanne sitting under the tree, kind of poking around with a stick; and though she did not seem to find my scraps of writings, I hurried out there the next chance I got and dug them all up and burned them at home. Still, I had noticed that the normally happy Julieanne had been crying out there; and it made me wonder how many of my classmates were being destroyed. Susan rarely smiled these days, and Hal looked disgusted. All of the Amys had formed a little group along with Sallee and Charlene and Janice, and they met regularly after lunch and compared outrages of the day. Laura had gone through more notebooks in a week than she usually did in a month, and Alvin was actually agreeing with Hal that things were more and more boring. Alvin!

Peter had moved and Robert was missing him. Holly looked grim. In sad and needless ways, Bernardo was the worst off, because Ms Skimme constantly expressed disbelief that anyone could be so stupid as to refuse to learn a new language. He who was normally so cheerful and friendly became quieter and quieter and stopped making things. "What's the point?" he would ask. "I am stupid."

Only to Bobby was none of this really new, and that too is very sad. I think all of us were learning something about Bobby's strengths during this terrible plague upon us: to struggle against one's own grain in an attempt to find some kind of acceptance in a society not of our making is terribly difficult; to persist in the face of constant belittling is a strength to be held in awe.

It is my own experience that I cannot do it, cannot even try acting against my nature, but I respect Bobby for every effort. I will give Ms Skimme this one credit: she made us appreciate Bobby for his unfailing good nature in a hostile world. But she plunged all of us into that world every moment of every day, and for what reason? No one will ever convince me that there is a *reason*; there may be a cause, but that is not the same.

Despite my knowledge that my classmates were still my friends, that I had separated myself from them for reasons and causes known only to me, I could not yet bring myself to speak out loud to them in words. I tried by shy smiles and small subtle expressions to convey some of my thoughts to them, but mostly I counted on their sympathetic understanding in our deep common misery. For personal companionship I had only the birch tree.

I would like to be able to tell you what all that tree came to mean to me. It was so perfectly formed, so delicate, so tender when the slightest breeze riffled through it, so seemingly sensitive to my every sorrow and my rare happinesses– it seemed to me that every twig and branch became a cluster of compassionate frowns or broke into a thousand smiles, and often I could make out the same lovely face. All summer her hair had been a mermaid green, but that autumn she wore her leafy yellow curls almost to the ground, and her eyes– formed in the smaller branches– were lined with care and concern by the littlest twigs. Her tears were frequent that fall, and her voice came through the soft winds and the bright birds and the deep rustling. I put my trust in the spirit clothed in that tree and felt safest when in contact with her delicate paper sleeves.

> *Tree, I know you can talk,*
> *Tree, I wish you could walk*
> *with us, with me.*

The day after I burned that new scrap of prayer, I went to my tree and saw Julieanne and Holly sitting there talking. I started to leave, but they called out to me please to come sit with them. I smiled but shook my head. "What can we do, Jody?" they called after me. I turned and looked sadly back, shaking my head in doubt but forming a little gesture of prayer with my hands. Then I shrugged and went on. Before I left the school grounds entirely, I looked back to see what they were doing; but they must have walked off in the other direction. I wished I could have stayed and whispered and planned and plotted with them, but I could not. I hoped that they would understand my sign language, but I had no hope that they could understand why I was unable to go join them. How could they when I could do so only partially?

. . . . after school today Holly and I biked back to the patio to talk about Ms Skimme. Maybe it was stupid, because she might have been looking right out at us, but Ms Skimme is usually one of the first teachers to leave, so we figured it was safe. All of us are so unhappy. Why would someone be a teacher if she doesn't like kids? We can't figure that out. Holly thinks that maybe there is some excuse if Ms Skimme was treated this way herself, but she seems to *enjoy* being mean. She *likes* to humiliate us. We saw Jody but of course she wouldn't come over. Jody used to be my best friend until she stopped talking. I guess she thinks we don't know why she stopped and that we don't like her any more. It isn't true. I mean, it isn't true that we don't still like her, even if it makes me mad sometimes that she won't talk. And I also mean that some of us do know a little about what happened.

Diary, why are people so mean? And why are parents sometimes so weird? My mother knows that Jody has been chased lots of times by the crazy boy with the knife, but she won't tell Jody's mother! Susan's mother knows and Laura's mother and Holly's; but all of them are afraid of getting Richard in trouble. Well, that's not exactly it. They would not mind getting him *help*, but they are more afraid of Jody's parents and how they would react. I heard my father say that he thinks Jody's father would kill Richard and Jody's mother would punish *her* for being some kind of cause of it all. So you see, Diary, all our parents are a little weird. I mean, we all saw Jody the day after he caught up with her and a chunk of her hair was missing. I asked my mom why she didn't call Mrs. Lewis and tell her about Richard. Mom just said, "Well, how can she not know? Look at the child's hair. It's not for us to tell her. I am sure she asked Jody about it." That was when Jody stopped talking. We all worry about her, but what can we do if our parents can't do anything?

You know, Diary, if I have a daughter someday and she comes home with a chunk of her hair missing, I can't imagine that I would *blame* her. I think at least I would ask her how it had happened; but in all the time that Jody and I were best friends, I never heard her mother say anything nice or loving. I only heard her tell Jody to stop doing this or stop doing that or to stop making things up. I bet she thinks

Jody cut her own hair off. We all know she did not. I wish Jody knew that we knew, but maybe she would be even more quiet and more embarrassed. I don't know.

Anyway, Jody did not come talk with us on the patio; but she did smile a little and when we tried to invite her to come be with us and asked her what we could do, she kind of folded her hands together as if she were telling us to pray. Holly and I went home then and all the way we talked about how we could maybe organize a little club or some other group and make a voodoo doll of Ms Skimme. I don't think Jody meant voodoo, but we wanted to stick a pin in that teacher anyway and praying for her to get sick didn't seem any better. I mean, if you want to hurt somebody back, you can't exactly be nice about it, can you?

I think all the Amys would be glad to join a club.

Have I mentioned that Daddy named the puppy Ex? Do you know why, Diary? It's because she keeps marking new spots on our rugs. I want to find a special new name, though, a nice name.

*Laura*

There was so much material for stories in those awful days. I could spend the whole day observing and the whole evening or a full weekend writing, and in that way it might have been a happy time. Of course, the reason for all the material was that we were being slowly murdered, so there was no possible joy. There is no more accurate word than *murder*, though we were stubbornly resisting the death; but there is only joy to a mystery writer if the victims are those she has made up. At least, that is my perspective.

I remember writing a story about Alvin, the mad scientist who is about to find a way to save the whole world, only to be destroyed by a new virus that he gets from drinking skim milk. And another about Bernardo, the inventor who is never granted a patent because he cannot find a name or write a description of his invention, which I think I wrote was a Book Skimming machine. There was one I wrote about Sallee, who whined and whined and whined all day and was turned into a skimmed pat of butter and put into a skillet where she melted away. I never did like Sallee. I also wrote one called "The Twins Who Talked to Each Other" and it got published.

I observed all of them but none more than Jody, who I felt sure was able to understand what was happening. I don't know why I felt that but I did. I guess perhaps it was because she seemed so strong behind her silent mask. I watched her walk every day to her desk

17

where she completed every single writing assignment but sat like a silent monk throughout the long and lonely days, refusing to yield to that force in the front of the room that aimed to mold her to an alien pattern, never once asking or caring if she had a pattern of her own, certainly never inquiring if she had a need of her own. I remember her silent stubborn stare on the day that Ms Skimme said to our class that she just might have to go ahead and recommend the Special School District for those with "speech disorders" and looked right at Jody, who we knew undoubtedly could speak and communicate better than any of us, if only she could be accepted for who she was. Both Bobby and Bernardo had thought she meant them, but the rest of us knew that she was striking out at Jody, working again to humiliate her. She gave Jody zeros on much of her work because, as she said, "I asked you to tell the class what you wrote, and you refused." Jody would sit there and shred the paper, starting with the area of the zero, and then she would walk to the trash basket and deposit the mass of shreds. Ms Skimme would be furious, and many of us would silently cheer our friend.

September passed in agonizing slowness. Most of our work was dull and all of it was accompanied by criticism. It was as if we would all too naturally assume we were perfect if any kind word of approval ever were uttered in our hearing. The plant on the window sill withered and it seemed to me that even the birds stopped lighting there. Once in a while there would be a yellow finch out in the birch tree; but as the leaves turned yellow, we could no longer be sure of the finch.

One day at the end of September, Mr. Filamon stopped in to visit. For all too short a time we stepped back in time. Mean Ms Skimme smiled thinly and said, "Very good," after Robert read his report. We all looked longingly at our kind principal, mentally begging him to stay. A drawing of Jody's was actually hung on the tack strip and a star was placed by her name. Mr. Filamon enjoyed the main lesson of that hour, which was a discussion of appreciating each other's strengths. Bobby said, "Why don't we do that?" and we all looked quickly to Ms Skimme, who lied in her icy way and said we all should, as she certainly did, and why didn't Bobby? Mr. Filamon seemed not to notice her tone of voice and smiled as he got up to leave, patting Bernardo on the back and inviting him to bring some new invention to show him– it had been a long time and he was sure Bernardo had many more by now.

"Sí, er, no. I will look," he stammered.

"By the way, Ms Skimme," the principal said as he walked to the door, "I don't believe we have had a chance to discuss the upcoming conference reports. Plan on spending some time with me after school today, and I will show you what you will need to do." She smiled that sliver of lip at him and said, "Of course." He left, and the drawing came down from the tack board and the star came down too. Later they would be found in the wastebasket, tiny fragments of silver sparkling in the heap.

We continued making lists of atrocities. At recess, where once we had run and shouted with the joy of being outdoors, we congregated in small trios and pairs and compared our battered feelings and looked for balm for our hurts. Most of the boys still kicked the soccer ball around the mud fields, but they had no enthusiasm. Mr. Rynne's class could have beaten us at anything and still we did not care about that. Sallee– for reasons never known– blamed all the boys and only the boys for not decorating the tree and yearned for Mrs. Autray to move back and rush into our classroom with hugs of forgiveness and grocery bags full of tinsel and an entire caseload of gold stars for us to paste all over ourselves– and if some fell on the tree, well who would complain?

I looked at Jody, whose eyes were sometimes red despite herself, and whose hands were raw though it was not yet cold out. I know she spent a lot of time scraping words into the dirt at the foot of the tree and then rubbing them out. Holly and Julieanne and Susan and I were often watching her, always wishing she would come back to us. We knew about Richard, crazy Richard, and we knew that Jody was terrified of him. We did not know then that there was someone else making her life a torment, though Richard seemed enough to us. He would stand behind a tree in the woods, holding his sharp knife, well hidden. You would think perhaps you would stop to pick some of the violets that grew there all spring and summer, and out he would jump. But most of us did not have to go home through the woods; and even if we had, our parents would have found a way to protect us. They would have found another route or met us at school or demanded that mean Richard's parents keep him indoors before and after school. They would have quickly demanded a different kind of crossing guard for the woods or an extension to the bus routes. Just knowing we had to walk that way, they would have done something. Jody's parents had to know about Richard, but they never did a thing except to criticize their daughter for being afraid. We all saw the haircut, but I may be the only one who saw the small jagged red scar on her back. I saw it one warm day when she was pulling off her sweater, but I never told her I saw it. Her parents surely had to know about that! I could not begin to imagine that she might not ever have told them. It was years later that I learned that she had been afraid to do so.

*Jody*

I wrote a lot of poems that year, although I kept very few. I had them in my head, though, and they gave me real comfort. So did my silence. It is strange to me to have learned by now that most people would have found their comfort in talking. They would have wanted reassurance and hugs and kisses and whatever tenderness was to be found in the sharing of their fears and concerns. Now I might seek that too, but then? No. There was no tenderness to be found; there was no reassurance to win. I found a quiet solace in my private knowledge that I was facing a dangerous foe with nothing and no one to come to my aid. I suppose I drew a romantic kind of thrill from knowing that I had such a secret and that it was a true one. No one could deny it if I did not tell it. No one could reproach me for my fears if no one knew what they were. But school had been my haven, my blanket; and now it was one more habitat of the enemy. I excuse none of those enemies. I concede them no right to their deeds. And, no matter what Ms Skimme suggested, I knew I was not crazy.

> *Hide, hide, little frightened child,*
> *run, run from the boys with their knives*
> *and the men with the words like spears.*
> *Fall, fall in the arms of your real mother,*
> *in the branches of the kindest tree.*

I grant you it was not the typical writing of a fifth grader, but it was my writing, and I buried all of it in the tree's dark lap and then I carried it all away to be burned as my sacrifice to the god who had decided that I would be tormented. *Accept my words, o dark and mysterious god, and take the knives away.*

*Alvin, from his* Youthful Notes, *bk. 5*

**Observation**: Girls cry more easily than boys, and people think that boys are sissies if they do cry.
**Hypothesis**: It is false to state that boys never cry unless they are sissies.
**Evidence**:
• Brett cried in music class. Brett is not a sissy.
• Bernardo did cry after school when Mr. Rynne called him a dummy for not hearing the whistle. He is definitely no sissy.
• Bobby can be a sissy sometimes, but he has never cried once that I

have observed, even when called stupid or when purposely tripped down the steps by one of the sixth-graders.

**Conclusion**:
• "I believe we are all complex beings capable of multiple levels of feeling and thinking and that what we react to is intricately related to our prior experience, leading me to the consequential inference that sometimes crying shows strength of response and recognition of trying circumstances."* Also, I have concluded from additional personal observation that sometimes crying feels really good.

*Edited by Arthur Ziggle, PhD, LLD, and numerous honoraria

Private comment written [several years later]: I wish Dad had just let me write what I could write.

**Observation**:
• Something is going on in our classroom.
**Evidence**:
• All of the girls are always making lists of reasons to be upset.
• My friend Jody is more silent than ever.
• Ms Skimme is always angry about something that none of us knows about.
**Conclusion**: to be figured out as time goes by.

*Laura*

I wonder how many of us remember that first report period that came so early that year. Knowing now about as many of the reports as I do, it seems to me that all of them must be etched in our minds and in those of our parents. Yet it is also a fact that many people can move right past the injustices that happen to them as if those misdeeds were simply a little swarm of gnats to be ignored, while others will perceive them as major hurdles in their way or at least as ongoing sore spots in their memories. For me, that was the worst report I had ever had or ever was to have, and what made it worst was that it was so one-sided and shallow and unfair. But all of them were– at least all of the ones I learned about.

You may wonder how any of us knew about each other's reports, but of course we talked. More to the point, our parents talked openly to each other about the outrageous comments Ms Skimme made to them about us. For the most part, our parents had every reason to look forward to good reports, glowing even. We had always been conscientious students, hardworking and responsible. We took active parts in all kinds of things, and we mostly had very positive attitudes. Most of our parents must have noticed a change in those attitudes, but I think no one was prepared for the reality in the classroom, let alone for the picture of that reality in Ms Skimme's hostile remarks. But the main way we knew things was that a lot of us were there. About eight of us belonged to a little club sponsored by Mrs. George, the principal's secretary, and part of our activities included helping her in the office whenever we could. Conference Day was a perfect time.

Mrs. Borwin was the first to have her appointments; and she stalked out of the room and headed for Mr. Filamon to discuss just why her lovely, gentle, industrious daughter was being described as a lazy nonreader! Susan! who read thirty books a week all summer long and at least three a week during the school year. And why was her work labeled "sloppy" when it sat there on the desk looking pristine and perfect, except for the circular brown stain from a coffee cup on *top* of the grade? Just whose coffee ring was that? It clearly could not have been there before it had been turned in; it certainly was not Susan's. More disturbing even than the complete ignorance that Ms Skimme revealed about her daughter was the basic fact that the teacher had had absolutely no idea that Hal was Susan's twin brother. Lots of us helpers could hear every angry word of her conversation with Mr. Filamon. "That woman asked me to keep an eye on Hal if he began hanging around our house, because Susan was the girl he most often talked to! The teacher thought that was *suspicious*! She didn't even seem to realize they have the same last name!" We laughed quietly among ourselves; but when Mrs. Borwin got home, she began calling other moms to come over for a little coffee of their own later that afternoon and to compare notes; and when I got home, I wrote that story I mentioned, the one about the twins who talked to each other.

It came out later that Mr. Filamon had admitted to several of the parents that he had been terribly upset about the reports the minute he had seen them, but he had seen them just too late to stop them. He wished he could have undone them and found a new teacher, but it was all beyond his ability to control.

Mrs. Patterson was disgusted to realize that Ms Skimme had no idea which Amy was her daughter and had been discussing Amy Betts the entire time. Mrs. Betts did not recognize her daughter in the conversation either, although in truth she did not recognize anyone's daughter in the ugly monologue. Who was the little monster who seemed never to know when to speak or be silent and who, to draw attention to herself, wore the most bizarre combinations of colors in her outfits? And, wait a minute, since when is clothing a category in a school report? And wait another minute, what about the work? It was true that Amy Betts was our fashion plate of sorts. She was the only one of us who got to wear expensive sweaters to school, but then her father manufactured them. None of us cared. We did not think she was trying to show off. Bizarre colors? We knew nothing of that.

Bernardo's father attended the conference since he spoke some English and his wife did not. Amy Patterson quite matter-of-factly listened in as she delivered a set of notices, but Ms Skimme seemed not to care what she said in Amy's hearing. She said that Bernardo might be retarded and was out of his depth. His father looked blank. "Bernardo is a good boy," he said to the teacher, "but I worry because he is not interested in making things anymore." Ms Skimme assured him that that was the first positive sign of anything in this incorrigible class. Mr. Ruíz seemed to think that *incorrigible* might refer to the fact that the class did less running out on the soccer field and murmured his sad agreement about not enough *corriendo*. Amy reported that Ms Skimme looked pleased at this very successful communication.

Five of us, I think, were working with Mrs. George that day. We all were helping make copies of notices and then stacking them in sets for each class and then delivering them. I remember walking past our classroom as Alvin's mother came bumbling out. She walked straight into the door first and apologized to it, then bumped into Mrs. Yore, Robert's mom, almost knocking her down. We all knew Alvin's mother and how rattled she always was. Of course I still know her and am aware of her many, many delightful traits; but, truthfully, she was and is the most absent-minded person I've ever known. In her defense, her family gave her just cause. She usually had her glasses on top of her head and around her neck a glasses chain that was always empty. She carried a briefcase of books that frequently fell out; but she was proud of Alvin in her way and devoted to her husband Arthur– a fierce, eccentric recluse whose "numerous honoraria" were self-awarded– who was absorbed in the study of fossils and the invention of fossil finders that he kept trying to patent. Alvin knew a lot about fossils, as well as his own favorite topic of snakes. I heard his mother mumble to Mrs. Yore something about being unusually clumsy under stress and "so sorry, so sorry" was repeated constantly. "Arthur will be so unhappy," she said, knocking her glasses to the floor and accidentally stepping on them. "We thought Alvin was doing so well. Here, let me pick up your glasses for you, Melba."

Mrs. Yore looked amused and handed the glasses back to Mrs. Ziggle, saying at the same time, "Nice to see you, Nadine; you do remember my name is Maureen?" Mrs. Ziggle looked confused but put on her glasses and brightened up. "Oh, Marlene," she said, "how nice to see you too! And how is Rupert? I haven't seen him for ages! I do hope you receive a better report on him than I just got on Alvin. I had no idea, just no idea. I wonder what I will say to him, but Arthur will handle it just fine. Just a minute here, just a minute– ," as she fumbled through the briefcase; "weren't you the one who asked me for the old recipe for fish paste?" But Mrs. Yore shook her head and swiftly and apologetically declined and hurried in for her conference on Robert.

Meanwhile I wondered about Alvin's report, not to mention my own, and mentally outlined my first adult character sketch that I wrote that night and am looking at now as I write these words. (I really do love my mother-in-law, not only for the humor she provides in our lives but equally for the way she has survived chaos.)

None of us saw or heard anything about Mrs. Lewis's quiet conference, but Jody was not at school the following Monday or even Tuesday. She was brought to school on Wednesday but was sent to the principal's office immediately for refusing to take off a large pair of sunglasses. She stayed there all day. Some of us worried about where Richard might be, and some of us worried about the Lewises; but all of us blamed Ms Skimme.

*Jody*

Things got very hard for me by the end of that first month of fifth grade, but I think the hardest was a bit later: being recommended for the Special District, when everyone knew that I had no trouble learning. I could not figure out how to make anyone understand what I was dealing with– without telling them, that is. I did not want to tell them. I thought I knew what would happen to me if I told, and what I imagined would happen scared me as much. But I always have to admit, too, that telling would have made me feel weak; and I did not need to feel any weaker than I was. I think Special District would have killed me; I know it would have– because it was really being threatened as a punishment for being me; and then what difference would it make if I knew I had a secret strength? Every minute of every day would be telling me I could not cope. And I would never see the people I liked, my friends who smiled even when they might never understand my silence. It was Mr. Filamon at first who kept Special District out of the picture, and I sincerely appreciated that enough to smile at him and leave him a thank you poem. I don't know if he got to read it before I got it back and burned it, but maybe he did.

> *You have kept me from death*
> *in a breathless place*

24

*and given me space to learn who I am.*
*Out of my silence I thank you.*

I think I first scratched those words with a sharp twig in the soft mud at the base of the tree. Some bright rustling and twittering of the yellow finch managed to convince me to share it with Mr. Filamon, but I was so afraid he would show it to Mrs. George or to my parents or to anyone that I just had to go back and remove it from his mailbox there in the office. Then I was sure it was safe.

As I write these words today in my studio, with my paintings and writings all around me, I see how important the recurring theme has been in my life: be who you are and yield your identity to no one. Run from those whose tedious refrain is, "Why do *you* have to be so different? Who do you think *you* are?" They never realize that it is not a matter of having to be different; it is a matter of having to be who you are. Sometimes you think you will break because people will demand that you yield to them in their misguided notions of love owed them. They are never to be allowed to win, for the cost will be your very life. It really won't ever be their lives, no matter how much they may try to claim so. Don't turn yourself over to them. Well, I guess I am just saying that I refuse to do so. But *"Do it for my sake"* is a major clue telling you to beware.

Things came to a terrible head that first conference day. No one was happy, except possibly Laura– just a little bit– because she got so many stories out of that day. But Laura was never one to be happy when others were hurt; the stories were kind of a little vein of gold in a mass of painful ore. I can remember watching Janice, so intelligent and calm, get more and more frustrated and agitated because suddenly she could do nothing right. Of course she was doing things as right as always, but there was that dreadful teacher marking her answers wrong because of some flimsy little technicality. I know one time Janice received a zero on a math test because she had left out a single label among the fifty answers. How many times do you have to write "37.632 average inches of rainfall" instead of simply "37.632" to indicate that you know what you are doing? She left out the last one because time was up and Ms Skimme had snatched her paper. My own string of zeros came, among other ways, from making all the labels rhyme.

> *Average rainfall, all in inches*
> *3 cups of flour and .2 pinches*
> *100 gadgets made per hour, 0 winches*
> *1 bushel (cardinals) and 2 pecks (finches)*

It was a way of salvaging some of the essential fun school had been for me before. Why should that have made my work "unacceptable" and "ostentatious"? I wasn't trying to display it anywhere. Even I had to acknowledge that Mrs. Autray was sorely missed. I know I would not have decorated my tree with tinsel, though. I just could not have done that.

When my mother informed me that I must be behaving even crazier than usual– *just having to be different–* and that it was my own fault if I wound up going to Lapidet School for Exceptional Children, I went kind of berserk and screamed for two days and stamped all around my small room, throwing all my clothes on the floor and jumping up and down on them, making huge ballpoint streaks all over those gross chartreuse roses and even peeling half a dozen of them off the wall. By Monday I had no voice left and my face was completely swollen, but I was sent off to school anyway. Instead, I went back and stayed in our apple tree, up higher than usual so that I would not be seen. Then on Tuesday I did the same but was caught in the act of coming down around the time that I would ordinarily be coming home. I had spent the two days crying and reading and eating very sloppy peanut butter and jelly sandwiches. I also had a stack of poems I had written.

> *You think that you know me;*
> *you think that you care;*
> *but here I am hiding in the bird-filled air,*
> *the leafy place, the secret nest. I swear*
> *I will stay here forever.*
> *You will forget me.*
> *What do you know?*
> *You will forget.*

Most of them were along those lines. It might have surprised Ms Skimme to know that some of us not only knew what *maudlin* meant; we could intentionally be so.

I think, too, of Bobby and vocabulary lessons and of the senseless belittling that he was made victim of. Bobby never got tired of trying to create the same sentence with each word; it was one of his two automatic sentences, though neither ever succeeded. "Maudlin is a good word," he would print, or "I looked up the word maudlin." The thing is, that he might really have opened the dictionary, but he could not really read. He could copy letters and phrases by rote, but it was not in him to understand the written word. It was a mind-boggling puzzle to him, but to the rest of us the puzzle was that he had been promoted each year without ever having learned much more. He was, as I have said, so good-natured and so good-willed in spite of the torments that I guess his previous teachers just figured he would float with the stream. Ms Skimme did what she could to drown him, not realizing that he was saved by the gentle raft of his own awareness that he was limited in the world of school. Her taunts could be shrugged off, because they brought him nothing new.

My public tears, when they came, overflowed from my own personal pains, but my private tears were for all of us. That has not changed much, except that my tears for us all will sometimes flow in public too.

Even though I had received a couple of really nice notes from Julieanne and Holly asking me to come back and also asking me what I had meant when I made the suggestion of praying hands, I went back unwillingly to school on the third day. I did know it had to happen sooner or later. I did all the classwork in the most commonplace way, but I had to do it (got to do it, thank you) in Mr. Filamon's office where I was allowed to keep my sunglasses on. At recess I went to my patio and my tree, and I leaned my head against the trunk carefully so as not to hurt the loose paper bark, and I deposited my most heartfelt poem from the weekend. A small flock of chickadees hung from the delicate branches; but a rushing wind whipped through, lifting them all in a cluster and hurling them far away. Nature imitates mind, for I had been feeling the way those birds must have felt.

> *I have rested here*
> *but now what comes to disturb me?*
> *What terror is this that uproots me,*
> *flinging me far from you?*
> *Let me cling to you now for safety.*
>
> *O tree, with your all-seeing eyes,*
> *so wise, see us now.*
> *Tree, with your all-feeling limbs,*
> *so strong and slim, protect us.*
> *Face that I see in you now—*
> *leaves for hair, twigs for eyes and lips and brow—*
> *smile upon us all. Be real for us all.*
> *We need you.*

When I had set the note under a pile of leaves and twigs, I got up to leave; but then I went back and tore off the top half, leaving the second part of the poem for Julieanne and Holly to find. I know they did, too.

## "Julieanne" ~ from her diary

Diary, an amazing thing happened today. Jody finally answered us. Oh, not out loud, but still she did answer. Holly and I wrote her a note asking about that prayer stuff, you know. We knew we did not really want voodoo, especially since we figured we might have to handle some pretty icky stuff. We thought maybe the prayer idea was safer. Anyway, she really answered! We found a scrap of her note paper under the tree with the words all written out for us. So the two of us quietly whispered it together and then we put it back under the leaves and twigs and put a couple of stones on top of that so it would not blow away.

I hope we get some kind of answer, any little sign will do.

p.s. I named the puppy Amiga. Bernardo suggested it. Brett is too busy with his music, and Bernardo is really nice. And handsome.

## Laura

What happened on Thursday after the conferences was, to put it mildly, unbelievable. It was so incredible! It was miraculous and, to use a word that one of our classmates later taught us to love, SOUP-PENDOUS! It took a little while to sink in and become real, but here it is in plain English:

Ms Skimme quit! Ms Skimme quit! She quit! She left. She resigned and moved away and never came back again. She really did DEPART Bell School permanently, and we could not begin to believe our good fortune. And her replacement? Well, I think that is Jody's to tell.

## Jody

I knew the very first minute. I sat in my seat at the back of the room in the middle row and a smile filled my whole being when a tiny yellow leaf skittered in through the door along with her. She was tall and pale with long blonde curly hair and a soft rustling voice that made you think of a refreshing summer breeze. You could imagine her as a pale Cinderella with the birds and the mice enchanted to do her bidding and flocking to her for love. She was so gentle and warm to all of us, and she wanted to know our names and what we liked and what we did not like and what were our hobbies and our favorite kinds of music. She said that out of all the grades, she had always been most partial to the fifth.

Tears filled my eyes again; and although I was still not ready to speak, at last there was someone who might bring me to want to, someone who would accept me for who I was and love the me I was; and she could do that for every one of us. Everyone looked awed and happy; and Holly and Julieanne kept looking at me too with their eyes wide open and their mouths the same, especially when she announced what I already knew in my heart: "Class, I am delighted to be your new teacher. My name is Mrs. Burch."

She mentioned a Mr. Burch who loved to help on all of the complicated projects and especially was fond of making things out of wood, but how did she know to look right at Bernardo when she said that?

And, "Lessons are fun, of course," she said, "but do you like special projects? I think they always bring book-learning to life. Don't you agree?" We would have agreed with her about anything, so dazed by our fantastic loss and by our more fantastic gain. At recess, Thomas perhaps spoke for many when he expressed his doubt that she could stay. But we hurried back to the class, eager for the break to end, so that we could see her and hear her and bask in her warmth and slowly begin to heal.


*"Julieanne" ~ from her diary*

I am speechless, Diary. We got rid of Ms Skimme and have a new teacher, Mrs. Burch. She is beautiful. Holly thinks we did use voodoo after all, but the name is just a coincidence. Besides, I am sure you noticed that she spells it b-u-r-c-h. Not like the tree. Everyone is smiling again. And I have Amiga right here smiling too. She is being very good, and the rugs are starting to smell normal again.

Diary, I need to know your opinion of Bernardo. I know he can't read or write very well, but don't you think he is nice? He is my amigo. He comes over after school and teaches me Morse Code, and I help him practice his reading. He says it's more fun doing things together. Most of the boys would rather play soccer again, which Bernardo likes to do too; but he also likes to walk me home. Can you imagine any of the other boys in my class actually telling me I am pretty? *Bonita*, he says. I am sorry he didn't tell me that name before I named Amiga. Oh, well, maybe the next dog.

Diary, you don't think we really did any voodoo, do you? I got 100 on my math quiz this afternoon, and so did almost everyone. Our new teacher told us we were very bright! I wonder if we need to tell her about labels on answers, though. She did not seem to think they were all that important, but even Mrs. Autray and Mrs. Pingleigh always required them.

BERNARDO      BERNARDO RUIZ
BERNARDO and [JULIEANNE]

*Laura*

For all my love of writing, I feel at a loss to tell you how everything went from gloom and horror to joy and renewed life. I want to include everything, no matter how small each thing seems; yet I know I cannot. The most immediate change, though, was in all of our eyes: we sparkled again. We found humor and laughter together again. We had hope and dreams again. All things were possible. Learning was always a part of our delight but sour preaching was not, hostility was not, soul-shattering criticism was not.

That very first day happened to be a music day, and we all paraded gaily to the music room. We stood quietly in our ranks there on the floor, and Brett stood wondering if Mrs. Burch could play the piano. He watched her walk to the old scratched upright and take her seat on the wobbly bench. He watched her put her hands on the keys, and he waited to see what she would play. She hit a terribly screeching non-chord, and we all squealed too. She turned to face all of us, her face a slightly pink color like a peach, and she stood up and said she was sorry but she would have to make a little confession. We all waited, puzzled.

"I am very sure that you would all be extremely patient with me," she began. "You are such kind friends, and so polite, but I am fully aware of my own limitations— as you would quickly be if I continued to sit here and try to play the piano. Surely there is someone here who can play?"

"Tell her," Hal whispered to Brett, who just shook his head.

"I suppose," she said, as nobody came forward, "that there are those who can do everything, but most people can only do— "

"Very little," Bobby said sadly.

"Why, Bobby, I was going to say that most people can only do lots and lots." Mrs. Burch put her arm gently around Bobby's shoulder and said, "I have admired how well you do so many things, and I think you are one of the few people I have met who never loses his temper." Then she looked again at all of us and said, "I keep discovering that all of you are fantastic at hundreds of things. . ." and we grinned happily; "thousands of things. . ." and we laughed; "perhaps even a dozen or so that you yourselves keep forgetting," and we glowed. "But I think you should know that 'lots and lots' is not everything; 'lots and lots' is not the same as all. I may be able to do a thousand things too, but believe me that I cannot play the piano."

"Tell her, Brett," Hal said out loud. Brett still shook his head.

"Tell me what?" she asked with a smile.

"Brett plays the piano," Bobby said. "Real good."

"I doubt if he still wants to, though," Thomas said, grinning.

"Want to bet?" Brett asked. Fearful that he had passed up his only two chances, he scrambled as fast as he could to the piano, and the whole class applauded. It was just one of the many well-modeled lessons we absorbed in the first few days. With Brett restored to his place on his bench, justice brought all of us peace.

On the next music day and on all of them thereafter, there was no hesitation or doubt at all: Mrs. Burch was clearly our teacher, but Brett was our music maestro. Did any one of us think less of her for allowing him to shine? Hardly! At last we were allowed to be proud of each other and proud of ourselves again. That first week especially, though, it seemed as if we had never known each other in the past; but now suddenly we each stood out in our very best light, and none of us put anyone down. Not even Sallee. We had had enough of that.

*Jody*

Once again in my life I could not wait to get to school each morning, nor did I ever hurry home. Fearfully, though, and shyly, I asked for my parents' permission to ride my bike to school as long as the weather was good. That way I could get there faster and not go through the woods. To my surprise, they said yes; and I began fixing my own lunch at night so that I could be ready at the earliest minute, even though we still could not enter the building before eight-thirty. Mr. Filamon was surprised to see me at the door first thing when he arrived some mornings; and after a few days, he stopped just saying hello and started asking me some question or other. "How are you this morning, Jody?" or, "Isn't this a glorious autumn?" or, "What do you think of the state of the world today?" But he never scolded me for not answering; he didn't lecture me on the politeness of answering when spoken to. He just said, "I can see the answer in your eyes, you know. You have very expressive eyes." And with my eyes I thanked him.

I rarely got there before Mrs. Burch. No matter how early I arrived, she managed to be there already, waiting for us all with a smile or a quick hug or little laugh wrinkles around her eyes. They too were very expressive. It seemed they were always thinking of ways to teach us and please us at the same time. They spoke with and without words, and their example helped me toward knowing that both ways were good.

I found myself spending less and less time at the tree on the patio and more and more down near the playing fields, silently cheering one team or another, casually moving nearer sometimes to Julieanne and Holly and Laura, sometimes to Susan and Janice. I liked to hear Hal tease Alvin, and I wrote little rhyming jokes and hid them in their desks. My pictures were always hanging on the tack strip next to everyone else's, and very few of my assignments got burned. Actually, none of them did.

I still did not talk. I think my classmates were surprised that Mrs. Burch seemed to understand that without ever asking. They were even more surprised, though, that she could call on an Amy and the right one always answered. "How does she do that?" was a constant question. Janice and I wondered how the Amys did it. Thomas was sure there was a trick, and Bobby said, "I doubt it," and all of us laughed. Bobby was pleased with himself for days and began saying I *doubt it* so often that Alvin wanted Bernardo to invent a workable Bobby-squelcher; but Bernardo was very busy teaching all of us Morse Code and learning a little more English in the process.

That particular project began for Bernardo the very first day that Mrs. Burch arrived. Ms Skimme had kept Bernardo in from recess every day until he could write a complete and perfect essay of apology for tapping on Julieanne's desk. When that first afternoon recess came, he quietly and automatically got out his notebook and sighed. Mrs. Burch asked him why he was not leaving, and he told her. He showed her the crossed-out sheet of paper, looking moth-eaten by his well-worn eraser, the paper that we had painfully seen hanging as a bad example on the tack board. Laboriously misspelled and missing things like essential verbs, it awaited Mrs. Burch's formal judgment. We all listened and watched as she called him over to her desk and asked what language he would like to communicate in.

"Spanish," he said. "Hmm," Mrs. Burch said. "That will be hard because I don't understand too much Spanish. We both have to speak and understand the same one if we are going to be able to communicate. What should we do?"

"Do you know Morse Code?" he asked. "Just a little," she

answered, "a little more than Spanish. Let's try it." He tapped
something on the desk. She listened intently and then said, "Try it
again, this time on my hand." He tapped his message, four distinct
letters, on her palm; and she gently closed it around his. "I got it," she
said, "and it is all right. No need to say it or tap it again. Now you
may go to recess. Tomorrow if we have a little time, perhaps you can
teach all of us more Morse Code." And after that, every morning after
the school announcements, we got to tap each other messages for a few
minutes. I tapped mine to Bobby, who never quite knew what I was
telling him but was always pleasant about it. It worked out fine for
both of us, because I could tap anything at all and still feel safe.

   After I had learned Morse Code myself, I realized that
Bernardo had tapped out "s  o  r  y".




*Laura*


   Our classroom began to fill with projects of all kinds, group
projects and individual ones. Alvin was back among us, no longer
counting holes in ceiling tiles or calculating the effects of more rain on
the shape of the water stains there. Hal was saying his favorite word
*boring* only rarely, if ever; in fact, he had actually been heard to say
"fascinating" almost daily– a word that we had associated only with
Alvin. Susan and Janice were leading the class again, although
Julieanne seemed to lose a little. She was briefly disappointed that
Bernardo's Morse Code lessons were for the whole class and that he no
longer would be able to tap on her desk unless he wanted the whole
class to know what he was saying. Sallee was content to dictate to the
hamsters in their cage and to allow Mrs. Autray to stay in Arizona
unpestered by further demands for her return, and Charlene looked a lot
happier without her best friend bossing her. Jody smiled more and
more and left little blue notes for many of us to find. The long window
sill held many treasures, but the best and most exciting project involved
all of us. It started one morning right after vocabulary sentences
(which were not restricted in length or kind or even in color) and right
before math. We were more than halfway through a hard unit on
decimals.
   "You all have been working so hard," Mrs. Burch said, "that I
think it must be time for some kind of change. What can we do with
decimals?" We all looked blank. "It needs to be fun," she insisted,
walking slowly around the room, "and it needs to be quite *fascinating*,
certainly nothing *boring*." We all grinned at Hal. "So, who has an
idea? Any idea at all will do to get us started."

"Decimate them," Alvin suggested, his library book of historic war strategies lying open on the floor. Mrs. Burch wrote *decimate them* on the chalkboard, and we were surprised.

"Eat them," Bobby giggled. That, too, went on the board. Bobby looked a little embarrassed but not for long. Many of us must have thought of what would have happened if he had said that a couple of weeks earlier.

"Burn them," Charlene snickered. None of us liked that stupid snickering, but *burn them* went on the board.

"We could convert them to fractions," Janice said. We heard a whispered "Boring!" and glared at Hal. *Convert to fractions* was on the board.

I had been deep in thought on this topic. I did not like any of the suggestions and was sure they were not what our teacher had in mind either. She wanted us to have fun, after all. All of a sudden, I heard my own voice blurt out, "We could turn decimals into characters and write a play!" I don't know where that came from.

"A play? We can't write a play," Thomas said.

"Why not?" I demanded. "We could too write a play. We could give all the characters numbers instead of names. Like .06 or .0000043."

"Spies!" Alvin said. "We could write a spy story. Agent .007."

"The grownups could have numbers like .02 or .9 and the babies could have cute little numbers like .0000000000005."

"Babies? Who wants babies? Cute little numbers on babies. GAG!" That was Robert.

"We could make it a puppet play," Holly suggested. "We made puppets at the Y last summer. It's easy."

"If we have spies, we will need a code," Bernardo happily pointed out.

"I don't think so," Thomas said.

"Sure we will," Bernardo insisted.

"Costumes, we will need costumes," said Amy Betts. Nobody asked if they would be sweaters.

"Sets," Susan said.

"A puppet stage," Hal corrected.

"It wouldn't have to be Morse Code," Bernardo said softly to Thomas. "We can make up a new one."

"A decimal code," Julieanne said.

"I knew we wouldn't be able to do it," Thomas said almost gloatingly. The class went silent. Everyone clamored for reasons. "Why couldn't we do it?" "Says who, Thomas?" "Why not?"

"See?" he said, pointing to the chalkboard; "Mrs. Burch did

not even write it there." We were stunned. Mrs. Burch looked startled.

"It sounded like so much fun," Amy Betts said mournfully; "why can't we do it?"

"Troops!" Alvin said, still in his own world rather than ours. "If we set it in wartime, we will need troops and then that of course accounts for spies and justifies the code. Yes, I think I see it now."

"Aren't you going to let us do a play, Mrs. Burch?" I asked almost tearfully. "Aren't you even going to put it on the board?"

"Why I thought it was absolutely settled," she said, truly amazed. "I was just so caught up in enjoying all of your wonderful ideas and more that you inspired me to think of! Of course I will list it!" And up on the board with all of the rest, but really wiping all of them out, with ornamental asterisks and underlining and all capital letters, went my suggestion:

### * PUPPET-SPY DETECTIVE STORY *
### *   WITH CODE IN WARTIME MAYBE   *

It was a soupendously proud moment.

"Do we need to vote," Mrs. Burch asked, but everyone cried out, "NO!"

"My, my," she said, "I am enormously impressed with your ideas and your enthusiasm. On a scale of 10, I guess I have to say I'm impressed 10.999999, although that's really an understatement."

The room went all a-buzz with whispered conversations going on all around. Bernardo was tapping and Sallee was hopping and Jody was already designing puppets. Thomas was looking enthused in spite of himself, although he doubted that he could tolerate Bobby's asking him one more time, "What is that thing, an *understatement*, Tommy?"

We did settle down after a while and we took out our math books, but then we were amazed again. Inside each of our books was an index card with a smiling face and a note that said, "I knew you would find something special! Thank you." Mrs. Burch was at the chalkboard, busily erasing and so we had no clue about her own feelings in that moment. Surely she knew we were impressed 10.999, again an understatement.

Without a moment's hesitation, she started us off on our play with a game: Name that Decimal! She would put fractions on the board and have us give her the decimal equivalent; but then she would say, "What do you suppose it looks like? What do you think it does? How might it dress?" And thus all of us, not just some, were led into the kind of thinking she wanted, the kind that would enable us to think in terms of a play, in terms of characterizing, of action, of costume. We were invited into our own creativity.

"Where might that decimal live?" she asked, and Bernardo raised his hand and suggested that it might live in a tree. She smiled at him and at us and said, "Why, yes."

"How come the little ones have the longest numbers?" Bobby asked repeatedly, and Mrs. Burch called on someone different each time to answer, hoping one of us would find the very words that would finally make sense to Bobby. I don't think that any of us did. "Why all those zeros?" he asked over and over again. "I don't see why .3 is any different from .0003." We were not really feeling patient with him, I must admit; but we learned to act patiently anyway. Our teacher always did, and so we learned to do so too. It became a challenge to us to see if we could find new ways to explain the same thing, and so our creative energies were put to many uses.

It was Robert who announced one day that square roots were something like cowboys. "Huh?" Hal said, blinking. "What do you mean?" Brett challenged him. Thomas cast serious doubts. Robert wrote a square root on the chalkboard and turned to us, saying, "See, it looks like the number is sitting in a saddle." Mrs. Burch was delighted.

"Fractions sit on fences," Janice said, carrying the idea along.

"Equations," Alvin started to say, but his mind went zooming out through space before he could finish his thought.

"What about equations?" Sallee asked, punching Alvin's arm. "Hmm?" he asked. "Oh, never mind. Well, balanced armies, maybe, something like that. Or the standoff at the OK Corral. You know." He disappeared into his space odyssey.

Mrs. Burch did not prod him for more.


### Jody

I watched her all the time for the pleasure of seeing that prayers can come true. I listened to her voice as I had listened to the wind in the trees. I wanted to give her my poems, just as I had buried so many at the foot of the birch. She was the embodiment of all I had sought.

> *I was a shadow on the grass*
> *and a small cloud in a gray sky*
> *with a voice so small beneath the thunder.*
>
> *You are a tree springing from the grass,*
> *soaring to the sky,*
> *a wonder to me.*

*You hear my voice,*
*a miracle to me.*

I slipped it into her math book. I was startled to find, the very next hour when it was our math time, that she had slipped notes into all our books, notes with a word or phrase of praise suitable to each of us.

*"Julieanne" ~ from her diary*

Diary, I have to admit that I was sorry when Mrs. Burch asked Bernardo to teach everyone Morse Code. It was kind of special until then. But we are working on our own new secret code, so I don't mind at all anymore. Besides, school is fun again. I still don't know what really happened, and I try not to think about it too much. It is spooky that Mrs. Burch knows some of the things that she does, and it is even spookier to see the happy light in Jody's eyes. It isn't surprising that she's happy, since we all are, but her expression is different.

I don't want to think about it; it scares me.

Amiga is growing so fast. She is just the cutest thing, Diary. She likes to be cuddled and petted and scratched, but sometimes she bites hard. Bernardo says she is just teething, but it hurts anyway.

This Saturday Holly and I are going to start looking for our Halloween costumes already. She wanted us to be witches, but I won't. I won't. That was not witchcraft, was it? We did not do anything so wrong, did we? I wonder where Ms Skimme is and what she is doing. I am sure she left because she wanted to, or because a lot of parents were angry, or because Mr. Filamon decided that she needed to. She didn't leave because of our reading that prayer, did she? I hope there was no foul play.

I don't want to think about it.

All of the class is nicer than ever, and even Sallee is being cooperative. Everything is better, so we could not have done anything bad, could we? I wonder if this is how Jody feels and why she keeps secrets from her parents. I hate this, but I don't want to tell anyone. This must be how she feels. Then why is she happy now and I am not? I am happy at school when I am not thinking about this, just enjoying all the things we are doing.

I don't want to think about this.

Perhaps a "puppet-spy detective story with code in wartime maybe" does not sound interesting to you. Perhaps you are wondering why we got so excited and how we could be allowed to spend as much time on it as we did. Possibly you might be among those who would consider it a waste of much valuable time, a way for our teacher to indulge us for no really good reason at all. I would like to tell you some of the ways it was so extremely worthwhile, so exciting, and how it managed to teach us not only some facts about decimals and their relationships but, far more lastingly, about us and our relationships. It improved our skills in communicating and planning ahead and making good use of materials and– well, I think I would rather describe some of the moments I still remember.

There was one afternoon in particular with Charlene. Now aside from snickering when she was nervous and being a kind of little slave to Sallee, Charlene was what you might call almost invisible, unnoticeable. She was there but never too real to us. Her main reality, I am sorry to say, was that irritating snicker. At the time I want to tell you about, which was right before music and therefore a time we usually were eager to get to, many of us were absorbed in our work on the play and no one more so than Charlene, who had joined the puppet-making committee.

Alvin, Hal, Bobby, and Bernardo were on the decimal code committee, happily whispering and tapping in one corner. Susan, Julieanne, Holly, and I were on the writing committee and were well along with our story. Even Jody contributed ideas to us. Robert sometimes came over to make sure we included realistic war details, and so did Alvin. Sallee and the Amys were designing a stage set, and others had their various jobs; but for once Charlene had chosen for herself and was oblivious even to Sallee as she made her Master Spy puppet. She was still at the design stage, and her drawing was truly fantastic: the spy wore a black trench coat, had a patch over its right eye, carried two guns (depicted only by bulges in the coat), wore a shoe that was to contain a combination short wave radio and miniature TV, as well as a tiny tape recorder that looked like a penny. The spy had a futuristic telephone the size of a thimble, a camera that seemed to be an innocent pencil; and Charlene was only getting started.

The rest of us had formed two straight lines and were at the door, and still Charlene was drawing and snickering to herself with great delight. You can imagine how shocked and startled she was when an arm draped itself gently around her shoulders and a rustling voice kindly whispered, "Music time, Charlene"

"Eeeeee!" she squealed and jolted, bumping her arm and

jarring her funny bone, making her squeal some more. I am sad to report that we all snickered. Charlene was very embarrassed and upset and started to cry; but Mrs. Burch just hugged her and held up her drawing, announcing to us all that it was no wonder Charlene had not known it was music time. "I just wish all of you could see this phenomenal drawing," she said to us. "You will later, but let me tell you that this is a master drawing of a master spy, worth all this care and loving attention Charlene has given her. And all of the details are so incredibly realistic. I just love this pencil! The eraser looks like a lens. Is it a camera? Charlene, you are our Rembrandt, our portrait artist." Charlene beamed and, still rubbing her elbow, joined one of the lines. We had new respect for our classmate, and it lasted. It did not last merely because, as you may be thinking, Mrs. Burch just piled on praise and we believed her. It lasted because what Mrs. Burch said was true– Charlene really was a master at details and a wonderful artist, and we had never known that before. I bet you have bought some of her unique cards yourself, but you don't know her by name. Charlene has never cared one way or another about being in the limelight, content then to let Sallee dominate and now to do work unsigned.

I might also mention that *phenomenal, incredibly*, and *portrait* happened to be on our vocabulary list that week.

### *Jody*

I had a hard time deciding what committee to be on for the Great Decimal play. I would have liked making codes or writing or designing. I would have liked being on almost all of the committees, but I knew there was one that I could not have stood. Sallee would have driven me crazy with taking charge, although Robert could sometimes keep her in check. I found myself working mostly alone and sending a lot of blue notes to each committee with ideas I had. One of them went to the coders. I suggested that they call themselves the D-coders. I heard Hal say, "That's a pretty good idea, you know. The D stands for more than one thing."

"What does it stand for?" Bobby asked. There was whispering and then, "But don't tell the rest of the class. We'll see if they figure it out themselves." Of course Bobby was soon telling Thomas what the D stood for.

"Stop that!" Alvin demanded.

"Why?" Bobby asked. "He wouldn't have gotten it. I know. Really, he wouldn't."

"It's more interesting to let people try," Alvin explained.

"It is boring to tell right away," Hal agreed.

"I didn't want him to tell me," Thomas assured them.

"Well, I doubt that you'd have gotten it," Bobby insisted. He didn't know why Thomas punched him or why the other boys laughed. Later I heard him whisper to Hal, "I wonder who could have made up D-coders. I can't figure that out." Naturally Hal, who was not boring, did not tell him.

We had a discussion one morning about how much time we could get to work on our play. At first we were allowed all of Friday morning, but that definitely was not enough time if we were to finish before the year ended, let alone by Christmas when we planned to have a dress rehearsal. Janice had suggested that one-tenth or .1 of our time was just too little and requested that we have at least .2 of the week. Mrs. Burch considered the suggestion but reminded us that we had quite a lot of other work to do too, work that probably did require more than .8 of our time. What kinds of ideas did we have, she asked, to solve the dilemma? (*Dilemma* was one of the words on our list.)

"We could skip writing essays," Bernardo suggested.

"We should give up the Morse Code time in the morning," Sallee countered. Sallee was still in an anti-boy stage.

"Cut out vocabulary sentences, since we are doing so much writing anyway," Laura said.

Mrs. Burch looked undecided and said she would continue taking suggestions for a day or so and then we would all make a decision. That afternoon I left her a little note on pale green paper (so she might not know it was from me) asking if we could take five minutes away from each of our subject areas each day– language arts, math, art or music, social studies, and so on– and have an extra half hour left over at the end of each day. It would not be a lot, but we would not lose a lot either. It meant we would have to plan carefully.

The next morning she asked the class what they thought of that plan, and it passed. "And I want to thank the person who donated this valuable idea to us. Who can tell us what *mastermind* means?"

Sometimes I think that vocabulary was one of the biggest building blocks of our education; and that suits me because, as I said near the beginning, words have always been my favorite food. Like a tall blonde mother bird, Mrs. Burch dropped words into our mouths and heads all day long and made sure that we digested them. They were no longer lists of nouns or verbs that we might read again sometime but rarely hear in the classroom or in our daily lives. She herself used them all the time and encouraged us to do so at every opportunity. She gave Hal every word she could think of relating to *boring*, and she was openly tickled when he used them in the negative– as in one of his first vocab sentences that second week: "I have had no feeling of ennui all week long." She would often commiserate with him when he growled about having to learn some geographical fact not formerly to his taste.

"Tedious, isn't it?" she asked him. "Not so bad," he said, surprising himself as well as the rest of us. Alvin of course could never understand how any fact could be tedious. We all acquired *voracious* in our growing list of friendly words. It dawned on us only gradually that the majority of the words she gave us told us about ourselves, and we felt more and more understood and valued. It was such a cozy nest she built, and such a simple one to construct.

"I looked up 'voracious'," Bobby wrote, hoping his formula would work at last. "And what did you find?" she asked him.

"Oh," he said; "I don't remember." And then she looked it up with him and had him explain it to her, and from the time she gave him and the bright eyes that held him in their warm gaze, he found new willingness to please. "Alvin is voracious," he wrote. "Yes, he is, isn't he?" she said, admiringly. "It can be such a *beneficial* trait." And then they looked that word up, and Bobby said, "that's good!"

"I am an educational *omnivore*," Alvin wrote in one of his briefest sentences on record.

I think we always knew which words were for us. I took great pleasure in seeing the simple word *poet* one day and then catching her smile directed at me. "Too easy," said an almost smug Bobby, writing "A poet makes rhymes." I knew it was more than that. Another time, she gave us the word *awestruck*, and we dutifully copied it down but applied it to nothing in particular. Mrs. Burch chose to write a sentence of her own on the board: *I am awestruck in the presence of so much ability.* All of us felt the thrill.

At home throughout those *breathtaking* days, little had changed; but it did not matter. I was riding my bike on the streets, not walking through the woods. I was intensely happy and at home my changes were not noticed or at least not commented on, unlike the earlier ones when I had grown silent. That suited me, not wishing to have myself *scrutinized* and criticized. I used all of the vocabulary words whenever I could, but only in writing, never in talking to my parents.

We became more and more puzzled by the Amy trick. For a while we thought that there might be an eye signal between the teacher and every Amy, but we could detect none. Not even Charlene's master puppet spy detective could invent any tool to catch them out. We listened for clues in the sound of her voice and for tapping on desks, but we never heard anything to let us know which Amy was being called on. Yet they always knew, and not once ever did Mrs. Burch have to say, "No, not Amy Betts. I was calling on Amy Patterson." It was one of the many mysteries we could not resolve, and so it added still more to our eagerness to be there and to be present if ever the veil might fall and the true solution be revealed.

Brett left the room one day, adding yet another mystery. He would not say where he was going, and we tried all kinds of ways to find out. Hal and Robert were especially aggravating to Brett, leaving him D-code messages and threatening to put footprint-detecting powder on his shoes. "Like you could," Brett said, unperturbed. Everyday for weeks thereafter he left for thirty minutes, but he never missed our music classes– except once, and on that day we got to hear Mrs. Burch attempt to play chopsticks and then we sang *a capella*.

Mr. Filamon visited now and then, delighted with the puppets, impressed by the stage, *mystified* by the code, *baffled* and *intrigued* by the complex plot, and altogether the most tremendously satisfying visitor. He asked us to be sure to arrange to give our show to all of the primary grade classes, and suddenly we needed to figure out who would be acting. Oddly enough, giving the play had never even come up! Even our intended dress rehearsal had seemed too unreal to cast. It just was an imaginary target, but now we got enthused about giving performances.

Finally I had a real part in our project: I got to be .001023, the child who listens to the others and says nothing but who manages to find an important clue that leads to the mystery being solved. I never knew which of us wrote that in, but we found the suggestion on some yellow paper at a time when I was using only blue and green. Charlene designed and made a small puppet that day, and it became my own.

I am sure that very real things were happening in all those other subsets of Bell School called classrooms; but to me, as to so many of my classmates, those other rooms might as well have been across the town or across the state or in some other galaxy. Our room with all its experiments prospering on the window sill and in each desk and in the air and deep within ourselves– our room was our reality. We might notice the quick coming and going of sparrow and finch and squirrel; we might still be squabbling with siblings; we might have our attention distracted elsewhere by a doctor's appointment or by a silly misunderstanding or by the stark threat of a young man with a sharp knife– by routine, by ignorance, or by the lurking evils of the outside world– but one brightly lit room in an off-white hexagonal building in the midst of mud fields and thinning autumn woods in a small town had become our truest home. One loving tender voice had brought us back from a nightmare, picked up our fragments of self and restored us to our safest place. Sometimes the cosmos comes down to us in one little narrow place. Every day of my life I thank whatever it is that sends such piercing messages, disguised as yellow leaves or finches or trees or as whatever else it wishes. So often it comes in human form.

I stopped dreaming of sharp objects gleaming starkly out from the dark; but I wondered what Julieanne was nightly dreaming of, for now *she* seemed to be drifting away. And so I could see myself across the room, see that something fearful had happened to another once-happy child, see that help was needed and be aware that I might have something to offer and not yet know what to say. I wanted to talk to her, but I did not know what to say. I spent a lot of time thinking about that, though– a lot of time.


*Laura*

Today I read Jody's words and I try hard to think back to what Julieanne was like then. I knew later that something was wrong; all of us came to know it. But that soon? I am sure we did not. Julieanne still took part in everything and seemed happy for all the changes. It seems strange to me that with so much good happening, so much happiness surrounding us each day like a globe of contentment, that there could still be new pain growing from the very cause that brought so many of us joy. It seemed to me that Julieanne's greatest, perhaps only, unhappiness was that Bernardo liked everybody, most certainly including her; but she would have been happier if he liked everybody *almost* as much but never *really* as much as her. She seemed a little jealous of the Morse Code lessons for all of us and of the fact that Bernardo would happily tap messages on everyone's desk.

And yet, as Jody says, the signs were already there. Beautiful Julieanne now carried more tissues and rubbed her eyes. She probably was crying, but I think I must have figured she was allergic. Maybe to Amiga. Holly might have known more, but I think Holly would have told us. Instead, Holly started spending more time with Susan and Amy Betts. That seems odd now, but back then friendships shifted and quarrels lasted a while before those friendships got patched. There was nothing unusual for us to see. Besides, none of us knew what could possibly be bothering Julieanne; she seemed to have it all: intelligence, pretty looks, a boyfriend already! and a puppy. We were unmindful.

When we heard that Holly had already made herself a witch costume for Halloween and that Julieanne had painted a large brown cardboard box to look like a house in which she would be hidden, all we thought about was how we would dress. We were so caught up in our play that October thirty-first came pouncing upon us, and few of us were ready. The day arrived, with its school parade (Mrs. Burch led us dressed as Mother Goose) and its night of trick or treat, but that year we were more eager for our special project than for all the candy in all the bags.  (I told you we were an unusual group.)


*Jody*


     That year, unlike the two before, I went out trick or treating alone (dressed as a silent ghost).  I did not go anywhere near the woods or anyplace I thought there might be real spooks.  I did not stay out long, but it was nice to feel that freedom.  My mother was so pleased that she gave me an extra-large bag, but then she was disappointed that I came back with only a dozen things or so within.  Yet again I was her child who was simply bound and determined to be abnormal, but this time I did not care.  I knew I had accomplished something big for myself, and that is what mattered.  My brother went with his friends and filled one bag and came back for another, so in some obscure way my mother was rewarded.  *Things* have never been my reward, but not everyone can believe that a child might feel that way.

     Book reports were due that week, and I had read Dickens's *Great Expectations*.  I did not understand most of it, but I had been drawn by the title.  One phrase became permanently part of my silent inner vocabulary– *"Ever the best of friends, eh Pip?"*  And I would think to myself each day at school, "Good morning, Mrs. Burch, ever the best of friends, eh?"  But I never said it out loud.  It was my private password, my reward for having read that long and complicated book.  It sits today on a shelf in my studio, and now I love it; but then it was too hard.  I tried to find a way to write a book report on it but gave up in great frustration and went for my usual preference, a poem.

Great Expectations

Here is what I have learned:
we do not understand
and often we get burned
by those who have a hand
in raising us.
We all expect some things
like love and friends and joy,
but then a Mag-Witch brings
great fear to the hero-boy
and also me.
We look someplace for hope
but it's not there.
Someone throws us a rope,

which turns to air.
But Pip could count on Joe
and also Biddy,
so friendship does exist, we know,
even in the city.

I was terribly unhappy with the last line, but time was up and I had to finish quickly. As I think about the book and my poem now, I think I understood at least a little more than I realized. The one thing I was sure I did understand in that book was how Pip felt about keeping Mr. Magwitch's terrible secret. Nevertheless, after all the years, I am still embarrassed by the last line.

When Halloween had passed, it seemed immediately that festive Thanksgiving was in the air; and so our class spent a little less time on our play and a fraction more time on understanding all the things and the people for which we were grateful. As I continued to notice and in a way keep track of Julieanne's distress, I tried harder and harder to find some words for her; but I also was learning something extremely important from her. I had thought that miracles were for everyone, that anything that was spectacularly good had to be so for all. But miracles may sometimes be for most or for many or for some or for a few. A miracle might be for one and only one and of no boon at all to others. It made me wonder if there were such things as miracles that existed for no one; and I came to believe in those too, for I can imagine that they exist, although I am not able yet to give you an example. I will bet, though, that they are not rare at all. Perhaps the flowers on a distant planet are miracles only for One, but maybe they are escaping even that notice as well.

One thing that Bernardo was grateful for, among many, was that he was allowed to speak his book report into a tape recorder, instead of having to write it. Bobby asked to do the same, but it did not bring about the same results for him. So again the message was clear: there are no solutions for all. We need to find what works for us but not to impose that solution on others; we need to think long and hard before mandating anything for all.

So, although Julieanne occasionally stayed in at recess and might still be talking with Mrs. Burch when we came trooping back, the fact is that for her the solution had yet to be found. It seems safe to say that the problem first had to be identified, and that was no easy task. I thought I had a clue; I thought that pretty Julieanne was jealous of the obvious love Bernardo felt for our teacher and of how much we all loved her. Julieanne had always been the most popular member of our class, and suddenly she was not. I thought of two very different possibilities for her to think about and wondered how to word them.

First, I thought, she could see that Mrs. Burch cared for all of us, including her, and that we all (including Bernardo) cared about our teacher. It was not an exclusive thing; no one was left out. But I did not really think that would matter to Julieanne. It might not have mattered to me.

The other thing I thought of, the one that might have made a difference to me, myself, came from some other books I was reading, books about legends and miracles that happened to children. After reading each story, I would find myself asking *And what next?* After the miracle took place, did life change forever? Was there really a happy ever after, or was that only in fairy tales? The thing that I kept noticing in every case was that no miracle lasts very long. It happens! and then its glory fades and you are left to wonder if it ever happened at all. What if it happened when you weren't even paying attention? What if you missed it? Such terrible possibilities, such losses! And those losses would last forever. One's life would never be what it might have been, and one would not ever know. That is when it first occurred to me that miracles might exist that no one even suspected. So what could I say to Julieanne about all this? I thought perhaps it would make her happier to know that this miracle of ours that made her so unhappy would probably end very soon. It just could not go on and on. I wrote her a letter explaining all this, and I mailed it to her at home.

She did not answer, but could that be a surprise to me?

*"Julieanne" ~ from her diary*

I had a crazy letter from Jody and threw it away.

*Alvin, from his journals*

.03  .122  .6  .85  .09354  .692  1.3  .77  .1510  .19  3.88!

Ha! Let's see if Hal can decode that!
I hypothesize that if I tell Bobby to tell Hal that he knows what it means, I can really get Hal this time! All Bobby can tell Hal is that he knows what it means. He can whisper some dumb nonsense to me, and I will say, "Right! How did you get it, Bobby?" Heh heh heh.

It's PAYBACK TIME! I predict that Brett will thank me.

*Laura*

November was another great month that year. The puppet stage had been made from donated wooden crates– we assumed from Mr. Burch– and the brocade that Mrs. Autray had left in one of the cabinets became the curtains. All along, the puppet-making committee had been reading whatever our writing committee had produced, and characters that came and went in the different drafts of the story simply changed their numbers and accessories at the clever hands of Charlene. The larger characters, with their larger numbers, grew more and more complex, with elaborate imaginary tools and supplies hidden within their folds. The smaller characters, with their *infinitesimal* numbers, often were reduced to mere finger puppets. Jody's character was one of these, while Sallee's was the largest puppet of all. She wanted to make it a marionette, but you might say that we kept her in hand. Charlene endowed that puppet with a tiara and a megaphone, and all of us had to giggle. Notice that we did not snicker.

We had one early snow, long before any of the trees had lost their leaves or even turned their usual fall colors; but the snow melted quickly and a warm autumn lingered, keeping the delicate birch tree surprisingly green and many of the small shrubs around the school blossomed as if it were spring.

Drawings of turkeys and Pilgrims began to line the tack board, along with vocabulary sentences based on seasonal words. The main ones were easy to remember: *appreciative, abundance, cornucopia,* and *feast.* It would be interesting to know what words we each might still recall. I looked in Alvin's journal of sentences and found this compact entry:

*On the chalkboard is a <u>cornucopia</u> of vocabulary words: a horn of plenty for us to <u>feast</u> (that is, to feed well) on and an <u>abundance</u> (lots) of erudition for which I am <u>appreciative</u> (grateful) at this <u>sacred</u> (holy) time of year.*

And if I remember correctly, that was the one time that Bernardo got to say his sentences in Spanish, for which he was truly thankful. All I can recall exactly, though, is that it began with, "Estoy muy, muy. . . ."

*Jody*

Julieanne avoided me after I wrote that letter. I didn't know if it made her angry that anyone noticed what she was trying to hide or if she misunderstood. It was good that we all had the decimal play to think about and work on; that way, we could each go on being as happy or as unhappy as we needed to be without irritating each other. I could see, though, that Julieanne and Holly weren't as close as they had been and that Holly seemed more hurt by that than Julieanne. Sometimes I saw Holly up on the patio, but I never saw Julieanne there. I myself was almost always down by the dome, watching the soccer game and listening at the edges to some of the clustered conversations. I know that Laura and Susan talked about Holly a little and thought that she was making a mistake in becoming better friends with Sallee.

Mostly it was pleasant to be near the field and quietly to throw or kick the ball back to Robert or Bobby or Hal when it came out of bounds near me. "Thanks!" they called, and that was kind of nice. Sometimes Janice would come and stand with me, not expecting any conversation. More and more, it was comfortable at school again. I was unhappy that it was not so for every member of the class, although it was for .95 of us. I realized fully for the first time how I had to have appeared to my classmates, and I was sorry.

Now I could stand there by the dome and look out to the dark woods, knowing that I was safe where I was and knowing that if any scary thing happened again, I now might have someone to run to. That was the biggest change of all for me, and yet I knew it could not always be so. Sooner or later I would be all on my own again, but I had been through so many scary times before. Now I was simply enjoying the respite. (*Respite* was one of our newest words.)

"I am taking a respite," Bobby called out to Hal, leaving the soccer game and shocking every classmate who heard him.

Robert developed an interest in gore along about that time. All of his sentences were filled with fights and detailed bruises and massive bleeding. Spies also were abundant, borrowed from our puppet play, and all of them met up with counter-counter agents who "beat each other to bloody pulps" every day. Mrs. Burch read his sentences and corrected only the spelling and grammar. In class and out, Robert was actually growing nicer and nicer, even to the girls. It seemed odd to us that his writing seemed so vicious. "Yes!" he would mutter out loud in the midst of writing his sentences. "Ha, ha! That'll put him out of the way for a while, won't it? Now we can invade the Kremlin and carry off the secret documents. They can't catch us now!"

I don't think that he ever once realized how much his glee genuinely entertained us. Of course, some of the boys couldn't help getting in on the act. Alvin, expert on so many things, would stop at Robert's desk with such vital information as, "Your gypsy disguise for a spy is nuts."

"Yep, nuts," Bobby would add, having no idea if it was or not. And Robert, who not long before would have thrown a punch or two and maybe kicked a little as well, simply ignored them and went on writing. "Aaargh, me hearties, methinks there is a spy aboard our pirate ship looking for doubloons and such, but we'll give him a royal doubloon in the mouth and no *respite!*"

Sometimes Robert would even turn around to Charlene and ask her to help him illustrate his pirate ship or make some spy puppets for him, not like the ones for the play but different ones just for him. Probably Hal and Alvin and Brett snickered then, but Charlene was thrilled: they were her first full-fledged commissions.

Her own puppet, the master spy, grew more ornate daily as November progressed. She found uses for the rickrack in the cabinet and she outlined the eye patch with the silver sequins found there too. Beneath the paperbag raincoat, the purple hem of an evening gown trailed out. Some of us may have thought the puppet more than a bit overdressed, but Charlene had a wonderful time and a unique vision.

Sallee, looking critically at her own large puppet, 876.9, turned it over to Charlene for added detail and was pleased with the results: her puppet now had an army cap and the five bright stars of a general, gold epaulets, and many medals. Occasionally Alvin would salute as Sallee passed by; and Robert offered to give her a purple heart, assuring her it was an honor. "The general is NOT wounded," Sallee informed him; "no more blood!"

There came a day in mid-November when Mrs. Burch startled us all. "I brought something in that I think you might want to hang on our tree outside," she said. We could not believe our ears– decorate the tree? Had we been hypnotized all along? Had this been Mrs. Autray and we in a trance unaware? NO, was the immediate shout.

"Not even these?" she asked, pulling from under her desk a large box full of bird feeders.

"Oooh!" we sighed and brightened and eagerly filled them all, some with thistle and some with cracked corn and then we hung suet and peanut butter balls. We never questioned the difference; we simply knew that there was one. Slowly at first a few birds came, and then some more, and then an entire classful it seemed. If one small bird stayed off to the side, not seeing a place for itself, well, that happened inside the room too. I thought about all the things I observed, and the little cardinal perched on a dry mound of fallen leaves told me some new things about myself; and they were nothing bad or abnormal at all. They were perfectly natural. I wished Julianne could see them too, but maybe that was not to be her message.

Then Thanksgiving was a few days off, and everyone was leaving notes of appreciation for others. It was quite a lot like an autumn Valentine's day, but the primary color was not red.

*Large birds soon on the table,*
*little ones flock to the tree;*
*I sing with the nearby cardinal*
*and thank you for hearing me.*

To my surprise, even I received some notes.  One was from the D-coders and was, of course, in numbers.  I translated it very easily and felt warm and happy.  Another arrived on lined tablet paper, often erased and laboriously printed.  "Gracías for yur help wit my sentces." And another, on yellow note paper,

*Who nourishes the tree?*
*The little birds who rest there?*
*The squirrel who hides his treasure there?*
*The rain of tears that fall?*
*The leaves that drop each fall?*
*All.*

*Who knows the tree?*
*Not all the birds who flock there*
*nor quiet creatures coming there.*
*She who knows why her tears fall,*
*who sees the leaves in spiral fall,*
*she knows the tree and senses all.*

I carefully wrapped the poem in tissue paper and kept it in my box under the bed.  I still have it, proof if any ever were needed, of the reality of those days

*Laura*

I know that we studied all our regular subjects with Mrs. Burch, along with the extra things she allowed; but I cannot remember them all.  Social studies is a blur to me, though I can tell you a whole lot I learned in that subject from just a short time later.  Our language arts periods were filled with stories and discussions and of course sentence writing, and all merged easily with our play writing.  Math of course was at the heart of the play, understanding relative sizes and measures; but what we were guided repeatedly to understand went far beyond the numbers.  All things had positive value; labels could be deceiving.  Bobby never could grasp the fact that the number 2 was larger than 1.99.  "How can that be?" he asked over and over again.  No one could get him to understand why the decimal point made such a difference.

"If your number is 1.99," Alvin patiently tried to explain, "it is the same as saying one plus almost one. Isn't almost one less than one?" Bobby would nod. "So that's how it is," Hal said, nodding at Alvin and turning back to his own work.

"I don't get it," Bobby whispered to Bernardo. "It says 99."

"No, it says *point*-ninety-nine," Bernardo said. "See, that point changes it."

"What point? I don't get the point."

Sallee still would have insisted that boys are stupid, but she rarely said so those days.

"Where is Brett, anyway?" Bobby asked one afternoon. We all looked up, hoping for an answer, because Brett had steadfastly refused to give even a hint of his regular absences. Mrs. Burch just smiled and said, "Some day you will know. That's not my secret to share."

"Secrets?" Sallee repeated. "I thought that grown-ups don't approve of secrets."

"Why not?" Mrs. Burch asked her, looking surprised. "Aren't secrets fun?"

"Well, yes," Sallee agreed, "but my mother always says we should have nothing to hide. She gets angry if I keep something a secret from my sister."

"But is there only one kind of secret?"

"A secret is a secret," Robert said. "How many kinds can there be?"

"A hundred kinds," Julieanne said, and then got back to writing up her science notes. The rest of us were still listening, though, and I noticed that Jody seemed very interested. I don't know anyone in our class who would be more familiar with secrets than she was. I wondered if finally she might join in a discussion, but she didn't.

"There are secrets that you have because you don't think others *ought* to know them," Mrs. Burch suggested, "and others that you might have because you think you will lose them. It is as if they will stop being real if others know them. What if you ask your mother what kind of secrets she means? Maybe she just means certain kinds."

"No, I think she means all of them," Sallee was sure. "She says that anyone who has a secret is guilty of something."

"Oh," Mrs. Burch said. "I see. I will have to think about that. If some of you are stuck for an essay this week, here is an interesting topic for you– what kinds of secrets are there? And how do you feel about them?"

"Thanks a lot, Sallee," Thomas said, thinking it meant more

work.

"It's not my fault," she snapped at him.

"And it is not an assignment either, Tom. I know you have already begun your essay. There is no need to change it. It's just one possibility for those who have not picked a topic yet."

I knew that Jody had already written her essay, but I saw her get out her notebook and write another. I don't know if she turned it in.

*Jody, from the box under the bed*

Secrets

I know people who have guilty secrets; I have met at least a few of them. I think a guilty secret must be very painful. It means a person has done something knowing it is wrong and is afraid that other people will find out. Perhaps then they will punish you, or perhaps they will tell others who will punish you. You would live in fear. I wonder if a secret can be guilty if you do not know right from wrong.

I have secrets, and I have lived in fear; but my secrets are not guilty ones. Just now, in class, you said, "There are secrets that you have because you don't think others *ought* to know them and others that you might have because you think you will lose them. It is as if they will stop being real if others know them." I understand that– all of it, but especially the last part. I don't want some of my fears to go away, because they tell me who I am. I want them to be real, and I don't want anyone telling me they are not.

I think Sallee's mother is just trying to know too much. She doesn't want Sallee to keep anything from her. My mother would like me to believe the same thing, that I have no right to secrets. She is wrong.

Some of my secrets have nothing to do with fear, either. They are things that have made me very happy. How would I feel if I told someone the best thing that ever happened in my whole life and she said, "So what? What's the big deal?"

It would be nice to find someone else to tell my stories to, someone who would know (without my telling) just the right thing to say. I tell myself my stories, and I always know what I want to hear. Then I know what to say. "Jody," I have said to myself, "you have some really great secrets!"

(DO NOT TURN IN)

## Secrets for the Box

*He drifts through the woods*
*like a ghost*
*and hides near the trunks of the oak*
*with sometimes a penknife and*
*sometimes a switchblade*
*and he threatens to poke*
*out your eyes.*
*Sometimes he stands and pretends*
*he is slitting a throat*
*and he points to your throat.*
*Or he says I will give you to five;*
*you can run. And I run,*
*but one time I slipped and I fell*
*and he fell*
*and cut off one braid*
*and he said, laughing,*
*this time you're lucky.*

## Secrets Out In the Open

*What are you wearing to the costume party?*
*she asked, and I said, Promise you will not tell?*
*I swear, she said, with her eyes big*
*and her fingers crossed behind her.*
*So I told her because I didn't see her hands,*
*and it wasn't any big deal;*
*but still it was supposed to be a secret*
*and so she should not have told.*

## "Julieanne" ~ from her diary

Today in class, Sallee said that if we have secrets it means that we are guilty of something. I thought I stayed very calm and I think no one knew how upset I was at that idea. I have always had some secrets, but I never thought there was anything wrong with that. Until now, all my secrets have been with Holly or Laura or Susan– and Jody before. We had secrets about who liked whom and what we were wearing to a Halloween party. Was that wrong?

Diary, I have never had a secret like the one I have now. I

can't tell anyone but you. And I feel very, very guilty, so it makes me wonder if Sallee is right. Diary, I think we killed Ms Skimme! No one has ever heard from her or about her. No one knows where she is. I think that the prayer Jody left for us to say was not a prayer at all. I think it was a letter to the Devil, and I am so scared. Sometimes at school I can forget for a while, but then it comes back. When Mrs. Burch is teaching or watching us at work, I am all right; but sometimes she stands by the window, swaying a little as if there were a breeze, and her face is surrounded by all those little yellow curls. Then I get very frightened again, and I want to run home and get under my covers and never go back again.

Mommy is taking me to see a doctor, but I can't tell anyone what I did. I won't tell anyone what I did.

I can't stand to go to Sunday School anymore either. Mrs. Graves talks a lot about the Devil and how he tempts us with promises of better things and too late we learn the truth. It is true. I thought I was only asking for Ms Skimme to go away, but look at all that happened! Maybe she is lying dead in the woods somewhere and nobody has found her. Maybe she killed herself when she realized how much we hated her. And now the Devil is happy that he caught Jody and Holly and me, but still I am the only one who is miserable.

Oh, Diary, don't ever tell! I did tell Amiga, but no one else.

*Laura*

It is difficult to read Julieanne's diary entries today. It makes me ponder long and deep about that subject of secrets, more so than I did back then in fifth grade when I wrote a short story, "The Boy Who Could Not Keep a Secret," about Bobby and his constant thwarting of all of Alvin's and Hal's great plans for secret codes. That was pretty much the extent of my own interest. I did not ever think about Mrs. Griswold's theory of guilt that she had passed on to Sallee, nor did I care that there obviously were secrets all around me.

Today I look upon secrets quite matter-of-factly: there are good ones and less good ones and terrible ones. If a secret eats away and hurts you, it is not good to keep it to yourself. If it spares others unnecessary hurt and anguish, why make yourself feel guilty about keeping it? It is not the secrets that are guilty, nor do they imply guilt. The content makes all the difference. I really don't see any other way to consider them. But it is quite clear to me now that making such arbitrary statements like Mrs. Griswold's can do secret damage itself.

Who knew how much additional pain it caused Julieanne? Who knows even now?

Fortunately, most of us remained unaffected. We lacked the experience to imagine guilty secrets except in the wildly exaggerated stories we might read or see at the movies. We lived in a much more sheltered environment that did not expose us to everything or even much of anything. Sin was a concept often mentioned at our Sunday School but lacking much reality for us, and I think we were far better off. We were the lucky ones, not Jody on her terrifying walks through the woods or popular Julieanne in her struggle with the meaning of what she had done. And after all, what had she really done? She had wished for a kinder teacher, and who can deny us that right?

*Jody*

I began getting a little nervous early in December. Every time we had music that month, a very small yellow leaf would blow softly across the music room floor and come to rest against Mrs. Burch's foot. She seemed never to notice it, and the rest of the class also seemed not to see it. It was a minor unsettling event down on the floor in the midst of the rising songs; but each time I saw it scurry out from its hiding place behind the door, I sensed a darkly disturbing rift in the air which dimmed the mood for a moment.

By the last day of classes before the Christmas holiday, Mrs. Burch looked taller, thinner, paler. She smiled as she invited Robert to select our first song. "Our first number," he corrected. All of the boys just loved tying everything to the play, but in fact so did most of the girls.

"Right," the teacher said, smiling more, and she took her customary spot against the side wall, swaying there gently out of time with the music. We sang– my classmates sang– a wide range of numbers: traditional carols, some old sentimental favorites, "The Gremlin Chorus" by Brett, our favorite version of beautiful *Greensleeves*, and finally *Red River Valley*. *"Do not hasten to bid me adieu,"* they sang; and the little yellow leaf quivered there against our teacher's shoe and seemed to cling to it.

Julieanne was invited to lead the class back to our room, and she did. It all seemed normal enough, except for the yellow leaf and the slightly pink eyes that I noticed. They were not Julieanne's eyes. Farther from the ground they stood, swaying almost in time to the music, closing now and then to allow their owner to imagine whatever she might wish to imagine or to absorb every moment of every song and our overwhelming joy.

I kept my eyes on her constantly, and more than once she smiled at me as if we shared a secret. The only thing was, I did not know what that secret was– I had only a few indistinct murmurings within my soul, but I had no definite idea.


*Laura*

All too quickly December slipped away, happy days charged with the democracy unit and workbooks and math and vocabulary and music, with some of the ordinary and much of the magical. Science experiments covered the back window sill; tissue paper "stained glass windows" blocked the view out of the backmost windows. Spanish magazines came regularly to the classroom; we worked hard on our many assignments and reports– Alvin wrote the first of his astronomy series then, Charlene researched famous illustrators, Hal brought us current events, and Bernardo brought us a different kind of *current* events. Robert and Brett treated us to their informal political debates, and Jody posted rhyming weather reports. One of the things that we repeatedly came to see and understand is that there are many ways of learning, and what suits one naturally will not necessarily suit another. Bernardo and I would never get the same value from long writing assignments; why should we have the same number of them? Where I would be thrilled with dozens, Bernardo would be overburdened with three. He and his father made a model of the eye for science class and it even blinked! He made more oral reports than I did, and Jody made none at all. Yet all of us learned.

So the month passed, hectic and intense and wonderful; and then it was that last day of school, the day before our long winter break.

I don't know which was most exciting that day– the morning, which began with one gift exchange and continued with us finally getting to perform our puppet play for the kindergarten and first grade, or the short afternoon with its special treats and other gift exchange. You might think that of course the play was more exciting for me; it was, after all my own idea. And it was very, very exciting; but now performing the play meant that it was over. No more wonderful half days and half hours of writing and then rewriting the dialogue; no more intense discussions of plot; no more joy at seeing the newest characters springing to life in the hands of the puppet committee. It was very, very sad.

But Mr. Filamon came to see us right after it was over, and he bubbled over with so much praise and enthusiasm that the pleasure did last all day and into the night as I dreamed of it again. Mrs. Burch glowed with pride in us and could not get over how well it had turned out, although she knew it would, she said. Mrs. Pirette, the ancient kindergarten teacher, had told her it was the first time the whole class had sat still and paid attention.

Then Mrs. Burch went around the room and asked each of us what we liked best about our play and she started with me. "It was your creation, Laura. Were you pleased?" But as I said, it was over. I am sure I must have surprised everyone when I said in a dull voice, "Yes, I guess."

"But was something missing?" she asked me. And yes, one thing was missing.

"I wish we were just beginning. I am sorry we did not make a movie of it," I said, surprising myself. I had not known I was thinking of such a thing.

"And a tape of the music," Brett added. (We did not have video cameras then; we did not have movies with sound in our cameras at home.)

"But you will find a way to remember and to keep your memory alive," Mrs. Burch said. "I have great confidence in your ability to keep finding new ways to keep all your stories alive. I imagine you writing stories and plays and new forms as well, and I think you will always keep finding more and more ways to keep your creations living." And I did feel better, hearing that, and began immediately to think of some ways.

I listened closely to what the others said about their favorite parts and paid attention to what Mrs. Burch said, thinking it would be another way of keeping fifth grade alive. She called on Alvin, who had slipped into a reverie somewhere in the universe. "What?" he asked, still calculating the distance between two new planets he had recently discovered in the galaxy he had been evolving.

"Your favorite part of the play?" she repeated.

"The play? Which play?" He was thinking about the flora and fauna right then, but he was fairly sure he had told no one about the vivid intergalactic drama he was cooking up.

"Our detective play!" Sallee snapped. "You might remember– just this morning; you do know that there was a morning this morning? You were in it. So were the rest of us. We put on a puppet show. THAT play."

"Oh, that," he said. (I was not happy.) "Well, what was the question?" he asked again.

Had he ever cared at all? Was it all so boring that it had been beneath his notice? Couldn't he pretend he remembered something and just say he liked it? I was angry with him.

"The part I liked best? Well, the battle scene of course, especially where .007 takes on the spies, except for the dumb scene at the end where it turned into a kind of Punch and Judy show. I think the code worked quite well, and I especially thought the use of the fake pencil was a perfect touch, but. . . ."

"At last!" Sallee muttered.

". . . the General was a pain." We laughed, and I think I fell in love with Alvin right then.

Mrs. Burch asked Charlene for her favorite part, and modest Charlene– with much blushing and shyness– had to admit that she liked many things but she loved her master spy best. "I guess that sounds pretty conceited," she said.

"No, it doesn't," Sallee said, sticking up for her friend.

"I liked my code the best," Bernardo said; "what's so wrong with that?"

Charlene smiled at him and said that she liked the code too, and the story. She had laughed out loud when Agent .007 got caught in his own trap and the big General sounded so very funny with Sallee's voice, but she could not deny that her much loved Master Spy was her single greatest accomplishment ever.

"You are right to value your spy," Mrs. Burch said in her rustling voice; "she is a masterpiece, and you made her with so much love and attention and care that she would *have* to be your favorite. It takes honesty and strength to share those deep feelings with us, Charlene, and I thank you." Charlene buried her head in her sweater arm, overcome with both embarrassment and pleasure. We could see the words sinking deep inside her to warm her inmost self. When she looked up a moment later, she saw us all smiling at her. She blushed deep red but no one snickered; she hiccoughed and we were truly overjoyed, giggling uncontrollably for quite a long time.

"Well, Mr. Hal," the teacher said at last, "what is your own unbiased professional opinion of our play?"

"Unboring, unboring, unboring, and also very good. I liked it," he critiqued. "I liked Charlene's spy's shoe the best, but everything was fine. And I do like Punch and Judy shows," he added, turning to Alvin, who was designing a massive new generator for his planets but who managed to hear Hal and to reply that real spies do not bop each other over the head with eye patches, much less sequined ones.

"Maybe they should," Janice suggested. "I liked that no one could really get hurt."

"And you, Amy?" Mrs. Burch said. Who would answer? We all looked quickly for any clue but found none. Amy Patterson said that she liked one of our mistakes best.

"Was she right?" Bobby asked.

"What do you mean?" Mrs. Burch asked him, not knowing how Amy could have been wrong about what she liked.

"Was Amy Patterson the one you called on?" he asked.

"Of course," she said, looking puzzled. "I'm sorry for the interruption, Amy. Please go on." Amy started again to explain her favorite part, but. . .

"How do they know?" Robert asked.

"Amy has the floor, Robert," the teacher reminded him.

"Please, puh-leeze, tell us the secret," Sallee begged.

"Class, I am terribly sorry to have to be harsh, but really this interrupting is not all right. There are times for questions and times for answers and times for telling your favorite part of a play. This is Amy's time to do that."

"And then will you tell us?" Robert pursued.

"Please think about what I just said," she insisted. "Amy, please continue."

And while Amy went on to inform us that we had accidentally given the same number to two of the soldier puppets and that she found that very realistic, some of us smarted briefly under the closest thing to an actual scolding we had received from our gentle teacher. Only later did I realize that she also had never answered the question.

Bobby almost got her. When Amy finished, Susan pointed out that it was a funny coincidence that one of the Amys would notice that detail but Tom doubted that that meant anything and coincidences were meaningless anyway. Bobby was about to raise his hand and ask again; but deftly she pulled us into her confidence to share her feelings about coincidences.

Without any of us moving, she managed to make us feel as if we had all nestled about her, that she had her arms around each one of us. "You know," she said in a soft dreamy voice, "I don't think I really believe in meaningless coincidence." We looked at her, not knowing what she meant. "I think there are no mistakes about the things we notice." Bobby beamed at the thought of no mistakes.

"I don't mean we don't make errors ever," she said, and his face clouded; "but I mean that what we see and learn are the things we are supposed to see and learn. And clearly the things that we ourselves have experienced have the most meaning for us. Amy, you could spot that repeated number, just like a repeated name, because you have to deal with that experience every day."

"So do I," said Amy Sanderson, "but I did not see it." Neither did Amy Betts.

"It doesn't always mean the same thing to you and Amy," she said; "you will be distracted by your many other interests, but I have noticed that both of you are often aware of things that seem the same but are not."

"My mother says I am too sensitive about that," Amy Patterson said.

"Mine thinks I should be more sensitive," Amy Betts whispered.

"What I like," the teacher said to all of us, "is that you each make these connections. True learning comes when you connect your own real experiences and make sense of them for yourself."

Bobby, whose hand was still up, forgot what he was going to ask, so that when Mrs. Burch called on him, he looked surprised but then in a spark of unusual quickness asked her, "Uh, what was *your* favorite part of the play?" Normally he would have just gone silent, and that little observation of change is not what I would have always noticed either.

Our teacher thought carefully for a moment, just as she wished us to do, and answered slowly, "My favorite part was and is and will always be the love and enthusiasm and spirit of yourselves that you brought to this project. I love HOW you did it."

"The best part for me," Janice said, "is just that we got to do it at all."

TAP-TAP TAP went one little hand, starting a code, and TAP TAP-TAP the class continued, making our decimal code linger on, and Mrs. Burch beamed at all of us and simply said, "You are welcome."


*Jody*


That day was like no other, and it started off in a special way. We arrived at Bell School that morning, not to the sound of the loud clanging bell but to the wafting chimes of the Bell Ringers, a group of students who met after school and now were performing just inside the front doors. We arrived with our lunch bags and mittens and boots and with two merrily wrapped packages, one for a friend and one for our teacher. The first thing we got to do, to start the wondrous festivities, was to exchange gifts among ourselves, each of us having drawn the name of a classmate a couple of weeks earlier. I had drawn Bernardo's. We wanted Mrs. Burch to open hers too, but she insisted on waiting. There was so much to do, she said, that she would open hers if we had time at the end of the day. She knew she would like everything and hoped we would not mind letting that be postponed.

It had begun to snow that morning, lightly at first and then more heavily so that by the time we had finished our shortened music class and our treat of a spelling bee instead of sentences and had come back to our room, the fields outside were solidly white. The tree outside our window had delicate ridges of snow on its branches, and each little twig was encased already in ice. It made our room seem cozier than ever, though we left it to give our puppet play. I leave that part of our story in Laura's hands and concentrate on what happened after lunch.

Brett left the room, but we were used to that. We talked for a while about the puppet play, which we all agreed was a great success. Even Julieanne looked pleased and excited, not strained or nervous at all. Holly kept looking over at Julieanne and smiling, and I wondered to myself if they were going to go back to being best friends. I knew that Holly had been unhappy with the loss of Julieanne's friendship, and I hoped they could go back to the way it was. I wondered, too, if I could ever go back to the way things had been.

Somehow Mrs. Burch got to talking about no such thing as a meaningless coincidence, and I thought about that a lot. There was her name and the way she had come to us; there was her hair as curly and yellow as the leaves on the autumn trees, the paleness of her skin like birch bark. There was her seeming to know each one of us, except really she did not know us all. Then too, for me, there were the other things– the leaf on the floor and the exchange of notes and poems as if we both had written them for both. And there she was, telling all of us that all of these things meant something, and I had to wonder if she was speaking directly to me. I believed she was, that however much the others may have needed to hear that same message too, it was for me. I felt again, in words I did not then quite have, that she was the exact embodiment of what I admired. She was herself; there was no one else like her. She was kind, gentle, tender. She loved us all without reserve or conditions. She did not fight us; she did not try to diminish us. She seemed to me to be a gift from a vast and loving source that permitted itself to hear us, including me, through whatever voice we possessed openly or hidden. She was my proof of wondrous miracles– and not mine alone.

And as I sat there thinking some smaller conception of what I now can express a bit better, a harsh and disorienting loud bell rang, jolting us all from our dream.

"Not a fire drill!" Sallee almost screamed. "Why would they do that today?" Mrs. Burch smiled and shook her head.

"Aren't we going to have our party?" Holly asked, disappointed.

"No, don't worry," Mrs. Burch assured us; "we will have time. That is just the signal for a special assembly, so put your scraps of paper in the wastebasket and off we'll go to the gym."

Laura will do a better job of telling you about the assembly.

*Laura*

I was going to retell the story just as I wrote it back then, but something came in the mail about a week ago that I think I would rather use.

*Mr. Filamon*

Dear Laura,

You wrote to me a few months ago, asking if I might possibly remember your class and the events that took place just before the start of Christmas break that year. You were kind enough to ask, assuming I did remember, if I would contribute my memories to the book you were proposing to write. There is no doubt, of course, that I remember that occasion, not only for its haunting results but also for the simple reason that I have told and retold its events through these many intervening years to my children and grandchildren. None of us has ever really understood all that happened, but no one has tired of hearing. I am sorry that it has taken me until now to be able to feel more comfortable in knowing what I could say to strangers; but in the final analysis I have decided to contribute my own account of the Christmas assembly, along with a few other notes and comments that you may use as you see fit.

Having enjoyed your stories all through the years, along with the works of many of your fellow Bell students, I have decided to follow your lead and cast my memories in the form of a story. Forgive me if my style is old-fashioned.

## The Assembly

Once upon a time there was a small school in a little village deep in the heart of the country. What it lacked in wealth of supplies and equipment, it made up for in the depth of its students. The school was run by a very young man who thought he knew good teachers when he saw them.

One day, in the midst of a very great need and without the young man's having had time to advertise, a young woman arrived at his office. She told him that she needed a job quite desperately, that she needed to help her father. The young man talked with her for a while and knew that she was exactly the right person for the job; he hired her immediately. Her class thrived, and everyone was happy. The young man felt pleased with himself and with all.

One day, just before Christmas, the teacher came to him and said that her father needed her to come home and asked could the young man find a replacement for an indefinite time. She was very sad and so was he, and they knew the children would be devastated. They both worried about this quite a bit and they pondered how to tell the class, but they did not come to an immediate decision. I should say that the man did not come to a decision; the woman just knew what she had to do. The principal was sure that he could never find any comparable replacement for her and hoped that she would be gone no more than a week. She gently said that that was a possibility, but she encouraged him to act as if she would not be back. That day there was to be a special assembly, and the teacher agreed that she would most certainly stay till school was out at three. Beyond that, she had no control of her time.

In the gym that afternoon, the whole school gathered and the excitement built. The youngest children sat in front on the floor and were clearly on their best behavior, at least in the first several minutes. The rest of the children sat behind them, in rows according to grade. The oldest had been to so many special assemblies that their behavior was not of the best, but on this day there was too much happiness to make much of a point of the extra noise. Still, some sense of discipline had to be maintained, and many of the teachers were wearing their whistles. Mr. Prendell, the sixth grade teacher, and Mr. Rynne of the fifth were in charge of the unruliest ones since both had served in the army.

All of the participants stood out in the hall, bouncing and jumping up and down, nervous and eager to begin. A few of the girls had on too much lipstick and some of the boys kept trying to peek into the gym. Mrs. Esquinoth was in charge of the assembly, and she was the most nervous of all. Anxiously she scurried from group to group to quiet them, but her voice got shriller and shriller. She tried to wipe some of the lipstick away but only managed to smear it. She ordered the boys back to their places, but they soon were back at the door. The young principal noticed all this, but he was busy with tasks of his own and was worried about the public address system (with good reason).

Nevertheless, at one-thirty exactly, he walked through the little knot of boys and went into the gym, acknowledged the scattered applause and ignored the low hum among the sixth graders. He cleared his throat and tapped on the microphone, but nothing happened. He tapped again and a shrill whistle, more of a screech, filled the air and everyone made terrible faces and laughed. Finally the microphone worked, thanks to the head custodian, and the principal was able to introduce Dr. Charles, the visiting Superintendent of Schools, who always appeared at the special assembly and who always got to leave immediately. Rank has its privileges, although it sometimes misses out on a good story later.

Dr. Charles was a dignified man, a tall man with white hair and heavy glasses, a man used to being listened to with respect except on this special occasion when he was listened to by kindergartners falling asleep and sixth graders making their occasional rude comments and was sharply interrupted a couple of times by the sudden blast on a whistle. Two dazed young first graders, in a drooling trance there almost under the nose of the speaker, further distracted our leader, who was starting his speech about how gifted our students were. Some of the older faculty smiled and some laughed, but a few were busy teaching correct assembly behavior. From the viewpoint of the young principal, no one right then looked gifted.

Of course the P.A. system went berserk, irritably buzzing and humming at inappropriate times, drowning out the speaker; but that is what happens at school assemblies, and that is mostly what we happen to remember. But this year the assembly was indeed quite special, and so I remember more.

Dr. Charles made his hasty escape in time to avoid being trampled by the first act in the assembly, the Parade of Pictures, which consisted of large murals being carried in by representatives of the classes that had created them. Mrs. Esquinoth took the microphone fearfully and began to try to announce titles and names. I think that the first mural was called *Winter's Little Creatures Eat*, but I no longer remember who carried it in. I have a vague memory of squirrels that looked like brown baseballs with footballs for tails, surrounded by red splotches for cardinals, gray things with pink spikes to suggest bunnies, and hundreds of spots to commemorate seeds and acorns. There was much applause from the second graders and an unfortunate catcall from the back of the gym. Mrs. Esquinoth, showing much quickness, announced that cats were not one of winter's usual little creatures and requested Mr. Rynne to look into the matter. She then tried to look into her wrinkled program notes but dropped her glasses and became quite pinkly flustered. I must relate that this incident did nothing to reduce the number of little creatures in the audience. Mrs. Esquinoth scowled quite ferociously, but two more murals marched past her and she got hopelessly behind. There were generous bursts of applause.

To the young principal these things were distressing, and yet they were also amusing to some special part of him. His professional self could not approve, but the man and boy in him could not punish. In general he was and is a happy man.

A few more anonymous murals traipsed past, while flustered

Mrs. Esquinoth adjusted her glasses again and the always perverse microphones, tired of waiting for her, shrilled out strange names of their own. The audience was restive.

While the custodian ran for the spare microphone, a group of tap dancers came out to perform. No amplifying was needed for that, and the staff breathed a sigh of relief, except for those few who were whispering furiously to one or another of their talkative children or the others who were dozing a bit. We never learned the identity of the dancers, nor did we fare better with the second microphone. TAP-TAP, the custodian experimented, and a boy's voice from the fifth grade section called out, "YOU'RE WELCOME."

Elizabeth Newton recited a poem, or so we were told; and a fourth grade trio presented a tableau. No one guessed what it was supposed to be. The finest musician ever to come out of Bell School, already a sterling young composer, sedately performed with several younger children and accompanied them as they sang a medley of his work. There was much cheering for this act, although Mrs. Esquinoth had wanted it to be last. Instead the finale was the sixth grade chorus, which sang lustily and loudly for fifteen minutes and continued their fifth encore while the audience exited. They were musically accompanied all the way to their rooms by the gradually dimming song of Bell's new School Anthem, also composed by Brett.

It was an unforgettable day in the life of that young man, the principal, and he has been pleased to send you this report.

### Jody

The assembly was over by two-thirty and we hurried back to our room. We wanted Mrs. Burch to have time to open her gifts, and we wanted the day to end with her, not with silly Mrs. Esquinoth. First, though, we had to cheer Brett and to let him know that of course we had not suspected him all along of cutting classes, of course we had not thought he was in some kind of detention, of course we would never think he had been caught doing something so terrible that he had to spend an hour a week down in the boiler room. And of course we did NOT think those things, but really we had had no idea that he had been preparing for the special assembly since October. We swarmed around him and told him how much like a penguin he looked in his tux, how wonderful his anthem was, how lucky he was that the P.A. system had not buzzed throughout his own performance, and again how silly he looked. Mrs. Burch beamed at him, and he made a formal bow to all of us. In fact, he looked quite spectacular in his tuxedo. He was the only boy I ever knew who had one.

Outside, the snow had piled up still higher and the windows were frosted in silver. The tree was out there, dimly, and it seemed quite far away. Under the radiators that hissed now and then, a tiny yellow leaf, barely visible, had found a warm place to rest. It worried me.

"Open the gifts, please; open the gifts," a dozen voices clamored. But Mrs. Burch looked at us all and said she did not know what to do. "Why not?" Janice asked.

"Well," the husky voice explained, "what if there are some gifts here not meant to be public? What if some are secrets?"

"Why would any gift need to be secret?" Sallee asked, still thinking that secrets implied wrongdoing.

"That's easy," Janice said, ignoring Sallee. "Let us each hold the gift we brought, and those who want you to open them will give them to you. If someone wants to keep a secret, he or she can give you that gift afterwards." For once, Mrs. Burch did not ask us to think about that or to write about it; she just smiled happily and said it was a wonderful idea. And that is what we did.

With our package in our hands, we gathered around her there on the floor, in the clear space up near her desk. "How shall we do this?" she asked, pulling us all in closer.

"Take a number," Bernardo said, tapping on the floor with his shoe.

"A decimal number?" Hal asked him. "I have another code."

"Bless you," Brett said.

"We won't mind what order," Holly said, worrying that the time would evaporate and nothing would get done. Almost all of us agreed.

"Yes, we will," Bernardo said, handing her his package. "Mine first." She opened the long rectangular lump in paper that promised nothing too wonderful, and yet inside was a plaque of wood, beautifully sanded and stained, carefully and lovingly made. Burned precisely into its surface was M R S. B I R C H, spelled out in decimal code. No one, especially not our kind teacher, would comment on the way he had spelled her name. It was ready for hanging anywhere, but she placed it tenderly on her desk.

"Part of me wants to open these all at once," she said, "and part of me wants this time to last forever."

"Can't be done," Tom said sadly.

"Have to compromise," Sallee agreed.

Bobby thrust a small box into the teacher's lap, saying, "Next." It held a smaller box, and the class groaned, but there were only two more littler boxes and then Mrs. Burch removed from its cushion of shredded paper a tiny rock. "See, there is a fossil in it," he said eagerly, pointing to a nearly invisible set of marks.

"And you saw that!" she marveled. "You found it when it could have been missed so easily."

"It was just down there in the creek," he said, suddenly a little embarrassed. "I didn't make it or buy it. It was just there." He looked and sounded apologetic.

"You found it and it is special," she said to him, giving it a place of honor by turning an empty flowerpot upside down to be a pedestal on her desk.

Holly had made a white loop potholder with a green loop handle. "I wanted to make a tree design," she sighed, "but I don't see how to do it."

"Paint or dye," Charlene said quietly. "Loops won't work."

"Not a single mistake!" Mrs. Burch said, setting it carefully inside its wrappings and placing it on that desk.

"Why did Charlene say 'paint or die'?" Bobby asked. Alvin took charge of that.

Laura gave a very long story complete with illustrations and a portrait and biographical sketch of the author. She would not let us hear the dedication.

Julieanne had made a set of candles, green and yellow. When Sallee objected that they were not Christmas colors, Julieanne turned a little pink. "The color of leaves," Mrs. Burch happily noticed, and the giver smiled again. She had included one candle holder, and Mrs. Burch found matches in the science cabinet and lit one yellow one. Brett turned out the overhead lights, and we continued in the smaller and cozier glow of that candle to hold on to that tremendous half hour.

There was an assortment of usual gifts— monogrammed handkerchiefs, a box of stationery with trees, two identical ornaments, a pin in the shape of a little heart, another that looked like an elf. There was an amazing puppet that looked just like Mrs. Burch, except that it wore a crown. A geode from Alvin, original audio tapes from Brett, a book of puzzles from Janice that measured an incredible one inch by one inch. "Is this to make me a *little* more logical?" the teacher asked.

"You are very logical," Janice solemnly said. "I just got it because I liked it."

"A lovely reason," Mrs. Burch sighed. "All of you are so very thoughtful."

We could tell that she meant it, that she could see in all of these gifts that we were expressing ourselves and were keeping our connections with her and with each other alive. Over and over through all these years, I have remembered that day and those gifts. They seemed to be saying, *Remember us, please. Remember us now and forever, as we will remember you.*

I did not give her the envelope in my hand right then, though Bobby asked me if I was going to. I just nodded yes but held onto it a while longer. We all snuggled in even closer, gathering like a crowd of waxwings struggling to sit in the very same tree. We chirped and begged to learn more about her and her family, more about who she really was when she was not with us.

> *What nests in the branches?*
> *Who tends the tree?*
> *What swirls all the leaves to the forest floor?*
> *What does the rain bring?*
> *How feels the snow?*
> *Tell us more, tell us more, tell us more.*

Really, we wanted to know that she existed only for us, and now I think that is true.

She sat taller, even there on the floor, and she seemed to hug us all. She got a faraway look in her eyes as she said, "My children are scattered far and wide." I cannot tell you exactly what those words did to me, but I burst into tears for the first time in a very long time and I cried and cried and cried. Everyone looked at me strangely, and Mrs. Burch was startled too. But I handed her my envelope then, right in front of everyone, and she opened it and read the first few lines. She read them out loud and I did not even care.

> *Her children are scattered far and wide;*

She paused to look at me with her clear, kind eyes, and then continued.

> *they hide, they hide*
> *in the earth,*
> *until some day in the bird-bright Spring,*
> *up they will spring*
> *from the Earth.*

The class sat silent and Mrs. Burch sat silent. Then she gave me a warm enfolding hug and I believe I heard through my sobbing, a softly whispered, "You *know.*" And finally I think that I did.

## Laura

It must have been one of those meaningful coincidences right there near the end. We were shocked when silent Jody suddenly cried, but that shock was replaced when Mrs. Burch read Jody's poem. The words would have meant nothing to us, but they were the identical words that Mrs. Burch had used; and we did not know who was more magical. It just seemed extraordinarily spooky, and Julieanne started crying too. But the bell rang and the spell broke, and somehow or other we were all in our coats and our boots and our mittens, carrying two packages each– one the gift from our classmate and the other a yellow envelope from Mrs. Burch. Our names had been ornately printed on each, and there was a sticker of a birch tree in the corner with the date in small letters below.

I walked home with Holly and Susan, but none of us said one word. We saw all the Amys and Sallee and Charlene; we saw Janice get on the bus. We watched all the boys slowly trudging home through the snow, but we heard no one saying one word. We scarcely noticed the children not in our class. We did not see Julieanne or Jody.

When I got home, I went straight to my room and got out my favorite pen and a large blank notebook and curled up to write; but it took a long time for any words to form. I went to get a cup of hot chocolate and a stack of graham crackers and returned to my room, but still no words made sense. I took a nap and when I woke up, I began to write it all down. Then I did something I almost never do: I threw it away! Me! I could not write it well enough, and so I threw it away.

It may sound odd to you, as it does to me now, but it never occurred to me that afternoon to see what was in the yellow envelope. I think too much had happened, so it was another day before I read my gift.


## Jody

I have never known such simultaneous happiness and misery. The bond that existed between Mrs. Burch and me was overwhelming. I can think of no word better than *glowsome*, which is how it made me feel. Yet, the certainty was within me now that she was leaving. I did not know when or why exactly; I did not know if we would see her again. But sooner or later, now or tomorrow or in a week or ten days, but surely sometime quite soon, she would leave us; and we would be on our own again. Not literally on our own– I knew there would be another teacher to take her place; but she had come– I was confident of it– to heal us from the scars and severe batterings of Ms Skimme, and she had done her job. We could stand on our own again. When we are granted our miracles, we must take them for however long they are given to us. We will not have them longer, and we are asked to accept that fact with a certain simple grace. It is very hard.

At three o'clock that afternoon, I was not quite ready to accept good-bye. I hesitated outside the classroom door and watched like some little puppet spy as Mrs. Burch put on her white coat, wrapped her yellow scarf snugly around her neck, touched with a lingering gentleness all the gifts we had brought but left them there on the desk. I ran outside quickly, to watch from a farther place. Julieanne was out there too, and we stood together near the old brown oak to wait and wave good-bye. Mrs. Burch did not appear. Her car, the shiny gray one down in the last space on the parking lot, stood there with six inches of snow on top. "Perhaps," Julieanne whispered to me, "she is looking for something to use to clean off her car."

Sadly I whispered, "Maybe." She looked at me with a smile of surprise, a small smile it is true but a very happy smile nevertheless, and a tear ran down her cheek. "But I don't think so," I added.

Suddenly I knew exactly where to look, and I quickly grabbed Julieanne by the mitten and started to run around the school to the patio. Just as we reached the corner, the first spot where we could clearly see the birch tree and our teacher standing beside it, Julieanne gasped and started to run away; but I managed to get her to come back. "Stay with me," I urged her.

Slowly we crept a little closer, afraid to go too close but also afraid to stay too far away. It started to snow again, and we could feel the large flakes falling all upon us and feel the magic hanging in the air. The clouds were thick and gray and pouring white down on us; and on the patio, every dried or soggy leaf that once had been on the birch tree fluttered up and attached itself, and the tree was clothed in green. We stood absolutely frozen in that warmest snow and could not move a muscle or speak a single word. We watched as Mrs. Burch removed her snow white coat and draped her scarf like one large leaf along the fifth grade window ledge. And then she stepped into the tree and disappeared.

Yes, it is the fact. She stepped into the tree and she simply disappeared!

The leaves so green and springlike seemed to welcome her bright spirit; they danced and whirled in a joyous mood and then they all turned yellow. Soberly then the tree stood there, while the air still crackled around us; and one by one those yellow leaves turned brown and slowly fell to the ground. The tree stood bare and wintry, and the snow still fell; but every single thing seemed as it had recently been, except for us: Julieanne and me. We stood in shock with the current running through our hearts and veins but with only numbness in our minds and legs. We could not take it in.

It grew dark at last, then darker, and the tree stood there like a tree. The two of us were coated with snow, but what could we do and where could we go? It was Holly who came and found us there, and the three of us walked home, silent sisters in bleak communion now, each in our separate directions. Like a penknife, a jackknife, a dagger, the cold wind blew through my coat and heart, and I felt scarred all over. But at home all was ordinary, and no one asked me where I had been or if anything was wrong, and I was glad of that.

### *"Julieanne" ~ from her diary*

Do not ask me, Diary, what happened yesterday. I do not know. Was it a terrible dream? It must have been a dream because in it Jody talked to me again. We were in this scene together and so was Mrs. Burch, but none of it makes any sense, so it must have been a dream. I must have come home from school and fallen asleep and dreamed those weird things. That is the only explanation. I wonder why I am so cold. Maybe I am getting sick and have chills and fever. That is the only explanation.

It seemed so real.

Tomorrow is Christmas Day, but that does not seem real. Holly is coming over this afternoon, and we will exchange presents if I am not so sick. I am so tired. I must be sick. That is the explanation. I think I will get back under the covers now, Diary. All I want to do is sleep.

### *Jody*

The next day I went back to the patio to see if the tree was still there. I was surprised, I guess, that it was. The scarf that had been placed near the window was gone, probably blown away; and yet it already seemed as if Mrs. Burch had never happened at all. It had been a glorious dream of ours, a mass hallucination perhaps, because people do not walk into your life and then disappear into trees. They may walk in and out of your life, but they don't disappear into trees. Mrs. Burch did. The more distant and unreal she seemed, the less I could really deny her. I kept wondering what was going on in the heart and mind of Julieanne.

Also I wondered what she had told Holly, so I decided to walk to Holly's house and see if I could find out. I am sure you can guess how surprised she was to see me, let alone to have me ask her what Julieanne had told her.

"Nothing," Holly said, after she got used to the fact that I was talking again. "She was quiet until we got to my house and she had to go on alone. She started to cry then, so I walked her home. I don't know what happened. What did?"

How do you describe what had happened? I was almost sorry I had spoken at all, for now there was no returning to silence myself. I said it was going to sound crazy, that I would understand if she did not believe me. I said that Julieanne would be able to tell her, though, that it was true, that we had witnessed something totally unbelievable together. Holly looked curious but blank. Then I told her what we had seen, and she just stared in my face. Long, long, long she stared at me and I stared at my mittened hands and at the ground and then looked again at Holly.

"Are you saying she left us?" she finally asked. I nodded. "And is never coming back?" I shrugged, not knowing. "Into the tree?" she thought to ask again, that fact slowly sinking in. I confirmed it. "Why?" she asked. I had no answer for her. "You are sitting here telling me that Mrs. Burch took off her coat in the middle of a heavy snowstorm and became a tree. . . ?"

"It sounds even weirder when you put it that way," I said, "but that is what happened."

"Does that make any sense?"

"No, I told you it was crazy." And as we sat there, working this through our minds, trying to bring some kind of order back into our small world, I realized that there is no way to make a miracle sound sane. A miracle takes us outside our world and turns it upside down and inside out and hurls us into chaos before it settles itself to rights and gives itself and us a shake and all too quickly "normal" seeps back in. Perhaps that is the worst of it all, that life too surely returns to normal and we are left to try the impossible, explaining to others what is beyond our power to convey. How can it help but sound plain crazy?

"I am going to Julieanne's this afternoon," Holly said. "I wonder if she will say anything."

"You can ask," I said hopefully. "It might not hurt to ask."

"She isn't the same as she was," Holly said sadly. "She never got over what happened to Ms Skimme."

"Oh!" I said, "what does she think happened to her?"

"She thinks we killed her," Holly whispered.

If I could make a single wish and know it would come true, I would wish that parents everywhere could know their children's true hearts– not that they could hear all their secrets and know all their acts but that they could truly understand their children's realities. Parents ought to be healing agents of Life, not mere mortals at all. If I were Julieanne's mother, I would want to let my child know that her change was a prayer for help, and all of us are entitled to that. And more, I would tell my child how happy I was that she could count on me and how much I do admire her for knowing so and trusting where to look.

Perhaps that is not what Julieanne needed to hear, and I am not her mother and, more than many, I know the appeal of silence. So I say again what I strongly believe, that it is our parents who should sense our inward truths and should strive to make us whole; but who am I not to realize that it isn't always their fault that they fail? Sometimes as children we cannot speak to let them know our needs, and sometimes our painful encounters with the world bury us far too deep. Then more than ever we need our miracles; and we should not punish ourselves for accepting them, nor should we be punished by others.


*Laura*


You may well imagine that the first day back at school in January was going to shock us all. It arrived to our totally unsuspecting souls, clouded and gray and miserably cold; but that was no clue to most of us. I was eager to get back, eager to see what new special projects would enliven our days, and I was not the only one to get there long before the bell. When I got to the front door, three separate and mute and heavily wrapped packages stood in a silent cluster. Three hooded and shivering sisters of the dark, each looking down at the ground, Holly and Julieanne and Jody stood, waiting for the door to open. "Hi!" I shouted when I saw who they were. I was happy to see them. No answer. "What's up?" I asked. Holly mutely shrugged but did not even smile.

Mr. Filamon came to the door to ask why we were there so early. "You girls will freeze out here," he said; "you know you aren't supposed to come in before eight-thirty. I can't let you wait in this cold for forty-five minutes!"

"I couldn't wait to get back!" I said, excitedly. Holly softly mumbled something too.

"Well," he said, thoughtful as always, "I suppose I can find things for you to do."

"We aren't having a substitute today, are we?" Holly asked,

unable (I realize now) to stand any suspense.

"Why do you ask that?" he said, looking surprised.

"We are, aren't we?" Jody asked, and he looked more than surprised and somewhat disturbed. I had no idea what was going on and said so. Everyone looked uncomfortable.

"I don't think anything is 'going on'," he said, trying to make nothing of it all and busily sorting out tasks. "Here is a list of lights to be turned on along the main hall," he said softly, handing me a printed diagram and a sheet of paper with numbers on it. "Do you think you would like to have that job?" It seems ironic now that he would ask me to turn the lights on. I was the one most in the dark, and was I able to turn any light on? He should have given that job to Jody, but I think he was so astonished that she had spoken that he wanted to keep her nearby for a while in case she had more to say. I suppose it was even more ironic that I had to use a numerical code.


## Mr. Filamon

You asked also, if I could remember that first day back at school in January. I recall that four of you were so eager to get back to your beloved teacher that you arrived while it was still dark out and I had to let you in very early. I remember being surprised, not only by the very different moods you all were in, but by one especially amazing event. Jody, our silent Jody, seemed to be back to her former self. She asked me a question– I don't remember what– and I thought to myself, "What a miracle Mrs. Burch has performed!" Perhaps I was doing Jody an injustice but that is what I thought, and I could not keep from hanging on to the thin hope that your teacher would find a way to come back much sooner than she had anticipated. I had not yet found a substitute to offer a long-term job, but really I did not want to. I did want her to return.

I think I found things for all of you to do, but then I had many responsibilities of my own. There were messages to put in teachers' mailboxes, lists of announcements to make, daily schedules to revise, and last-minute requests for substitutes to honor. I went into my inner office and got on the phone, while out in the main office you all worked pretty quietly except that occasionally I could hear one or another of you, and I marveled each time I heard Jody. I wondered if anyone knew just what might account for the previous two years and what now had accounted for this change. I did not have a long time to spend thinking, though, and got busy making phone calls first. It may come as a surprise to you to know that I never did know personal histories.

We simply didn't get involved in those days.

When Mrs. George arrived, I could hear her surprise at seeing helpers already there. She looked in on me and raised her eyebrows, asking an implicit question. "It's all right," I mouthed to her; "they need to be busy." She did not mind of course and immediately set you all to sorting out welcome-back letters, counting out enough for each classroom. I heard Holly ask if Mrs. Burch was coming back, and my secretary said, "Why wouldn't she?" I had never told her about Mrs. Burch's conversation with me, the one that I have already described.

I left the office to make sure the heat was working, double-checking radiators in every room; and by the time I finished, it was almost time for the first bell. I got on my overcoat and gloves and went out to meet the first bus and to triple-check the sidewalk for slippery spots that might have been missed. Our custodian was just reentering the building with his shovel and a wheelbarrow of salt and ashes, and all seemed well.

The buses were running late, so I hurried inside to get warm a little and gulp down a swallow of coffee. You all were watering plants in the office, and Mrs. George was talking to Jody, who was answering. I believe Mrs. George was in a state of shock, but she acted as if Jody spoke to her all the time. More and more teachers arrived, but I did not see any new faces. I wondered what Mrs. Burch's temporary sub was going to be like; he was new on the list and I had never met him.

Children were lining up at the door and I had a call from the bus company that they could not get any of the four buses started. I called the PTA officers to start our phone tree going. Now children would be straggling in all day, and the strain would tell on all of us.

I remember a couple of hundred smoky white puffs that greeted me when I opened the doors. All of the children were jumping and chattering, and each word they said sent out a new little puff of vapor. I had the amusing illusion that all the native tribes in the west had descended on me and were storming my gates with smoke signals. Promptly at eight-thirty I opened the door and was engulfed in a frosty mass of children, eager to gain the warmth of Bell School or at least the warmth of the front hall. I tripped over a six-year-old body mittened and scarfed and coated-over-sweatered and booted, to boot, and totally unable to rise. Puddles of water were everywhere, all over the well-waxed floor.

"Move along," I said foolishly.

"Can't," came the faraway voice. I looked around and I scratched my head and peered down into the hood.

"Who are you?" I asked, unable to recognize anyone under all that wrapping. He was Joey, one of the first-graders, and I offered to give him a push. "Want a push?"

"Lots of them," he said, giggling. I picked up this rotund red bundle and set him down in a relatively dry spot, then pushed and guided him in an intricate line around the other more movable bundles stalled voluntarily there in the front hall. At the door to his classroom I left him. "Thanks," he called out. (Perhaps it is strange that I still remember these details, but they are clearer to me than yesterday. You will, I fear, discover this vagary of memory yourself.)

Most of the morning, most of the day, was just as it began. All order and serenity were thrown over; we simply had to survive. At ten-thirty that morning, I found my way to room 5B, but no substitute had arrived.

## Jody

That first day back was strange. Order and serenity were overthrown, and we simply had to survive. (I had written that sentence long before I ever saw Mr. Filamon's letter to Laura, and I almost took it out. But our inner networks are so much wider than most of us ever know, and I was both shocked and thrilled to see that little-known connection. It is one more lesson in my life.)

All morning long our classmates tramped in, so that it was almost lunch time before we were a full class. For me, it was a day of trembling anticipation; but no new substitute arrived, and some were getting frantic. "What could possibly have happened to Mrs. Burch?" they asked, but who would tell them? Holly would hardly claim to know first-hand; Julieanne was silent, and so was I. Tensely we sat at our desks, drawing or doodling or talking, while the others waited restlessly and constantly looked at the clock and out the door.

Mr. Rynne came in often to give us assignments and to tell us to be quiet, even though we were not being noisy. We looked at the list of dull words that he put on the board for us to define and use in sentences: *quandary, inconsequential, definitive, prosaic, impersonal, determine, factor, scoff, felon,* and *detrimental.* Those were the words he gave us. How did they apply to us? We might have been in a real quandary, but nothing was prosaic; nothing could be even somewhat inconsequential. His assignment was impersonal, and we were inclined to scoff at it. Nevertheless, we dragged out our dictionaries and our tablets and pencils and sluggishly tried to work.

"Why don't we all do them together?" Amy Patterson suggested. We looked at each other and grinned. Why not?

"I'll look them up," Susan offered.

"All of us can make up sentences and we'll pick one," Laura

suggested.

"The one that fits us the best," said Amy Betts.

"Who will write them?" Bernardo asked.

"All of us," Sallee said firmly. "We all will turn them in."
We were so pleased with ourselves that we ignored her tone, and I
happened to look out the window where it seemed to me that the birch
tree was not quite standing in its usual spot but was closer and leaning
in. It was as if it were listening to us, and its twigs seemed to smile.

That was the morning that I learned that one can make any
word one's own.


### Laura

I am looking at all of our sentences. I wrote them down and
kept them and have them here before me, as well as the names of their
authors. We took those insignificant words and made them our own:
quandary, inconsequential, definitive, prosaic, impersonal, determine,
factor, scoff, felon, and detrimental.

Quandary: puzzle, predicament
> If Mrs. Burch does not come soon, we will be in a real
> quandary. (Laura)

Inconsequential: of no importance
> No talent is inconsequential. (Brett)

Definitive: conclusive, convincing, precise
> The dictionary is the definitive book of word meanings.
> (Janice)
> So far, there is no definitive answer to the question, "Is there
> intergalactic warfare?" (Alvin)

Prosaic: ordinary, commonplace
> The last few months of school have not been prosaic. (Hal)

Impersonal: detached, impersonal, cold
> We all know what it is like to have an impersonal teacher.
> (Holly)

Determine: to fix upon, to decide
> Today I did determine we would do our sentences together.
> (Sallee.)
> Who can determine what is a dream and what is a nightmare?
> (Julieanne)

Factor: cause, agent
> We wonder if the weather is a factor in Mrs. Burch's absence.
> (Janice)
> Our play contained a master factor. (Charlene)

*Scoff:* to jeer at, to ridicule
> *Mrs. Burch never did scoff me. (Bobby)*
> *We wouldn't scoff you, Bobby. (Robert)*
> *Never scoff at others' fears. (Julieanne)*

*Felon:* criminal, wrongdoer
> *Sooner or later, a felon will be punished. (Julieanne)*

*Detrimental:* harmful
> *I doubt that anything will be more detrimental to us than having another substitute. (Thomas)*

As we wrote our sentences and made our selections, we formed another bond. Cooperating on assignments like this could be fun, although I certainly would not want to write too many stories this way. I looked often at Jody, wondering if she would contribute out loud, but she did not. I kept feeling at any moment she might, but she stared out the window and chewed on her pencil and now and then smiled at nothing visible.

I think I am glad that I knew nothing then, for the morning would have been unbearable. I was protected by the same quiet childlike faith that sustained most of us, that our teacher was simply delayed– at worst had the flu– and soon would be among us. Had I been in on the terrible secret, I am sure I would have blurted it out. That would have been all wrong. As it was, two of the three who knew a little more, were skilled at keeping secrets; and Holly was never quick to speak. She waited until she had to.

## Jody

I heard all the definitions and sentences and wrote them on my tablet; but my eyes kept going to the birch tree, which I swear moved closer and closer. Was I the only one who could see that it now was pressed hard to the window? As if it had ears to strain toward us and hands to cup those ears, the tree seemed anxious to join us and to share our strange transitional moments. It seemed to straighten a little each time that Mr. Rynne entered, but then it would bend in closer again and the twigs would crinkle in pleasure. Part of me thought I was making it up, and part of me knew I was not. No matter if anyone else paid attention, that tree was right in the window. I wondered what Julianne was thinking, but I could not tell.

Every so often, the wind picked up and we could hear its soft scraping moan. The branches tapped a delicate code, but no one else seemed to notice. *I am here, I am here*, the tree tapped in code. "I know," I whispered. "I know."

By lunchtime we still were on our own, though several teachers dropped by. Mr. Filamon paid us a visit too, and while he did apologize for the lack of a substitute, he seemed to share our desire for none but our own teacher. "We are doing our best," he said.

"So are we," Bernardo assured him.

"I will go ahead now and give you your next social studies assignment," he said, opening the book to the start of the familiar democracy unit. None of us wanted to say that we had studied all of that chapter. He wrote the numbers of the pages on the chalkboard, encouraged us to be on our best behavior, and left. We all looked at each other, many growing more and more openly concerned about Mrs. Burch. Sallee was getting increasingly distressed and was afraid there had been an awful accident.

Janice thought car problems were more likely. "Her car was in the parking lot with a whole lot of snow on it," she said. "She must have had trouble that last day of school and had to get a ride home. Maybe she just could not get a ride back here today." Some agreed that that must be it.

"Wouldn't she have called?" Susan said. "Wouldn't Mr. Filamon have known?"

"Did he say that he did not know?" Janice asked. "He just said he does not have a sub."

Laura looked from Julieanne to me, raising her dark eyebrows as if to say that we knew more than anyone and when were we going to share? Julieanne looked away. I wanted to see what was going to happen. There was no yellow leaf under the radiator, no leaf behind the door. The tree, pressed close to the window, had no leaves on it either. There was no electric current rippling the air, but the tree had moved. I waited to see what would happen.

Tension mounted. Finally Holly said to all, "Can we take a vote? You know, we are a democracy. Can we vote on an idea I have? At least it is something to do."

"On what?" Sallee asked suspiciously.

"How many of you would be willing to tell the rest of us what you got from Mrs. Burch?" There was a jolt or a shock that went through us, and the tree strained ever closer. I thought the window might break.

"Why?" a dozen voices asked as one. "Yeah, why?" And again, "Why?"

"She isn't coming back," I said in a hoarse voice; and all the eyes around the room turned to stare at me. Sallee scoffed, but then she stared at me again.

"You *sound* like Mrs. Burch," Bobby said. The class stared

then at him but quickly looked back at me.

"How do you know?" Hal asked. And all of them except two repeated, "Yes, how do you know?"

"She isn't," Julieanne said too. Eyes flashed instantly to her. "What do you mean? What do you know? Why? Why not? Says who?" a bunch of voices cried out to us.

"I think there is a way that all of us can know," Holly said, standing up. "I think that in a democracy," she went on, struggling to keep her voice calm and trying to keep to the subject, "when all of the citizens work together, they can know the right thing to do. They can know the answer." I saw the little twigs crinkle again, and the branches seemed to applaud.

"I got a poem," Bobby said. So had we all. Did we all notice back then that Bobby was a little bit sharper, quicker?

"And did your poem say goodbye?" Holly asked.

"No," they insisted. "No way."

"I think mine did," Holly admitted. It was so brave of her to take this act upon herself, to spare Julieanne and me from having to tell what we had seen. What good would have come of our telling the class specifically what we had seen? The miracle would not have been theirs then at all; it would have been ours. So we went on, and I remember every word that was said, so indelible is that day.

"What did your poem say?" Janice asked, but Holly had done all she could.

"Someone else first," she whispered and sat back down.

"Footsteps!" Robert warned us. We all froze. The steps came closer and the doorknob rattled, and Mr. Rynne walked in. "What's going on? Why aren't you working?" he asked.

"We are," Laura said sweetly. "We were just about to share some sentences." The rest of us nodded.

"Hmm," he said, "well, go on. I will be back."

We breathed a sigh of relief and Robert quickly closed the door again. Imaginations had all been stirred and we wanted no more interruptions. "Who's first?" he asked. I think Holly was relieved but surprised that everyone showed interest. No one laughed or got out a book or turned to anything else.

"But they are private," Charlene said and all the Amys agreed.

"But we need to make connections; remember?" Susan said.

"My poem did not say anything about leaving, and that is that!" Sallee said, but her voice sounded a little frightened. She stood up and said, "I remember all of it and I will tell it, and then you will see that she said nothing about leaving.

*'Right and left, up and down,*

> the branches balance out the tree;
> short or long, thick or lean,
> they make their own fine symmetry.
>
> I am point-five and you are a half,
> to put it now mathematically.
> Different we seem, though equal all,
> I balance you; you balance me.'

Nothing about leaving! Nothing!"
    We agreed that there was nothing about leaving. "Not mine
either," Alvin said and recited in a faraway voice,

> "'All twigs are bent by forces
> into their secret ways
> but twist and spiral toward new suns
> as in some complex maze.
> Galaxies will open;
> stars will fall into the seas
> on distant moons and planets
> where live fantastic trees.
> You will see them, find them, know them,
> and make them all your own.
> You will write your name across the sky
> and etch it deep in stone.'

Nothing about leaving." Many worried faces began to relax.
    "I'll do mine," Susan said. "It doesn't say anything about
leaving either.

> 'The world has many branching paths
> and leafy doors in unexpected places.
> Our minds were made to wind and twist
> through vast and unknown spaces
> that call to us in many ways,
> enriching dreams, enriching days.
> The books that lure us pull us there,
> like birds that fluttering in the air
> make our hearts want to soar.'"

    "Nope," Thomas said, "nothing about leaving." Holly was
beginning to feel very foolish; but now we were enjoying the poems, so
we did not stop. The Amys went one after another.

*"'I am myself alone,*
*no matter what my name.*
*My leaves are mine, my flowers too,*
*though I may seem the very same*
*as other trees that you have known.*
*I am myself alone.*
*and yet am not alone.'"*

And then another Amy:

*"'The sun smiles bright upon the tree.*
*You cast your special light*
*on all your friends including me;*
*and when I smiled back at you,*
*you knew whom I was talking to.*
*So take this smile, this gift,*
*and let it shine on you,*
*then let it gleam when clouds grow dark*
*and mysteries start to brew.'"*

"So it was smiles!" Hal said.

"Signals," Brett mused.

"Tricks with mirrors. Smiles are a kind of mirror," Laura reflected.

"Don't be so sure," Amy said. "Mine is different.

*'In every forest there is one*
*whose job it is to find the sun,*
*to grow in peace toward one bright ray*
*and lead the ones who'd go astray.'*

You are all astray," she said, "but that is all of my poem I am sharing."

"Well, lead on," Brett said. "How are we astray? How did you do it?"

"That might not be my job," Amy said, blinking coyly.

"Footstep alert!" Robert called out, just before Mrs. Esquinoth stepped in to ask how we were doing and what we were doing.

"We were just reciting some poems Mrs. Burch gave us all to memorize," Laura said. We nodded again.

"How nice," Mrs. Esquinoth said and sat down. "I'd love to hear them too."

"Oh-oh," Bobby said.

"I think we're finished," Holly said, managing to seem sorry.

"Oh dear, I should have come sooner," Mrs. Esquinoth said.

"Well, I am sure you have plenty of work to do and if you run out, I imagine Maestro Brett can conduct you in song. A merry cheerio! to all of you."

Outside the tree was quivering, and I believed it was amused. Inside, we too were quivering but with a greater variety of emotions.

"Hurry," Laura said, "before someone else comes and also wants to stay."

"I think I could say part of mine, if I could stay sitting," Bernardo said. "My Dad helped me to memorize it."

We said he could, just hurry.

"Could I keep my eyes closed?" he asked. "That would help."

"Yes, yes, just say it."

"I might make some mistakes."

"We don't care; just say it!"

"Okay.

> '*One purpose of a tree–* '

you won't laugh?"

"Bernardo!"

"Okay.

> '*One purpose of a tree is duty*
> *and you will mind it.*
> *One purpose of a tree is beauty*
> *and you will find it.*
> *Life hides its reasons all encoded*
> *all around us–*
> *some dutiful, some beautiful–*
> *they all surround us.*
> *Some work with head*
> *and some with hand*
> *but all with heart*
> *who would astound us.* '

I got it all right!" he said, sighing heavily. "Now you go, Hal. See if you can get all of yours right."

"Hmmph!" Hal reacted but stood up. We noticed he did not add, "Boring."

> '"*Endless patterns in the trees,*
> *infinite patterns on earth, in skies,*
> *innumerable patterns on every shore.*
> *I wish you all the seven seas,*

*journeys afar and journeys near,*
*where with your eyes you'll scrutinize*
*this complex life that holds in store*
*for minds like yours, for souls so dear,*
*the truth that life's enchanting, not a bo–."'*

and he stopped short, making a flashy slicing gesture with his hand.

"How did it end?" Bernardo asked.

"You can figure it out," Hal insisted. "It's easy, and it rhymes."

"It's not easy for me," Bernardo said. "You get things that I don't."

"Me either," Bobby agreed.

"So what?" Brett said to Bernardo. "You got all those decimal codes, and I never did get them."

"You would have, though, if you hadn't been out of the room. You are fast too," Bernardo said.

"Stop it," Sallee ordered. "We want to hear all the poems. We don't need an argument about who gets what. Bernardo, you are smart in your way. Now let's keep going. None of the poems is about leaving."

"But they might be saying goodbye," Janice sadly pointed out.

"What makes you say that?" Sallee demanded.

"The ones about us were in future tense, but some of them are switching to past tense."

Again the tree applauded, though the smiles in the twigs were not there. A tiny chickadee resting in an upper branch dropped down to the ground like a tear. But the face that the big branches had always formed was clearly there. Even without its curly leaves, the face was visible and perfect.

Thomas stood up abruptly and stiffly said his poem.

*"'Although the tree*
*stands stark and bare,*
*who doubts that magic*
*haunts the air?*
*Not Thomas.*

*And though the day*
*grows long and grim,*
*who says no warmth exists?*
*Not him.*

*Believe in what you see and hear,*

*believe in what is strong and near;*
*but don't dismiss and don't leave out*
*the things that you might want to doubt.*
*Believe in me, as I believe in you.'*

I'm not sure what the 'me' is, but I guess I can think about it some more."

"I think there is a change now," Hal said. I smiled at him. Yes, I thought there was a change too.

"I don't see it," Brett said.

"Magic in the air," Hal observed. "It does feel that way, doesn't it?"

Laura stood up to say hers.

*"'Words are the seeds*
*from which our stories grow,*
*in which we share with others*
*the things that now we know.*

*Words are the leaves*
*that we swirl through the air,*
*to circle and to skitter*
*and to say that we are there– "'*

and Laura would have continued except that at that absolutely precise moment one small beautiful yellow leaf pirouetted from behind the dented wastebasket and came to rest at her feet. Everyone saw that leaf. Two more chickadees tumbled down, and the air was charged with awe and pain. Laura bent down to pick up the leaf and repeated the words, *the leaves that say that we are there.* Sallee trembled and Julieanne appeared frozen, and all of the boys looked pale. Hal leaned forward to get a clear view, and Alvin ate his eraser. Janice looked horribly confused and the Amys hugged each other in fear. Charlene hiccoughed. Holly looked at Laura, then at Julieanne and me. I turned my face to the tree outside where the face was nodding yes. Yes. Yes. Someone was crying, but I did not turn to see who.

In a stuttering, stammering, halting voice Janice began saying her poem, calling us back to a common concern and focusing our attention.

*"'Nature has its logic:*
*a tree will be a tree;*
*a soul will be a soul.*
*The two can grow to one*

*and be a greater whole.*
*It is a mystery*
*but nature has its magic.'*

and I don't understand it at all," she cried in obvious pain.

"You will," I whispered to her. I don't know if she heard me.

"Footsteps!" Robert alerted us; but this time the footsteps came toward us and went right past our door. We breathed again.

"Mine isn't a poem," Brett said. Bernardo was astonished.

"It must be a song," Hal said.

"It's no fun if you tell," Brett reminded him.

"But it was obvious," Hal insisted.

"Anyway," Brett continued, "it is written in numbers, but I finally decoded it. It goes to the tune of "Greensleeves". He softly sang it for us, hoping to attract no more visitors.

> *"'The trees have mu-usic of their ownnnnnn,*
> *and they play their melodies gai-aily;*
> *each rustling leaf and each numbered twig*
> *will remind me of all of you dai-ly.'*

There was more, but why would she need to be reminded of us, unless she was leaving?" he asked sadly.

"A bigger clue," Hal said. "This is not looking good. I really thought Holly was wrong until now."

"It does not have to mean good-bye," Sallee still maintained. "She could have just been saying goodbye for the vacation time."

"Right," Brett said. "She would have to be reminded of us over vacation time. Sure."

It was growing clearer and clearer to almost all of us that, whatever the poems said individually to us and about us, taken together they spelled out a farewell. The random order in which we seemed to read them was more than a coincidence. They began as love notes, and they never lost that quality, but with each added poem there was a little more weight in the balance. Each poem acknowledged something of who we were but together they were a mounting kind of message, a gathering transition to that terrible word *goodbye*. In scruffy little yellow curls, that fact was blowing clearly through more and more minds. Our teacher had been telling us goodbye, and she was not coming back. At least nothing so far had indicated that she ever would come back

"Mine is not about leaving," Charlene said. How could that be? I wondered. Why would the pattern be broken?

> *"In every crowded wood*
> *the branches interlock;*
> *a tree grows out to others*
> *and flowers, unlike rock.*
>
> *So too it is with us,*
> *with every human soul.*
> *In friendship and in courage*
> *each of us grows whole.*
>
> *Rejoice in what you do*
> *and what you learn;*
> *lean on each other when you must*
> *and be leaned on in turn.*
>
> *Life calls on all our art*
> *to master all our fear*
> *to be ourselves.*
> *Take heart.'*

It isn't about leaving," she said.

"It is about going on," Susan noticed. "It's about us needing to keep being willing and able to go on."

Far out on the snowy field a couple of classes were building snow figures. No one came to send us to recess, and that was fine with us. We were not finished sharing. "What about yours, Robert?" Alvin asked.

"I didn't think I had to memorize it," he answered defensively. "I can't say it because I read it and put it away. I don't know it. Sue me."

"Whew, that's great!" Bobby said. "I thought I was the only one." Robert did not look pleased. He knew his had had something to do with making a solid argument for things that were not solid. It was something like that, he said.

Holly, the one who had started this, stayed quiet, no doubt hoping we would all forget about her. Julieanne and I were the only others remaining, and neither of us volunteered. Bobby happened to look out the window and said in a very loud whisper, "Wow, look at that!" We all turned and for the first time everyone saw the tree. There it was, right against the window, and we stood or we knelt on the chairs at our desks to stare at the glowing birch. Something must have taken strong possession of Julieanne, who suddenly went to the window and nervously recited her poem directly facing the tree:

87

*"'There is a time for every bud,*
*for every leaf on every tree;*
*there is a time for children now to learn,*
*now to play, now to grow from me.*
*There is a time for trees to vanish*
*and for leaves to drift and spin.*
*There is a time to give each other gifts*
*and a time to move within.*

*There is a way to love by holding on*
*and a love that must let go.*
*There are times to guess at secrets,*
*but now it is time to know. . . .'"*

And just as Julieanne uttered that last word, there came a wild rushing whoosh at the window, a roar as of a great storm. Julieanne screamed and Holly jumped and our class let out a fierce howl, as the tree which had been wildly waving at us burst into green and then disappeared. Then what a dismal and deathly silence fell on our shaken selves. We stood or sat or hunkered down, frozen in disbelief and some began to sob. No one came into the room, and certainly no one left. Sallee was the first to make her way to the window, frantic to touch the panes. "Come back," she called, though she could not again command. "Oh, please don't leave us. Please!"

"It is very hard," Janice said tightly, "to have so many people constantly entering and leaving your life."

"I think she knew that," I said. Again all eyes turned toward me, some wondering what I could know and others assuming that I had all the answers, but I did not. I only knew what I knew.

"What do you know?" Hal asked. "And how?" There was no scorn in his voice.

"Clues everywhere," I almost said to him; "no fun if you tell." But this was no day for teasing nerves already shattered. "Really," I said, "there really have been clues; it just takes eyes that are willing to see them."

"Like the leaf?" Laura asked, and I nodded.

"Like her name?" Janice asked, and I shrugged. That might have been a coincidence, if one believed in them.

"I need to see clues," Laura said sadly; "if I want to be a writer, I need to see the clues. But I saw some things now and then and never thought much about them. I guess they did not prove anything to me."

"You may not ever have proof," Alvin said. "Scientists follow the clues for a long time and may not have proof in their lifetimes. You just have to have faith in your clues."

No substitute ever came that day, and we spent the rest of the afternoon crying a little and talking about things we might have understood sooner. We were a solid little unit that had been put to a test, and now we needed to learn if we would stand together. On that afternoon, from the fire and ashes of all of our pain, our strengths began again to emerge. I stood long at the window, looking for more clues, seeing nothing but the gray sky until Bobby said that I should tell them my poem. I turned around to face them all, and I said with my heart full of growing gladness,

> "'My father calls and I will come,
> a tiny sparrow winging home
> with gifts of love left in the nests
> like seeds to sprout in Spring.'"

"That's nice," Charlene said.

"Uh, I was not finished," I said awkwardly and also somewhat apologetically. Some laughed.

> "'My children will lead and I will follow,
> until we meet in April Hollow
> where gifts of love rise from the earth
> and grow to trees in Spring.'"

"Is that the end?" Charlene asked, and I nodded. "So you think she will come back?" and I nodded again.

"How?" Laura asked, wanting more clues or possibly plotting many different stories.

"I don't know," I said.

"So, then how are you sure?" Sallee asked, still red-eyed and swollen-faced.

"I just believe, whether I am sure or not."

"What if she comes back and we don't recognize her?" Amy asked.

"Hmm, interesting possibility," Hal murmured.

"Quite fascinating, really," Alvin agreed.

"I don't get it," Bobby kept repeating to Thomas.

I went back to my desk, weary from all the talking and most especially tired of repeating to Sallee, "because I just believe, and that's all I can tell you. I just do." Suddenly I felt exhausted and just wanted to go home and curl up under the covers. So much had happened with so much intensity, and I needed a separate place to go to absorb it all.

All of us would need time and space to make our own sense of what had happened, but forevermore we would have each other as fellow witnesses and sharers when doubt and disbelief would descend upon us. I put my head down on my desk, thinking that the day was all but over. I still would make one trip to the window that day, but I thought there could be no more.

*"Julieanne," ~ from her diary*

Diary, I know that another terrible miracle happened today and that all of us shared it together. That is my only hope and my only consolation. I did not cause it. I did not ask for it. I do not have to hide it from my friends at school. All of us saw it. All of us trembled and shook and were scared when we saw it happen, and all of us stuck together. Thanks to Holly. Thanks to Holly. If she had not spoken out and asked us to talk, we could not have gotten through all that happened.

But now what? Who else can we ever tell? Can we tell anyone outside of ourselves– our parents? our neighbors? our penpals? our doctors? new strangers? I don't even really know what happened and if I tried to describe it, who would believe it? Why would they believe it? But where is our Mrs. Burch? That one question may always haunt me. What happened at that tree? How does a person become so real and then all of a sudden, she is not there at all?

So I have lots of questions, Diary, but you have no answers. Someday I may marry and have children. Will I ever be able to tell them? Someday, maybe, I will talk again to Jody like the old days, and we will whisper our secret together. Maybe. But I do know now that it happened for all of us, not just to Jody or to me. I will keep reminding myself of that when I get scared or dream of what happened. I have been upset and nervous whenever anything drops or breaks, but I am getting over that. Someday I will be over it completely. I really think that I will.

Amiga is here, my closest friend, and she has not disappeared. I tell her things that happened and she wags her tail and licks my face and stares at me with her bright black eyes. I lift the flap of her left ear and I tell her bits and pieces of what really happened, and she seems to smile a little more and even a little to laugh. I don't laugh, but I think it is all right, Diary, and that I will be fine. I really do.

## Mr. Filamon

Finally, Laura, I want you to know that Mr. Lemphill, the substitute who never showed up that day, called from St. Innocent Hospital in Blumette. He had been in a very minor accident that morning and had waited all afternoon in the emergency room. It seems that at first he got stuck in a large snowdrift on his way to school and when he finally got himself extricated and was on his way again, a tree branch crashed into his window and one bit of flying glass cut his hand. He says it was a miracle that that was his only injury and that even the windshield was minimally broken. Still, he did require a few stitches. The phone lines were down in that part of town, and that is why he could not call until sometime around three that afternoon. I don't think your question about why you had no substitute is silly at all, but I regret to say that the reason is pretty mundane.

You also ask me about the birch tree out by the fifth grade patio. That is the one thing that is blank in my mind. I don't remember a tree. And you ask what I remember of the rest of the year, but I will have to postpone the answer to that. I am a little more easily tired these days, but soon I will write you again.

Good luck with your book— and my regards to all of you, my very fondest regards.

William Filamon

## Laura

I will leave the final words to Jody, who saw farther than the rest of us. She says she saw only a little more, that she was only a little more used to searching for clues, and that may be so. To me, it seemed as if she saw all, but things like that are relative. I knew that I needed to learn from her new ways to see and new ways to think and new acceptances to make— not only to help my writing but also to deepen me.

It wasn't going to happen overnight and in fact took a long time, but the best of my work comes from the Jody in me and the Alvin I live with— the parts that feel deeply and observe closely and seek always to understand. In turn, I believe that Alvin might say that the best of his work comes from the Laura in him, the part that sees not only the intricate and fascinating possibilities in life but loves to make a coherent story of them all.

What Mrs. Burch told us has stayed with me: it is, for me, very important to make connections. Thus there will be a Part Two to this book, the story of the link that we had to make between what we were on that shattering day in January and what we became by Spring. I cannot tell you just when it began, just when we stopped peering in every cranny searching for Mrs. Burch and began to accept our daily routine. Nor can I tell you precisely when, in the midst of that daily routine, we found ourselves without even knowing it in search of April Hollow.

*Jody*

By the end of that day Alvin and Hal were quietly comparing notes on the likelihood of trained soldiers being able to disappear spontaneously. Bernardo was whittling his pencil. At whatever speed we were settling toward normal, all of us were permanently changed. At three we were dismissed to home, as on any ordinary day. After all the others had left, as I have already mentioned, I went again to the window to try to retain a sense of what we had lost. I had to look twice, because I caught a sudden glimpse of yellow and assumed it was Mrs. Burch's scarf. It was not. Tucked into a shelf of snow there on the window ledge where the tree had recently been, was a sheet of yellow paper with an intricate drawing of a tree. I could not see more than that, but again the wind howled low and lifted up the damp paper, splatting it forcefully against the window pane so every word on the sheet was there before my eyes. I read the perfect letters, precisely etched in black:

> *Through little melting clumps of snow*
> *in every patch of every woods,*
> *leaves are rustling, branches stir,*
> *the world is bright beyond;*
> *and in the earth, silent and dark,*
> *untouched as yet by light,*
> *seeds are swaying toward their spring*
> *and in their sleep they smile.*

Down in sunny spots near the creek, narrow new-made rivers ran and carried those clumps of melting snow a little farther on. What would carry us on? "Goodbye," I whispered to Mrs. Burch and, "ever the best of friends," and watched the ink seep into the snow and the words then seep away. I stood and watched the wind take up the yellow sheet and rip it to tiny shreds. Confetti mingled with snowdust blowing from the roof of school; and the poem was lost forever, except in my mind and heart. I smiled, recognizing what I had already known, how it could become necessary to destroy one's work to protect it from all the wrong eyes. Then I promised that I would never stop looking for that giving spirit who wrote it and that I would never forget her. I asked for help in knowing whether April Hollow was a place or a time, but it was too soon to know. Then it was time for me to go home, and I put on my coat and mittens and slowly walked outside. A few of my classmates were standing together there, quietly talking and crying. I said goodby to my friends, walked home through the falling snow, humming a little of *Greensleeves,* and wondering who next would teach us.

# IN SEARCH OF APRIL HOLLOW

*Laura*

If you have continued reading all the way to the end of *The Tree In the Window,* you know what the new year brought us. The days that immediately followed were a blur of substitute teachers, none memorable. Our class was sorely tested in its desire to stand together and to grow together, and we shrank into irritability and gloom. Verbal fights broke out at every recess and even an occasional fist fight. The snow lay in thick gray patches around the soccer fields, and the cold air held us prisoners in our extra clothing so that we could not run free and dispel our pent-up feelings. None of the work held any pleasure; and in the constant presence of outsiders, no one would utter a single word of what had occurred in our lives.

The patio was deserted all the time; no sign of a tree's having been there was remotely visible. Not a root showed nor a leaf remained in the sodden brown grass; no birds fluttered in for a familiar landing, and no meaningful scratchings in the dark wet earth could ever again be traced. In every way, when we looked out the window, we felt bereft and troubled. Not even Jody was immune to the sadness, although she held out hope. "What kind of clues should we look for?" we asked her.

"It is too soon," she said. "It is way too soon to be looking for her. Remember, she said in the spring?"

But it was only the first week of January and we were only ten– mature tens, but still children after all. Spring might never be coming again, and already it seemed forever since that traumatic and aweful day. "It was just a couple of days ago," Jody reminded us; but how could that be real? It was centuries ago; it was eons ago; it was back at the beginning of time. "Really and truly, just two days ago," she repeated. It was not at all real, however much it was distressingly true.

I think the string of substitutes went on for a couple of weeks. Following Jody's guidance, I tried looking for clues in each one of those teachers who entered our class. Surely, I thought, there would be a clear sign. I watched for skittering leaves and I listened to each of their names and I paid attention to their complexions, but nothing said, "I am the one." Yes, yes, I knew it was January; but surely we would have a new permanent teacher before spring.

One thing that became clear in that dreadful waiting time was that each of us responds to fantastic events according to our own lights and perceptions. I don't think that a single one of us was in danger of forgetting The Day; but for some it receded quickly into a memory of the past, and they were most easily able to go on. I believe this was the case with Robert and to an extent also with Thomas. Of the girls, I think perhaps Susan and Holly came closest to letting go quickly. Along with Janice, they were the most practical among us; but they had been changed too.

For some, the void and the pain and confusion was too raw and too immediate to bear. They regressed in their various typical ways– Sallee became more of a nag than ever, Janice appeared lost in doubt, and Julieanne stayed red-eyed and depressed off and on for several weeks. It was odd, because in between her bouts of crying, she often seemed happier and more at peace than ever. Of the boys, Bernardo suffered the most, longing for the totally warm and loving consideration he had received and feeling, I am sure, thrown back on the unlikely mercy of a stranger. Bobby seemed only confused.

More of us felt as I did, I think. We were not disabled for coping. We could do all our work and go on with our play, but not as if nothing had happened. There was a lonesome void in our days and a mist of uncertainty lingering. We wanted Mrs. Burch to return, but we held in our thoughts one part of the Christmas poem to Jody– not sure exactly just what it might be or if it really existed, we held fast to the hope of oncoming spring and the haunting promise of April Hollow.

## Jody

It seems ironic to me now that it took Mrs. Burch's departure to seal my new sense of safety. In that burst of tears when I heard her say the same words that I had written for her, I felt another kind of burst as well. I could speak again without fear and then could wonder why it had taken so long and what had made me take that silent path within. But, really, I knew that the inner path was my only way of coping with the daily path through the woods. I knew that I was no safer physically, but I learned that I had an incredible guardian within who would accompany me through all the difficulties on every path. My loneliness began to disappear.

## Laura

We did not have to wait much longer for our new teacher, although at the time it seemed forever. That Mr. Lemphill arrived with a bandaged hand and a fondness for stroking his mustache and beard but with little idea of how to teach fifth grade. He told us he really was waiting for a part in a play and that he would be with us just for a few days. I was glad, because he kept using the wrong hand to wipe his forehead and always had bandage lint all over his face.

I think the next sub either was a frustrated librarian, because she had us spend all our time reading library books and doing book reports, or else she just did not expect to have to follow lesson plans. We knew there were plenty of plans, because Mr. Lemphill had often mentioned them and had said that he was almost sorry not to be able to stick around to see how we did with some of the units.

Mr. Filamon kept checking in to see how things were going and looking sad at the fact that he had not been able to find anyone permanent. But the town was small and spare teachers were few, and it was rare that new people moved in. Mr. Lemphill came from two towns away. I think some of us wondered if he was traveling toward Broadway a couple of towns at a time. If so, I hope he has made it there by now.

But the day had to come at last, and it did. I woke up to nothing strange in the air and had no hint as I entered Bell School. But when our class had settled in, no teacher present yet at all, some dry leaves blew across the window panes; and a few of us perked up at the sound and the sight. Then Mr. Filamon came into the room and said he had an important announcement. I sat up straight, my shoulders tense, my eyes wide open, my ears alert, every sense waiting to hear a name and see a face and make a connection. A short woman came in, not a thing like Mrs. Burch. She had straight brown hair, cropped close, and had glasses half dangling from a chain. Her eyes were bright and friendly; she carried a shopping bag full of books; there was a smudge of ink on her face and traces of paint on the back of her well-scrubbed hands. She reminded me in first appearance more of Mrs. Autray, and I sank back, more than disappointed, though really they were not alike at all. "Class," Mr. Filamon said with a big smile, "this is Mrs. Green."

*Jody*

A buzz of excitement went through me and many bells rang softly; and my own voice whispered to me, "Jody, did you hear that? Jody, listen! Jody, her name means spring." And I shrugged to that voice within myself and said, "Could be." I was not so sure. I was hesitant. I was willing to wait and see.

She took off her gray coat and put it on the radiator, not yet knowing which cabinet to use and obviously not caring too much. She smiled and began talking to us, and her voice was not rustly at all. It was cheerful enough, but it suggested not one thing of trees or magic, and I remained prepared to wait.

Oddly to me, the rest of the class accepted her right away, and we were immediately in the midst of a discussion. "I have to catch up," she told us, "and I need to know who you are." So we spoke of our interests, and she spoke of hers; and quickly we gained a sense of each other. Charlene was thrilled to learn that Mrs. Green was an artist, and Laura was happy to know that Mrs. Green also loved to write.

In turn, our new teacher was excited to know what talents we possessed, especially Brett's, since she, like Mrs. Burch, had no skill in music at all. But she asked every one of us, not just Brett, questions. And when Bernardo started talking about making a computer, her eyes grew very bright indeed. As he talked and she listened, she pulled out of her shopping bag a Spanish newspaper. It was as if that blue bag did bring magic, kind of like a large floppy hat that needed its amoeba-like shape to hold far more than rabbits. She pulled from its incredible invisible depths books of logic puzzles, books of art, picture books on astronomy, books of various science experiments, collections of mazes, hundreds of post cards of distant places, pictures of stamps, lists of possible pen pals. Not all at once, but almost every day, she pulled something new from that bag to entice us to learn and to kindle our interest, to help us to know what we loved.

We asked if she was new to our town, and she nodded yes. "I didn't expect to find a job so quickly," she marveled out loud; "but sometimes things work out for the best." We asked how come she wanted to teach if she liked to paint and write. "I needed a change," she said quite simply; "I needed a new challenge." She drew a stick figure on the chalkboard and said that used to be her. "But now I am ready to make her more real," she said, quickly adding shapes and curves and pattern and texture to the outfit she had drawn on the figure, which suddenly had become a small portrait. It happened so subtly and quickly– as if from a bare stick a tree had burst into life.

A cardinal lighted on the window ledge, pecked on the glass, and flew on. But it dropped on that ledge a dry yellow leaf, and I knew that we had our own teacher– that whether or not she knew the way to April Hollow, she definitely knew how to take us into the green bright spring.

*Laura*

We soon were enveloped in work and play, almost as if we

had never known much of either before. We galloped through high mountains of paper and rested by fantasy streams. Bernardo and Bobby were hard-pressed to deal with all of the writing we had to do, although Mrs. Green assigned Bobby paragraphs where the rest of us had to do pages. She allowed Bernardo some leeway with the tape recorder and encouraged us all to contribute ideas that would help anyone else in the class learn more easily. It became a goal for us to find those ideas, though there was rarely a tangible reward– no parties, no candy, no stickers, no stars. "Those things can mean little or even nothing," she said. "Joy is the ultimate reward. Love all the things you learn." Alvin understood immediately.

Special projects and small group clubs formed and flourished all over the room. I cannot begin to describe all of them, but one stood out from the others and took over our daily life. It was not like the decimal puppet play; it was bigger, more encompassing. It did not require .2 of our week; it required our constant attention.

It began as a social studies unit. We sat around Mrs. Green in a circle on the floor, as we came to do every morning and whenever there was something major to discuss. "I would like to make these social studies lessons more real," she began. "We need ideas; what can we do?"

"A puppet play?" Bobby asked, but we shouted that down, explaining why it would not do. "You liked it back when Laura suggested it," he said sadly.

"But it's time for something new and different now," I said. "We're ready for something more."

Mrs. Burch would have put her arm around Bobby and made him feel important for having remembered that it was my idea. Mrs. Green was not like that, though. She was warm and friendly but she did not express affection the way Mrs. Burch had. She seemed to assume that there were disappointments and frustrations and that of course they were too bad but hardly fatal. Unless she saw evidence to the contrary, she assumed we could cope. "Yes, I think something new to all of you is more what I hope you'll find," she said. "But a puppet play sounds like great fun," she said, "so no wonder you wanted to do it again." Bobby smiled a little. She might not be one for warm hugging, but she did not want anyone to feel put down.

I need to mention before I go on that sometime that first week back at school, a new boy joined our class. His name, he said, was Ian– he pronounced it to rhyme with "lion"– and then he introduced himself as someone who liked to learn about almost everything. Bobby sighed, but Alvin sat up and grinned, happy that here was a new friend.

So when we were sitting in that circle, creating our small stick figures of a plan, Ian suggested that we build a computer and Bernardo immediately became his friend too.

"What does that have to do with social studies?" Janice asked.

"Computers have to do with everything," he answered. I noticed that he did not sneer at her for asking, the way some boys would have. I noticed, too, that Julieanne was looking at him quite often. One more thing that I noticed was that Jody was watching me notice, and she gave me a secret smile.

"I don't like computers," Sallee said, and Ian looked puzzled. How could anyone not like them? It was a mystery to him. "I think we ought to make our own little world, a new city or a new state. Maybe a country."

"I know who will want to run it," Thomas whispered to Hal and Brett; but they didn't really know this new boy yet.

"What are you thinking of, Amy?" Mrs. Green asked, noticing that Amy was working something out in her mind.

"Nothing," Amy Patterson said.

"I didn't have my hand up," Amy Betts assured her.

"Yippee!" Bobby shouted, "at last! No more of that secret mirror stuff."

"It was signals," Hal clarified.

"No, it wasn't," Amy Patterson reminded him. Then the whole class, in bits and pieces and with nearly constant interruptions from someone or other, told how Mrs. Burch had always called on an Amy and the right one always answered.

"Very interesting!" she said; "perhaps later today the four of us can meet?" she asked them. "Right now, though, we are getting some very wonderful ideas for a project. Let's go on."

"Not signals," Bobby insisted to Hal.

"Okay, a system. Is that all right? A system? They had this special *system.*"

"Fine," Bobby said. "What's a system?"

"A computer can be a system," Ian said, eager to get back to the subject of special projects and ignorant of Mrs. Burch. "It can be as big as we want."

"I bet we can't make one that works," Amy Sanderson said; "but I was going to say that Sallee's idea would let us do all kinds of things. We could have a city that is run by a giant computer but not everyone would have to take part in working on a machine. We could each do the parts that we want to do."

In my mind I could imagine Ms Skimme telling Amy that it was no surprise that we would think we could do what we wanted to do. I could see Mrs. Burch before my eyes, too, swaying and openly admiring our many ideas. Mrs. Green smiled and her eyes grew bright, and she pulled from that blue magic bag of hers a story of a boy and a

99

girl who are left on a desert island and have to fend for themselves. She read it to us, and I still remember how I loved to hear her read. It inspired us with many ideas for how we ourselves would cope, and that night I went home and wrote a story a little bit like that one myself. I wanted to see what I would do if I were left in that lonely, frightening situation; and so it was that I learned fairly early that writing is one of the most straightforward ways of coming to know yourself. When Mrs. Green read my story, she pulled from her inexhaustible bag a copy of *Lord of the Flies*, asking if I would like to read it. It depicted, she said, a very different way of reacting.

Our discussion of a special project was ongoing for several days. All kinds of new words appeared in our daily assignments, and we were encouraged to use them in every setting. *Spelunking* was one of those words, and Hal really liked it. "Going spelunking," he would say, taking the new library pass shaped like a doughnut and coming back with a book about caverns and caves. "I am just spelunking in my mind," he would report, if asked if he was daydreaming. One day he brought in a smooth river rock for part of his science experiment. He had come across it while cleaning his room, spelunking there in his closet.

"I am very impressed," Mrs. Green said.

"That I had this old rock?" he asked.

"No, that you clean out your closet!" she said.

I am getting away from the subject, though. I want to get back to the Project. Little by little we all agreed, each as we found a place for ourselves within the larger plan, that a new community could be exciting; but we did not know where to start.

*Mrs. Green, from her private journal*

I got the job at Bell School. I was hired to teach for the rest of this year a fifth grade class. I had a very long meeting with William Filamon, a genuinely fine man who cares about the kids and wants them to achieve as much as they can. When he finished telling me what all had happened in the first few months of their year, I felt that I had fallen into a huge trap. I wondered how I could possibly help these children who had been through loss, hurt, excitement, and more loss. I was afraid of hurting them more, and yet at the same time I knew that I had moved to this small town in order to heal my own hurts and losses; and I was tremendously sympathetic from the start.

Now after merely two weeks, I really believe I was led to this class, that in some deep and mysterious way some force brought me right here, right now. I do not know if I can help them, but I am sure that they already are helping me. Last night I had a new version of my recurring dream. Mostly in these dreams, I see a distant small tree and gradually it comes much closer, sometimes because it comes to me and sometimes because I walk toward it. The branches wave and beckon me; and as I get near it, the leaves whirl and spin and seem to try to tell me things in words. All I can usually make out through the rustling is something that sounds like *a chance, a chance.* I wake up wondering what is that chance? Is it perhaps something being offered to me, or am I supposed to give a chance to someone else? I believe that my decision to move has something to do with the dreams, that I am offering myself another chance at life if I can just pay attention to cues and follow my own best instincts.

This time, it was as if a tiny yellow leaf had turned into a minute elf and had come to dance right next to my ear and to whisper gentle words of welcome. In the dream I reached out to pick up this tiny creature or leaf and to hold it in my hands; but it shied away and danced out of reach, saying, *"No, you cannot hold me."* Then it turned into a yellow bird, not a canary but perhaps a goldfinch, and it soared in a bouncing motion and glided on delicate wings before it flew away. I feel that all of these tree dreams are meaningful, but I cannot quite understand them. Last night's dream, though, suggests to me that I am on my own right track.

This class astonishes me. Perhaps I caught some of their infection from that second teacher Ms Skimme when I was shown the reports she had written on each member of the class. I was alerted for problems, even though Bill assured me that the children were not at all as they seemed in those terrible descriptions. I may have thought he was simply trying not to discourage me. Now that I have met the class, have worked with them, listened to them, and observed them, I find myself disgusted by Ms Skimme and wondering what destiny drove her. Surely if destiny operates for one, it must operate for all. Who guided her to these children and made her want to destroy them? What chilled her heart to the talents and gifts they offer? Probably it is not just their gifts she spurned. Who denied her own? Who made her what she is? Who or what? I will never know, but these children I will get to know to whatever degree they let me.

I want to win them over, I admit, and I hope that a special project will be the key. So I have already introduced the topic, and already I am the person won over. With no prodding at all from me, they came up with the concept of a brand-new community in which they could incorporate all of their learning and all of their loves. They allowed instantly for all kinds of offshoots and special activities. I could not have equaled them had I planned this project for months.

Sallee suggested it; Ian adapted his own pet idea to it; Amy Sanderson made it more appealing; and then, one by one, each of the others saw ways to expand and contract and make a simple concept into a vast potentially living and breathing organism. It was simply breathtaking to observe.

Things broke down a little bit when it came to the actual first steps, but it took only a few suggestions and little pointers to get them on their way. Already with this second week barely over, they have named their future community and have formed committees of many sorts to undertake a vast expedition. Alvin, Ian, Bobby, and Charlene are the designated advance scouts. They will "visit and explore" this new place and report back to the others where it is, how to get there, and what are its principal plants and animals. Charlene, I am happy to see, is not letting the boys confine her to drawing the flora and fauna or to rewriting their notes to pass on to the newsletter committee. Laura and Susan and Jody are writing numerous "memoranda" to the crew, listing supplies they will need for a long journey, anticipating all kinds of emergencies and making suggestions on dealing with them, serving as scribes to all of the other committees. I gave them the word *liaison* this week. They seem comfortable with the way I like to bring in new vocabulary.

Robert and Sallee and Janice are writing an outline for their proposed constitution and drafting possible laws. Tommy, Bobby, and Bernardo are setting up a plan for a communications system and are deciding on the need or not for a code. Brett is trying to make a real public address system from a kit. Both Amy Betts and Amy Patterson are designing residences– looking up information on various kinds of dwellings from huts to barracks, while Amy Sanderson has decided to learn all about first aid so that she can be the community doctor. There are still a few who are undecided about their role, but it will come to them. Janice puzzles over each possibility but cannot reach a happy conclusion. Julieanne and Holly want to work together but can't decide between planning the new national holidays and outlining forms of celebration or developing nutritious meals for the crew. Hal is busily researching currencies and will propose how to deal with finances, but he also wants to explore for caves on their new planet and see what treasure awaits him.

*Planet*, I said. They were not content with a town or an island. On their own time, Alvin and Hal and Ian and Bernardo constructed a cardboard spaceship ten feet long and painted silver, ornamented with special insignia whose meaning I do not yet know. Named *Skybound*, it is suspended from our ceiling in the back of the room, and the whole class absolutely loves it. They want to add another one, a little smaller, on the floor, to use as a reading nook. The boys are working on that this weekend.

All this accomplished in a matter of hours! Probably a total of ten, not counting the work on the spaceship, spread out over the last six days. I worried ahead of time that even a medium-size special project might not get finished by June; but these children have taken on a monumental project, and will they complete it even before spring? I worry now that they will finish it too soon, and what will become of the last weeks of school?


*Laura*

We named our planet Haminox, and I will tell you how that came about. We were gathered for our morning discussion circle, and Bobby said he was starved. "How starved?" Ian asked.

"Really starved," Bobby said, rubbing his stomach.

"Hungry enough to eat a whole pig?" Bernardo asked.

"Mmm," Alvin said, "ham and eggs sound good."

"I'm hungry enough to eat an ox," Bobby said, holding his arms wide.

"Mmm," Hal said, "ham and ox."

Mrs. Green had just called for suggestions for a name for our planet, and she assumed that Hal had suggested Hamandox.

"It doesn't sound right," Susan said; "it needs a change."

"Hamorox?" Janice suggested. "You wouldn't want ham *and* ox."

"Hammerhocks," Robert offered, pleased with himself.

"Hammerclocks," Thomas said, "'cause last night I was trying to fix my alarm clock and I hit it a little too hard."

"I did that once," Charlene sympathized.

"Herclocks," Sallee said, giggling.

"Haminox," Ian said out loud; "it sounds like the name of a computer. Haminox 5000."

"Just plain Haminox sounds good," Julieanne said.

"Okay, we will call it Haminox," Sallee announced. There was a flurry of reaction from all of us.

"What do you mean, we will? This is not a tyranny," Alvin said.

"Not an aristocracy, either," Amy Patterson put in.

"Sorry, sorry, sorry," Sallee said, more than a little huffily. "So, vote."

We held a semi-secret ballot and the results, as nearly as I recall, were 15 votes for Haminox, one for Haminox 5000, one for

Hamorox and one for Hammerhocks. We were a democracy.

## Jody

I have never been good at judging people's ages, least of all back then. Mrs. Green might have been thirty or fifty, for all I knew. If she had had gray hair, no doubt we would all have thought she was old; but she didn't. Her hair was brown. She mentioned her three children sometimes, but she didn't say if they were scattered far and wide or if they lived with her and went to some other school. She was not a mysterious figure like Mrs. Burch; but even though she told us many things about herself, we did not get to know a whole lot about her private life. I think it was still too soon for us to know that teachers did indeed have real lives of their own, apart not only from us but from their children as well. In all the time I kept my secrets from my family, I rarely considered that they had secrets they kept from me. We live in the cocoon of our own imaginings; and whether we see with a clear and rational far-ranging eye or with a blurry narrow one, we cannot help limiting all others who exist in the entire universe or expanding our own selves to fill all the universes in creation. We can't cope with All.

Mrs. Green made every effort to help us expand our minds and ourselves. She brought us more of the world and wanted to take us out into it as well. To us, this meant field trips, but she had a bit more in mind. She sent us on plenty of library trips with specific missions. Sometimes she put on a little tin sheriff's badge and deputized us all. "Deputy Jody," she might say to me, "our community needs protection from the wild carnivores that Charlene has sketched here. Mosey on down to the library, please, and bring us a report on carnivores." Each of us would receive our assignment, and we each received a badge.

Sometimes she put on a General's cap and would salute us as we accepted our semisecret orders. "Sergeant Alvin, invade the enemy territory and let us know the exact terrain. This is a dangerous mission; I look forward to seeing you alive here in my office at 1400." Alvin would salute back and head off to his desk to draw a map of the wild uncharted area closely surrounding our colony on Haminox. The "enemy" we grew to realize was ignorance. We were set to vanquish it.

She brought in a typewriter and established it in the back corner, letting us know that we all could use it sometimes but that Bernardo had first dibs. "Now, Señor Ruíz," she said, "you are our Spanish correspondent. I want you to take these notes from our scribes and translate them into Spanish." Bernardo did not know whether to salute or not, but he took the notes to the typewriter and made the best translations he could. He thought he was finished, but no. "Bueno," she said, "and now for your assignment." Poor Bernardo was less than thrilled. "I want one single paragraph for the class newspaper, a good paragraph about what you have written here. It needs to be in English, and it needs to be good enough for the Managing Editor to accept. Bernardo groaned, knowing that Laura was not going to be an easy editor to please. Still, he liked typing instead of writing, which always cramped his hand, and he also liked translating things into Spanish. He took more care with his assignment, knowing that he liked the outcome.

We saw that there were many ways to approach our learning. That was the constant message: don't ever lock yourselves into little boxes. Think of ways to enjoy what you do, if simply going ahead and doing them is not a joy in itself. She let us see every day that the most helpful thing we could learn was to discover the *ways* that we each learned best.

Finally– in the sense that this is the last thing that I am writing about this minute, not in any final sense at all– she welcomed all of our improvisation and striking out on tangents. She did not hold schedules sacred, not if new somethings equally important or more important happened to come along. Thus it was that we encountered a very strange creature, one who might easily have been passed by. Quite by accident, purely by chance, we stumbled across a Grizzim.

It was at one of our morning circles, and we had been calmly discussing the need for public institutions. None of us felt the need for a school, but Charlene had fallen on the ice and badly twisted her ankle and so we established a hospital. (Robert in a burst of philanthropy offered to donate it and, in the least real part of our world, finished making it out of a stack of shoeboxes within a few days.) The topic, though, was public institutions. We included a library and a small post office, and we debated the need for a jail. It was in the middle of that jail discussion that Julieanne, with her eyes large and sad, said, "What will we do if a Grizzim comes?"

"What is a Grizzim?" we asked, puzzled.

"I don't know," she said. Still, she had been inspired to say it and had no wish to back down. "What do you think it is?"

Mrs. Green could have steered us back to the topic of real institutions; but she waited and watched, her eyes as sparkling and alive as Julieanne's. None of us had any answer, though, nor really a whole lot of interest. "I think I know what a Grizzim might be," the teacher said. We looked at her, waiting to hear what it was. "Well, no, I'm not telling you what it is," she said, very, very amused. And then in that way she had, the way that Bernardo and Bobby just writhed at, she had us get out paper to write what we thought a Grizzim might be and what on Haminox we might do about it. More than a few groaned and glared at Julieanne, who shrugged as if to say, "I didn't make the writing assignment."

"The author of the top idea will get excused from one big assignment this week, not including tests," Mrs. Green cheerfully announced. That brought Bernardo back to a smile, though it did nothing for Bobby. "You have fifteen minutes, and then Julieanne will get to judge. Sometimes a definite reward is worthwhile, as long as it's reasonable."

"Can we draw it?" Charlene asked. Yes, but there still had to be some description in words.

So we sat on the floor with our crayons and pencils and stared off into space. We pondered the possibilities in that strange word *Grizzim*, and we doodled and scribbled and thought. After a while, some were done but others had barely gotten underway. Those who were finished handed their short papers to Julieanne, who read the contributions out loud. I still remember several: Amy Sanderson thought a grizzim was a monstrous plant that had claws and teeth and was designed to wave and threaten anything that moved within a radius of thirty feet.

"A defense plant," said Alvin.

"I thought it was more of its own scarecrow," Amy said, laughing.

"That's also a defense plant," Ian said. Alvin grinned.

Thomas, openly doubting that his would win, had described a magical all-purpose box that cooked and cleaned and made general repairs. "You mean a grizzim is a Mom?" Bobby asked. Neither Hal nor Susan could see any connection. "Isn't that what your Mom does?" Bobby asked them. Not that they had ever noticed, they said.

Janice protested that a cooking and cleaning box did not really sound menacing enough since the question was, What would we do when one came? Hers was a purple bogeyman with devil's horns and her answer was that we would either destroy him or hide in a special place. Ian did not think the question required a monster Grizzim at all. His was a rare and magical creature which allowed its owner to look into its eyes and see what was happening anywhere in the universe. "It's the only one of its species," he proudly announced. The Amys saw no great value in that, but Alvin did and so did I.

Bernardo's Grizzim was a writing robot. All you had to do was tell it (out loud) what subject and what kind of writing assignment and it would turn out reports or themes or stories or articles perfectly spelled and typed. Hal's was a colony of frog-like creatures that made wonderful pets but in a food emergency were delicious. Sallee was disgusted. Her own Grizzim was something like a teddy bear and was to be a standard feature of every hospital room.

Holly's grizzim was a cloud that regularly visited Haminox to put out fires, fill swimming pools, and drown enemies if necessary. Brett's was a mechanical device that created music from the movement of the stars and projected colored images across the skies of Haminox, which were, by the way, pale yellow by night and a luminous charcoal by day. "So now we can have concerts," he said, happy.

"And we don't need television or movies," Amy Betts added.

"Can I make the popcorn when we have those Grizzim concerts?" Bobby asked. "I make real good popcorn."

There, as I look back upon it, was a true measure of how real our planet became for us. We were sitting in a small circle in a vast universe, conjuring up imaginary creatures and fantastic appliances and inventions. We could drown our imaginary enemies in the outpouring of our imaginary cloud, defend ourselves against implausible invasion, feed ourselves and entertain ourselves from the depths of our creative wells– and our thoughts could become not just an exercise in fantastic creativity but realities unto themselves. And when we spoke of our grizzim as a machine capable of delighting our minds and souls with a phenomenal light and music show, one of us could ask in simple, pure seriousness and anticipation if he could be the one to make the pop corn when we watched the show. *When we watched the show* was to him an inevitability. Friday afternoon of that week, Mrs. Green brought out from her magic bag a corn popper, Bobby popped the corn, and we listened to records of symphonic music while swirls of color danced in our eyes. We learned that we can make some fantasies come true.

Brett was excused from one book report.

And yet, though Julieanne of her own free will selected Brett's concept of a Grizzim, the rest of us made a different decision. We thought of her question– and she could not deny our reasoning– *What will we do if a Grizzim comes?* And since that did sound menacing, nothing like a light show at all, we pretty much forced her to change her mind, even though Brett won the prize. All of us thought together then and what we came to decide was that a Grizzim was an alien being who blocked our paths, who frightened us, who threatened our entire community. What we would do about it, we thought, was to use Amy's idea of a grizzim and make it a Grizzim-guard. The Amys volunteered to make one. It evolved to look like a scarecrow of sorts but with elaborate antennae to pick up signals from afar and a walkie-talkie to relay us the news. They gave it a badge and a cap and a ferocious expression, and Sallee gave it its name: Teddy Grizzimgard. Amy Patterson donated a large lazy susan that was in their basement so that Teddy could rotate and never miss a thing. They added a mirror, as a back-up device, and Alvin looked suspicious. "Signals and mirrors. Do you think that they're giving us clues about that trick with their names?" he asked Hal.

"Hmm," Hal said, "very interesting."

They debated about giving Teddy a gun, but the class council voted against that. "But then what can *it* do if a Grizzim comes?" Julieanne asked again. We agreed to think about that, and then something happened that forced us to make our decision.

## Laura

Our classroom began to look like an animated version of Mrs. Green's magic bag. You could have walked in any day and plucked at least a thousand items from the sills and shelves and extra tables, not to mention corners of the floor and a good large area of the ceiling. But one day we arrived in class to discover the spaceship lying on the floor, badly dented. Coming down, it had brushed some of the latest science experiments off one table. After we cleaned things up and rehung the spaceship, we discussed the possibility of vandalism and that led to a planetary council on crime and punishment. We talked about all kinds of crimes, from trespassing to murder, and we debated all of the dire consequences we thought were appropriate. Some of us were more bloodthirsty than others– Bobby wanted to toss everyone into our live volcano. Robert contemplated drawing and quartering, but the rest of us were aghast.

"You can't do that!" Sallee nearly screamed. "Boys are monsters. Jail is enough."

"Why jail?" Janice asked. "That doesn't make sense if you are talking about trespassing. Just tell the person to stay off your property."

"But vandalism? What about vandalism?" Holly asked. "You can't just tell people not to damage your property and expect that to work."

"We aren't going to damage our own property," Bernardo said.

"Well, who knocked the spaceship down?" Bobby asked.

"Maybe it just fell, Bobby. Did you ever think of that? Maybe it just was too heavy for the wires and it fell," Brett said. "Things can just fall." Charlene nodded sadly, rubbing her ankle.

"I think the volcano is a good idea," Bobby retreated.

"People aren't marshmallows," Susan said. "I think we should be humane." Susan had been horrified to learn about cases of capital punishment a few days earlier when watching the news.

"I think whoever did it should just confess," Sallee said.

108

"Nobody *did* anything," Brett said; "I still think it just fell."

"Give one warning the first time, and then boom! into the hot volcano," Bobby said.

For a while our discussion continued along the same few paths, until Robert proposed that we forget about the spaceship and just use the list of laws that he and his committee had drawn up. If the class wanted to add to them, fine; "But, gee, really," he said, "we already have a long list. Theft is on it, and so is vandalism, and a lot more besides."

"Oh," we said, having forgotten. So we got out our planetary newsletters together and read the pages and pages of laws that he and Sallee and Janice had written, though they had never agreed on the proper punishments for any of them. It was disturbing to see just how many things might be considered crimes. Eating someone else's food was on there right next to asking to borrow scissors and not returning them. Clearly a great many of our own experiences were playing a part in the list, but was every single thing that we did not like going to be a crime? And would we punish every crime as if all were alike?

"Volcano," Bobby whispered, but we just had to ignore him. We established a plan of repayment with services, no plan of revenge at all. It became a more simple problem to us when Mrs. Green asked us to consider what the outcome should be– should we be most interested in punishing, most interested in preventing, or most interested in the chance to move our community along? With a lingering farewell to the volcano, even Bobby voted for moving Haminox forward. We rejected prisons and executions, favoring fines, with banishment being our most severe punishment. We hoped that by making a fair system of laws, we would decrease all interest in breaking them. We didn't know how to prevent people from stepping on a neighbor's lawn or bumping into their spaceships. We understood that glue bottles would occasionally disappear from the shelf and our writing tablets might by mistake end in someone else's desk, but was every mistake and every misdeed always to be regarded as a major offense? We did not know how to make every distinction, and we did not really care to. We did know, though, that what mattered to us was to make our community succeed. We allowed ourselves, all of ourselves, one supreme freedom: the freedom to learn from our mistakes.

We stationed Teddy Grizzimgard beneath our newly rehung spaceship. We gave him no gun, no power to kill or maim. He had the walkie-talkie in his hand that could be used at any time to signal an alarm. We allowed for no accidental justice; each case would come to all of us to hear and then to consider and act upon. Communication was our best defense.

109

*Mrs. Green, from her journal*

I never get over how much some children are capable of taking on. They might be the very ones who can't get around to taking the trash out at home or who just can't be bothered to make their beds. Perhaps they would rather sleep through breakfast and might even be accused of evading helping with dishes. I would not argue with any parent who says, "That can't be *my* child you are describing, that young person who does extra reports and reads extra books and helps you to straighten the room after each council session!" All I can say is that I have been privileged to see another side of your children, the one who has stored up all that you gave and silently taught to make each the person that is. We each know part of the complex being your child is, and isn't it wonderful that there is a whole lot more than either of us fully knows?

I am thinking of that odd little episode, the Grizzim, that may have reflected Julieanne's fear of all the unknowns we were tackling. It initiated a lively set of drawings and several paragraphs, but it led to something bigger. Now, in addition to all that they have been doing– and they have been doing a lot– eight of them have formed a subgroup that they call The Mad Inventors' Club. Ian and Bernardo started it off, but others have followed their lead. They meet after school in the area of the basement outside the supply closet– there simply was no more space in our classroom. I watch as their ideas mushroom, thinking each time that here is where they run into a wall. Sooner or later, they will try to stretch too far. So far, I have been wrong.

The boys started with a desire to invent the computer that would govern all the various mechanical functions, including the clocks, on Haminox. It is to be programmed to know all the laws and dispense the appropriate compensation due any victim. It is not being taught the word volcano, but it knows the word *story* and can, thanks to Bernardo, write any assignment and guarantee an A. When Jody and Laura asked to join the club, they set to work creating illustrated stories on rolls of paper towels. A pair of holes was cut into the cardboard computer's sides, allowing for a dowel rod to serve as a scrolling bar. Then, when anyone wanted a story, or so the original plan presumed, they could use the scrolling bar and an illustrated story would issue from a slot like those on certain mailboxes.

Julieanne joined their club because she was interested, I think, in Ian– or perhaps it was Bernardo. (She seems to like both of them.) Hal and Alvin soon were hanging around, and they have added a number of secret things of which I as yet have no clue or knowledge. Susan, staying late after school to wait for a ride, came down to see what Hal had been talking about at home and got hooked. She began writing more paper towel stories, and she offered to ask Brett for music tapes to add to the computer's possibilities. I think Brett is making new ones for this magic computer, but he has no other interest in it.

It is, for reasons I cannot explain, an intriguing group. They work together so well, and they are so calm as they proceed to make fabulous modifications– they are so delighted with their results– that I see this group forming a solid bond that may well last them a lifetime. I hope so.

Sallee tried setting up a different club, based on the same idea of an inventors' club but with a different goal, and so far it has not gone anywhere. I think that her irritation with boys is not shared by many, if any, of her peers; and so when she sets things up in a way to exclude the boys, she finds her ideas rejected. She had decided to make a small machine, a weather-forecaster, which I think quite a few of the others would or could have enjoyed. For a short time she had four with her, and they met a couple of times to make plans. They could see the other group working, and they could see how smoothly it could run. But Sallee was insisting on all her own ideas and rejecting theirs. She had seen the other group's scroll and had worked out a way to use a tinker-toy crank and an oatmeal box. If you turned the crank, she told me, it would rotate inside the box and push a slip of paper out. The weather forecast thus was based, quite realistically, on chance. (I think it was Hal who asked why not just use a dart board, but then where was any scope for invention?)

That crank was her  undoing– for after all, in a group project, who likes a crank? Sallee not only had one; she was one. Nothing that Thomas suggested was deemed worthwhile. Nothing that Charlene designed was quite right. Sallee fussed and fumed and turned that little crank, pushing herself right out. The forecast was gloomy.

I have confidence that she will see what is needed and that she will work to make changes in herself, but that task is a very hard one for anyone, let alone for a fifth grader. I think she'll do it though; I think right now for the first time she is seeing what could be. She is seeing an ideal group in action, and it is not limited to girls. She may be cloudy for a while longer, but I think the sun will smile again.


*Laura*

No matter how busy we were, Mrs. Green made sure we had some time every week for listening to a story. We could close our eyes and listen, could draw or drift or dream, could relax from the pressure of all the work, and let her read to us. Who would not look forward to that time? Of course, most of the time the weekly reading would somehow have a connection to at least one thing that was happening on our planet or in our daily struggles, and the nice thing was that we did not *have* to discuss it. We could, but we did not have to. I remember one short story she read about a pioneer boy and a girl who get left behind in a wilderness when their parents are victims of a raid. They had been traveling in a wagon, which gets burned. The horses are taken. The story of how they reached a settlement a hundred miles away, how they each brought different skills and strengths to their terrible ordeal, caught our own imaginations and made Haminox even more real to us. Yet I was into noticing all I could by then, and it seemed to me that she looked a little more often at Sallee than at any of the rest of us.

When she finished reading, Bobby said something about the story being dumb. A boy and a girl could not do all that by themselves, he said. Ian and Alvin thought it was very realistic and were sure that they could have solved the various problems too. Julieanne expressed doubts that she could have survived. She thought an adult would have to be necessary too, but Robert agreed with Alvin's comment that we all can do more than we think. Amy Betts wondered what would have happened if there had been two girls, instead of a boy and a girl; and that sparked a big debate. Sallee stayed quiet, but I said that I thought that having a boy and a girl made it much more realistic. Hal agreed that it made a better partnership, and Susan nodded too. Ian said that he thought if it had been two boys or two girls, half of us would not have liked the story. He thought the author wanted all of us to like it. I have remembered that often as I have written my stories, to make them for more and more people. Perhaps the most memorable thing about that discussion, though, was that Sallee did not say one word.


### Jody


We made our computer from a pair of refrigerator boxes that we got from the appliance outlet downtown. We each had different ideas about what we wanted to include, but we just decided to use them all. Laura and Susan and I wrote tons of short, short stories and poems. Julieanne added her own short descriptions of books she had read so that our classmates who were looking for a book to do a report on could have some suggestions. We were hoping Janice would join us and write some puzzles, but she didn't really want to. She made some suggestions every now and then, and I understood her.

Bernardo got some wires and white blinking Christmas lights

to attach to the top of the computer, which made Ian happy. Mr. Ruíz showed Bernardo the best place to put an electrical outlet strip inside so that we could have all sorts of attachments but only one plug to run to an outlet in our overly crowded classroom. We placed a small tape recorder inside, along with a radio tuned to the weather station. We cut a half door, like an igloo entrance, on one side of each of the two large boxes so that two people at a time could enter our computer and use it as a getaway spot or a resource center.

For a while we called our computer Grizzim 2000, because we tried to make use of all the Grizzim ideas we could. On one side of one of the boxes, we painted a cloud with rain falling into a volcano. On another side, we painted musical notes and wild abstract designs. We attached cardboard tubes sticking out at odd angles to suggest another scarecrow, and we donated a few of our old stuffed animals to represent Sallee's teddy bear Grizzim. Mrs. Green offered us the use of the corn popper, but we decided agaist it.

"It's not complete," Ian said. "My Grizzim is missing."

"I have a play crystal ball," I said. "You can have it." So I brought in that plastic globe and gave it to him, and he took it and added with softly glowing markers pale suggestions of distant mountains and faint streaks of lightning. He reverently hung it from the ceiling of one of the boxes and painted a fake electric switch on one of the interior sides. He pretended to go into a trance for us and in an eerie voice he asked to know what was happening right then on the planet Haminox.

Every one of us listened in silence, fully expecting an answer.


*Laura*


With all that we had put into our computer, we had a hard time giving it a final name. We thought about having a contest for the whole class, but really we wanted to name it ourselves. We decided to put all our suggestions into a jar that we put in the computer under the hanging globe and to see what happened. I think we expected the computer to tell us its name itself. It did not. But we opened the jar a few days later and read our own names. These are what we had written:

The Dream Machine
The Cave
Experimental 1000
Roll-a-Scroll
Pioneer 8

Máchina One
Guardian
Tomorrow's Chamber

We each voted for our own. Hal looked around and said, "Now what?"

"New names," Susan said.

Mrs. Green, sitting nearby looking through a dozen or more catalogs– despite the story she had read to us, she would not let us work after school without an adult supervising– asked us if she should order a film series on computers or a series of travelogs through primitive countries. "Trave-Log," I said. "How is that for a name? If we would separate the syllables and capitalize 'Log' and give it a number, wouldn't that be an okay name?"

"Trave-Log One," Ian said out loud. We all repeated it. Jody wrote it down.

"I think Roman numeral one," Alvin suggested. "Make it Trave-Log I."

No vote was needed.

"I guess I will make my own decision about the film series," Mrs. Green murmured.


*Jody*

A few days after we named Trave-Log I, we had a wondrous surprise. We arrived in the basement to see it rocking and all its lights running around the top rims of the boxes. Brett's music was softly playing and the crystal globe was glowing. For a moment we were stunned at our gleaming and pulsing creation; then we broke into excited commotion. *"How could this happen? Who did it? When did this happen? Isn't it beautiful? Who did it? Bernardo? Did you?"*

Totally enchanted, we were eager to bring it upstairs to the classroom. I looked around for yellow leaves, even though it still was early March. I searched the floor and behind the doors, but the truth, not leaves, came out: at Bernardo and Ian's request, Mrs. Green had invited Mr. Ruíz to come in and rig the surprise. He had wired the globe and installed more lights and all of those lights and the tape recorder came on as soon as anyone came within five feet. Then we knew why Mrs. Green had led us down there instead of following us. Usually she had to run to catch up with us, but not that day. She got within five feet of Travie before we reached the door into our special workspace there in the basement. We oohed and cooed and purred in perfect pleasure. We wanted to take and install it in the classroom immediately, even though we still had mock switches to paint and other minor details to add.

"I am a little concerned," she said, "because someone will always be within five feet. We can't have this on all the time."

"We don't need to keep it plugged in, do we?" Ian asked, thrilled at the results which he had not seen before we did; "the wires are hidden, so no one needs to know; and then we can make it a big surprise sometime for all the others. We can make it our group secret, can't we?"

Of course we could, though we could hardly wait for the class to see the full effects of our masterpiece. For a little while we would revel in our secret and contemplate the awed reactions from Sallee and Robert and all of the others. I don't think it occurred to any of us that they would be jealous, and the amazing thing is that they were not. Perhaps Trave-Log I was not nearly so special to anyone else as it was to us. But to us, oh so definitely to us, it was incredibly, phenomenally stupendous.

"Soup-endous," Ian declared. "Stew-perb." We had not paid much attention to this quirk of his, but he regularly mangled quite a few words, despite his great love for them.

Mrs. Green suggested that we rearrange some of the tables in the room before taking the computer up there. We ended up changing the entire room, with Trave-Log I in the center of the back wall and all of the science experiments on either side. Our space ship hung in the front, not directly over the teacher's desk but near it. We ranged our desks along the other two walls, leaving ourselves a satisfying large space in the middle of the floor for council meetings. You may well imagine the radiant effect on our classmates the next morning: it was as if they were really stepping onto a new planet. Well, not a new one but a renovated one of our own.

It was March and birds of all kinds were returning. Snow lingered in spots on the mud fields and rains washed the spots away. The trees were almost beginning to bud; the crocus and jonquils in the front of the school had bloomed already and were starting to fade. The grass was starting to turn a little more green, though we still had bouts of intermittent snow and blustery days. The worst of winter, though, was past; and I looked forward with all of my heart to what might come in April.

Still, I told myself over and over, April might not be a time. For I was really thinking of April Hollow, and that might be quite simply a place. *Don't count on April*, I told myself. *Be patient and wait and see.* Perhaps you think that was easy for me, but I assure you that it was not. *It has to be coming closer,* I said to myself each night before I went to sleep. *It has to be a little bit closer,* I said each early morning when I awoke. It did me no good to say not to think about it; it was always in my mind. I looked for every leaf that blew, before there even were leaves. I watched each bud unfold on any tree that I thought might hold an answer; but all of them seemed quite determined to remain silent. Then I regretted my own past silence, feeling that it came back to mock me. What kept me calmer and happier and able to get through each March day was the focus we had in our classroom and our work on Haminox. More even, I knew that I was not alone. I had real friends with whom I worked each day and a bright and shining cardboard friend that we had named Trave-Log I.


### Mrs. Green, from her journal

We spend a huge amount of time on Haminox, but everything we study works right in. I am eager now to find an appropriate reward for the children, a reward that will tie in with our special project but will also let them know that their hard work made it possible. I keep searching for ideas and have not yet found one. I do believe what I say about joy, but I want to find a richly satisfying way to bring the project to a memorable end. I want them to know that sometimes work itself builds in tangible rewards itself.

Bill tells me that report cards are due in another week, that no one wanted personal conferences again after the grim, miserable results of the last ones. I am sorry about that– I want to meet these children's parents, know a little more about their families. I plan at the very least to call all of them, invite them to one of our council sessions, let them visit our "planet" and contribute their ideas if they wish. Bill is trying to discourage me from doing so, but he is not forbidding it. It's a good thing, because the fact is that I began already. So far, no real problems. I haven't had much interest in visiting from most of the parents I've contacted, but I think Thomas's father plans to drop in. Julieanne's mother let me know about the visits to the child psychologist, and that was helpful. I have tried to connect with Alvin's mother at least five times, and I do get through. She answers and then there is the most awful screeching, a burst of apologies, and a disconnect. I am intensely curious and find myself imagining all kinds of exceptionally bizarre possibilities. It does sound as if a treeful of chimps might live in the phone, but then there is also occasionally a hissing sound.

I myself am wanting a reward and a break, not from the kids, just from the intensity. I called Peg to see if she could drag herself away from her grandkids for a long weekend and come visit. She will be arriving Friday around dinnertime. I hope that in between all our catch-up conversations she will be willing to help me scout around for a memorable field trip for the class. It needs to be close enough so that we don't spend the whole morning getting there but far enough away to seem like a real adventure. It needs to be more than exciting, more than exotic, it needs to be. . . to be. . . hmm, I wonder if next week I can give them the word *numinous*. That's what I want our field trip to be– filled with a divine presence!

. . . .

My God, I just reached Mrs. Ziggle! I hope I can recall and capture the conversation word for word; it would be such a pity to lose it. I dialed the number and got the familiar small voice.

"Yes, who is calling please?" she chirped. In the background I could hear that screeching sound, somewhat like a demented parrot. Mixed in was a new eeeeeeking sound, and Mrs. Ziggle was telling someone to stop teasing Citadel.

"Are you there?" I yelled into the phone.

"Why, yes, dear, who are you? Oh, oh, just hold on a moment while I try to calm Citadel down, and Grandma is getting extremely flustered." There was a clunk as the phone was set down, giving me time to wonder what Citadel might be. I pictured an elephant-sized Dalmatian, though I can't say why. I could hear the screeching recede and the eeeeeeking sound likewise subside, but the hissing was now audible. I found it more than a little unnerving. I heard a slightly muted version of Alvin's voice saying, "Down, Citadel!" and wondered what the creature was doing. Perhaps it had been resting on top of Grandma's shoulder or on top of her head and was still suspended in air, though Grandma had been carted away. I was in a state of suspense myself. Then came an abrupt silence.

For several minutes I calculated the amount of interest I owed on my car, the state of the national debt, the number of papers I still had to grade, and the probability of hearing from any of my own kids in the next few days. I came to no sure conclusions. Finally the Ziggles' phone clunked again and the small voice said, "Who did you say this is?"

I introduced myself. "Well, then," she piped, "you will want to be talking with Alvin I guess."

"No, no, I want to talk with you about Alvin," I said. "Report cards will be coming out soon, but first I wanted to talk to all of the parents."

"Why?" she asked, sounding anxious. I quickly assured her that Alvin was just fine, that I had no complaints, no concerns. I just wanted to talk with her. I mentioned that it sounded very lively in their household.

"Lively," she repeated. "That is an interesting word. It never occurred to me, but *lively* does sound nice. I guess that is why it didn't ever occur. Hmm, lively. Well, I will try to keep that in mind. Thank you so much for calling," and she hung up. Hung up! I dialed again and got Alvin, who called his mother back to the phone. "Yes, who is calling please?" she asked.

I apologized for bothering her but explained that I had not yet gotten to my point in calling.

"There was more?" she asked, emphasizing that last word to make me feel very guilty about imposing.

"Did you get my note?" I asked.

"I don't recall a note, my dear. Possibly it went into the trash, and unfortunately today was our pickup day. I doubt that the trashmen would have known to remove it."

I had no idea what to say to that so I tried to ignore it, but I do want to remember to use it sometime myself. "I sent a message with Alvin saying that I would call," I tried to continue.

"Well, then, and so you did. And now all is well. I trust that no signature is required or anything. Thank you so much. It is so exceedingly delightful to hear from someone who follows through, so rare nowadays. And so that is that, and you have fulfilled your own goal and promise. Good-b– "

"No, no," I shouted frantically, "not good-bye yet. I thought you might have some questions and I wanted to invite you to one of our class council sessions, and– "

"No, no," she said quite calmly, "no questions, none at all. Nothing. 'Less and fewer,' those are my mottos. 'Less and fewer.'"

"I don't understand," I said.

"You would if you lived here, my dear," she said. "Around here, what with Arthur and Alvin and Grandma and Citadel, not to mention Adlai, life is full of questions and even fuller of answers. I would dearly love to know nothing about something for a while. It is so very wearing, so constantly and utterly wearing. Down, Citadel!"

"What kind of dog is Citadel?" I asked, struggling to know something definite.

"Dog?" she asked, surprised.

"Yes, that screeching, eeeeking, always up thing that you have to keep saying *down!* to."

"The screeching, eeking thing you refer to is Grandma," she said.

"Oh, I am so sorry," I began to apologize again.

"Perfectly all right, quite understandable. It really gets very wearing."

"Then what is Citadel?" I tremblingly asked.

"Citadel is Alvin's snake," she said. "It used to be Adele, but Alvin has been training her to uncoil and hiss on command– he calls it sitting– and he is doing a remarkable job, but the snake now thinks her name is Citadel. She terrifies Grandma and we have to call her down. So very, very, utterly wearing. I would like to have a nickel for every minute I want to know nothing. I would be extremely rich then and perhaps could learn to enjoy it."

I could say nothing.

"Well, Mrs. Bream," she said, "or did you say Grimm? Well, by whatever name you call yourself, I am sure Arthur might welcome a call if he were not in his study with the new piranhas. So much of life is predatory, so he may well indeed enjoy a call, not that he likes to be disturbed. I will send his office phone number with Alvin, who is a very good boy and always remembers to deliver messages. Probably you will be more careful than I and will manage to keep it out of the trash. They don't often rescue items, you know, and I appreciate that."

She said good-bye and the phone clicked, and I was left more than astonished. Now my head is coiling and spinning, but I can hardly wait to tell Peggy. She is coming, as I said, to pay a little ssssocial coil, and I will be able to entertain her. I wonder if I can ask her to ssssit. How do they know that the snake thinks her name is now Citadel? And did I say Bream or Grimm? Am I classed now as a predator? I think of myself as tame.

Thiss was pricelesss, and to think that I would have missssssed it, if I had listened to Bill. No more calls tonight, though; I don't think I can take any more. I wanted to learn a little more about the families and in that way more about each of the children. I don't know what I know about Alvin, but I am awed by him all the same. I think I will reword that– I don't know what I know about Alvin, but I am awed by him all the unique.

*Alvin, from his youthful notebooks, 5G*

Goal: to train Adele, my snake, to sit

Method:

- I will first attempt to learn which is her favorite snack:
  - Sudomice, a synthetic round golf-ball-sized pellet Dad made
  - real mice, which are harder to come by (cats in

neighborhood)
* Mom's St. Patrick's Day frog cookies

* As I place the favorite snack about six feet away from her, I will shout "Sit, Adele!"

* I will then see if she will uncoil and reach out when I shout, even though no snack is available.

Expected results:
* If snakes can hear, Adele will learn to uncoil on command merely by hearing the word <u>Sit</u>.
* I will be able to answer the question, Can snakes hear?
* unless Adele is deaf

Anticipated problems:
* Grandma will probably get more upset
* Mom will be unhappy if Adele likes the cookies– she will not want to bake more often
* Dad will be unhappy if Adele does not like the Sudomice
* Mom thinks the snake may get confused about her name
* Hal will not want to come over after school for snacks
* I will have to keep Adlai out of the training area


*Mrs. Green, from her journal*

The weekend was great! Peggy and I talked all night Friday and had a totally wonderful visit. I demonstrated the act of "sitting" and almost knocked out a tooth on the coffee table, but we laughed so hard that I did not care. We ate breakfast on Saturday at noon and then drove fifty miles to the Garden, a fantastic arboretum that I know is going to make a great field trip. I am eager to start planning several activities toward that goal. I tentatively set a date with the education staff there for April fourteenth, and now I have to see if Bill will approve and order buses and get all the essential permission slips and whatever else is required.

I spoke with a Mrs. Landwahr, who told me that the Garden offers some choices of field trip schedules. She recommended that we arrive about ten and go directly to the small theater where they show a film on plant evolution and then plan to ask questions of Dr. Herbert Randle, whom she describes as scholarly but very good with children. He is an authority on rare plants, which should make Alvin happy, and on using the computer to study possible future evolution. That should please quite a few. Then we can tour the grounds by ourselves, with a picnic in any of the many designated areas that we choose. She says there is one section where the children may climb the trees and explore the paths without any danger of getting lost, that all trails lead back to the starting point and are free of poison ivy. There is a phone to the office at the picnic area if we should require anything.

Mrs. Landwahr also gave me a catalog of science products, recommending I look into something called a plant haven, sort of a small hydroponics kit that we might have room for by the back-most window. If not, we will move something. I phoned the order in already.

All the way home from the Garden, I could not stop telling Peg about the class. She laughingly said, "And you wanted to drag me away from my grandchildren!" but, in fact, I could see she was very interested in the kids, especially when I told her what a horror Ms Skimme had been. She asked about Mrs. Burch, too, but I know almost nothing about her other than the fact that Bill said she was outstanding and had a difficult time giving me a contract for the rest of this year. He admitted that he really kept hoping she would return, even though she had told him to look for a permanent replacement. For some reason the children never talk about her, and I find that odd.

*Laura*

Mrs. Green often spent our extra working time in the basement either grading our many, many assignments or else hunting through catalogs for ideas. She also did a lot of writing, but I didn't know if she wrote stories or what, because we didn't usually get to see the results. I do know now that some of it was her own personal journal because, as you can tell, she was kind enough to allow me to use parts of it in this book. It was not easy to find her– she moved away from our small community about the time we went to junior high– but Mr. Filamon was a big help in tracking her down.

Anyway, one of the things that she bought for us provided our class with a real crisis on Haminox. It was a miniature hydroponics lab in which we were to develop a whole new bunch of experiments before our big field trip in April. Our major experiment involved mold and was partly a joke, though not entirely.

The lab was a plastic tent-like structure, enclosed all around but with armholes so that we could put things inside and take things out. There were four armholes at waist level and there were two additional larger holes at the bottom so that water could more easily be added when necessary. It was big enough to hold two big pans of water and had a built-in shelf unit that could hold lighter objects. We held a planetary council to decide what experiments we would conduct. After a lot of noisy discussion, we agreed that we would each bring in two identical objects of our choice, putting one in the lab and one on the window sill. We would wait a week and compare the amount of mold, if any, on each of our test subjects. We would then write up our observations and put them all in a notebook as part of our Haminox archives.

*The Haminox Files*
*Science Notes*
*Mold*

page 37. Our class has recorded the following observations:

Thomas: I have observed that both slices of white bread have turned green, although the one in the lab is more completely green. I believe the additional moisture makes the difference.

Holly: I have observed that both radishes are definitely uglier, filled with black spots and little white beards. After a few days they could have been used to make tiny Santa faces, but not anymore. Ick.

Robert: I have observed that rocks do not mold. I have seen rocks with moss on them, but not here in our experiment. I do not think that mold and moss are the same.

Susan: Lettuce turns slimy and brown and sickening in a surprisingly short time. I thought that only happened at home, but it happened here on the window sill too.

Charlene: Cheese molds very fast, especially mozzarella.

Jody:  Leaves curl about the edges;
          into themselves they fold.
          Dark spots appear upon them,
          and then they mold.

Class conclusion: extra moisture may increase but does not decrease the presence of mold.

Additional observation from Alvin: my father said we did not account for the difference in temperatures.

Additional observation from Brett: jars with different contents make different sounds. (I already knew that.)


*Jody*

All that March, the weather was constantly shifting. One day we would be sure that life was about to burst into buds, and the next it would be snowing heavily. Out across the mud fields, through the bare woods and over the icy trickle of the creek, in and among the trees in the subdivisions as well as the trees in the woods, violets peeped out from patches of snow and squirrels pawed nervously in the sodden leaves, looking for something to eat. Birds scouted the territory for nesting sites and flew away. We still wore heavy coats and boots, but the promise of new small shoots and stems seemed to insist that spring really was on its way. But was *she* on her way? Were we on our way?

The April field trip held all kinds of hope and all kinds of promise, and we prepared more eagerly for it than Mrs. Green could possibly understand. One whole week, all of our reports were geared toward exotic plants. The flora and fauna team on Haminox was especially busy with new drawings and written descriptions. Ian and Alvin were swamped with short articles for the *Haminoxian Gazette*, our science newsletter. Nurse Amy created herbal cures for planetary epidemics, and the hospital that Robert had so generously given was a hotbed of radical theory on new kinds of transplants. Two of the more mangy teddybear-grizzims received pale cabbage heads.

In the midst of all our experiments and preparations, when we barely had time to do every assignment and still take part in all of our extra activities, a most unwelcome, irritating interruption came– a new mystery for us to solve. Ian discovered it first. "There is a big problem with the Plant Haven," he said one morning, pointing to a small puddle of water on the floor by the haven.

"That's not good," Charlene said. "I wonder how that could have happened." She went to look inside the haven and reported to us that all of the water was out of the two pans. We thought that was odd, but Bernardo volunteered to refill them. No big deal.

"Teddy Grizzimgard didn't do his job," Bobby said, and we

smiled.

"Maybe we need another master spy," Charlene suggested. Somebody snickered.

The next day and the next and all that week, the problem kept recurring: a small puddle of water on the floor, no water in the pans. Janice was stumped and Laura was mad. "We have too much to do," she said to me; "I am going to follow the clues and solve them."


### Laura

On the second day of the mystery, I decided I had to approach the problem as if it were one of my stories. I got out paper and pencils, sharpened them all extra fine, and began making notes. I listed every member of the class and wrote down any motive I could think of. Who would want to get our attention? And why? I scribbled notes about everyone and I studied the puzzle hard; and then a light went on in my head, and I was sure that I knew who did it. But I wanted to catch that person wet-handed, and so I made my plan.

I would hide in the room before school, if Mr. Filamon would let me in, and I would wait for the crime to happen. I would leap out from my hiding place, capture the villain, haul that person to justice. I would turn the person over to the class, dust off my hands, and take my bow to the class. Then we could get on with our work.

Mr. Filamon would not let me into the room early. Curses, foiled at the start! But fate was on my side. That third day the water disappeared twice– the second time during our lunch time– and after telling Mrs. Green my plan, I got her permission to stay in the room while the others went to eat. I squeezed into the narrow space between two file cabinets and waited, pretty sure that I knew who was taking the water. It seemed as if I had been stuck in that cramped space forever and I was getting very hungry and miserable and bored, when I heard the door to the room creak slowly open. I watched as the very person I had suspected crept in and tiptoed back to the Haven, using one of the custodian's buckets to pour the water into. As always, some spilled on the floor.

"I see you!" I shouted and the culprit screamed once, dropped the bucket and fled. I was stuck between the two cabinets and could not get out. All I could think of was that everyone would come in and find the water and the bucket and me! They would think I had done it! I would not be the heroine of this story at all; I would be laughed at and then they would all be angry with me, as I was angry with the person who now was running away from the scene of the crime. I sobbed in total frustration and red hot anger and my foot was asleep and my shoulders hurt. And then the door opened again, and I cringed.

"Laura? Are you all right, Laura?" Mrs. Green asked, holding the guilty person by the hand. I did not know what to think. "Sit here, please," she said to that person, pointing to her own chair. What! I did not understand. But she came to get me out of my tight spot, and that mattered first of all. Once I was free, I was able to get very angry in words with that pale someone. Mrs. Green neither stopped me nor encouraged me; she just waited and let me say what I needed to say. I stopped abruptly, hearing the rest of my classmates coming down the hall toward our room. They arrived to find three of us sitting there. Jody was the only one who knew that I had wanted to solve the mystery, so I was sure that the others (if they were thinking of the Haven) assumed I had at least a part in stealing the water. My face was fiery with anger, but they'd think it was red from embarrassment.

I wondered what Mrs. Green would do, what would happen to the guilty party. Would we really have a planetary council? Would the principal be called in? I wanted Bobby's volcano, but we were a planet of peace. We happened to be studying letter-writing in language arts; and probably I need not tell you, though I myself was astonished, that Mrs. Green jumped on this opportunity to have us all write business letters. Business letters!


*Mrs. Green, from her journal*

. . . to the manufacturer of the Plant Haven today, and all of them were annoyed– even those who like to write. But I put all of the necessary information on the chalkboard and then waited eagerly to see what each child would write, hoping to see what to do. I simply suggested that they write to inform the Haven company of the problem we were having and to inquire about solutions. And since that assignment turned out to be quite simple, quickly accomplished, I gave them the more difficult task of writing the response they expected to receive from the manufacturer. Then it became very interesting.

I have those letters with me here. I brought them home to read again and to make me smile, for they are so completely characteristic and therefore to be treasured. The letter to the company was pretty much the same, but here is the body of the letter that Janice wrote:

*Our Plant Haven has developed a problem. The water keeps disappearing. We have checked but seen that there are no leaks, and we do not think that the water would evaporate in hours when it did not evaporate at all before. Before, the water stayed in the pans. Can you help us solve our mystery?*

Now for a few of the return letters: Ian's suggests that the class return the Haven for a free replacement. The writer is sure, he says, that the corporate lab would be very interested in the opportunity to examinine this unique haven, though he was also very sure that they could find no more clues than such a bright class had succeeded in discovering on its own.

Thomas's note expresses his sorrowful doubt that the haven manufacturer can do anything at this late date. Perhaps if the class had returned the Plant Haven sooner. . . .

Alvin's shows interest in this fascinating Haven. It is a first, he says, for the company, which has never had complaints before. If the class members wish to return the product at their own expense, the company would be happy to look at it and bill them for the time, or perhaps new experiments would be appropriate.

Janice, as company president, regrets this illogical turn of events but can see no reason for the company to be involved.

Bobby seems to be suggesting that the class think about hiring a guard. His first letter had mentioned Teddy's failure [to prevent the problem]. His second recommends tossing the Haven and the guard into their live volcano. At least, that is how I interpret his new efforts at writing.

Amy explains that not all Havens behave the same; the haven company could take no responsibility.

Hal's letter recommends the additional purchase of an adapter kit ($98.95) which will convert the Haven into a water vanisher. He acknowledges that we have stumbled onto a water vanisher on our own, but who knows how long it will last? The problem might go away at any time and we certainly would not want to miss out on this extremely interesting opportunity to have a double-function Haven. ($95.25 if we will act quickly.)

Sallee admonishes the class for making an unwise purchase, saying that the company has been taken over by new management and offers to sell us a new model.

Julieanne proposes that a mischievous spirit has managed to take possession of the Haven and urges the class to exorcise it.

Holly matter-of-factly offers to replace the product.

Jody writes, *"problem: invisible crack in the water pans; we'll send replacements in our vans."*

Susan offers to send literature on better models.

Charlene did not pass hers in to me with the others. Without a word, she brought it to my desk, laid it there, and returned to her seat. I read it and asked if she would read it out loud to the class. I know she was uncomfortable with that request, but she did it anyway.

*Dear Class,*

*We at this company believe that you have a mystery there worthy of a master spy. It is our opinion that someone right in your class is responsible, not out of meanness but because he or she enjoys that kind of mystery. We suggest that you go around the room and ask each person directly. We know that he or she will be honest and will admit that he or she did it. He or she really did just want a mystery worthy of a master spy, and she is, we know, very extremely sorry. She just didn't think.*

Charlene then sat down, looking at no one at all. Laura, who had written no letter, looked at her hands and looked at me. I waited to see if she would say anything, but she did not. She busied herself with stuff in her desk, rearranging things more neatly. She still seemed achy from having been squeezed between the file cabinets, but I think she was feeling even more squeezed by her thoughts. She opened her desk again, took out her paper, and hurriedly wrote a note, somewhat subtly placing it beneath a book on top of her desk, pointing to it when I was looking her way. The rest of the class sat quietly, except for Bobby, who began to whistle softly.

The children looked at each other and at me. I think most all of them knew the problem now and they knew there was no need to send out their letters. The wall clock said one o'clock. They looked everywhere except at Charlene, and then they put their tablets away and without any need of direction got up and went to gym. I went over to Laura's desk and found her folded letter there. It said, and I quote in full,

*"We are not in the business of solving other people's mysteries. We leave that to fiction writers and real detectives. If the Haven has no leaks or damage of any kind, we cannot be held responsible. Please take better care of your Haven in the future, and it will give you a lifetime of trouble-free service."*

And so I sit here at my desk at home, pondering anew all the complex strengths we are capable of, what bravery, and what honor. I say this not only of the way in which Laura handled herself but fully as much of the way in which Charlene came through her ordeal.

"How did you know?" I asked Laura after school today.

"How did you figure out that Charlene was the one?"

"She was the only one who had said anything that could sound like a motive," Laura said meekly. "She has always wanted us to need her spy. She has to know it can't really do anything."

"You were very kind to Charlene," I said.

"No, but some things are very real to me that are not to others. I understood that."

I did not know much about the spy or the puppet play until today. It is one of the rare times that anything has been mentioned about the children's time with Mrs. Burch. As Laura told me about that play, and I saw the light in her eyes, I knew that my predecessor had found her special way to reward this class, and I felt even better about the upcoming field trip.


*Jody*

The last week of March teased us cruelly. We had three days of spring and tulips and light sweaters, and then we had a major ice storm that threatened to kill anything that had dared to try to grow. Mrs. Green was out those days with the flu, and once more we had a sub. He was nice enough, and he stuck strictly to our teacher's plans, which included a lot of extra time working on Haminox. I think she figured it would be a lot easier on the substitute and it would allow us to keep getting ready for the trip to the Garden. We polished our long list of questions and we held all kinds of council sessions.

Our planetary nutritionists gave us recommendations for our picnic lunch, and we ignored them. Ian brought to our council the question of whether we should go to the Garden dressed as native Haminoxians. A few pairs of eyes lit up at the thought of going in costume; a lot more did not. We decided that we could not make that decision in Mrs. Green's absence, although it was tempting to think of surprising her.

Because of the lighter work load, we had several short periods of recreational time. Ian and Robert were playing chess. Susan and Laura were using Trave-Log to listen to tapes. Brett was playing a tune on the science jars. Janice and Hal were working at the puzzle table, solving logic problems; and they were both giggling. Apparently they had found a few that Mrs. Green had made up and left for them. Hal and Janice whispered together and then both asked the sub if he would give the problem to everyone. We all wrote the problem down for ourselves and several of us tried to work it. I only vaguely remember part of it, but it went something like this:

*Five farmers among themselves own six cows, each of a
different breed. The cows' names are (in no order) Albina,
Miss Bossie, Cowdoyoudo, Dewdrop, Flower, and Mudder.
One farmer owned three of the cows, none of which he had
named for his mother. The other three cows were owned by
four brothers, who named the cows after each of their
sisters– this was a family tradition.*

A long list of clues followed and wound through a kind of word maze,
but most of us thought it could not be solved. In fact, Janice got it
quickly.

It was not my favorite activity, although sometimes I did enjoy
riddles. I preferred what I thought of as larger puzzles, more real tests,
and I knew that we were in one. So while much of the class frowned
over cows, I stared out the window. A few small birds hopped along
the ledge and then took off for the woods. One tiny chickadee stayed
near the window, gazing brightly in at the sub as if checking to make
sure all was well. I let my mind conjure up Ms Skimme and thought of
how our class had been shattered. Half of us had grown to hate the
place where we had been happy before, and a few of the most outgoing
among us had grown as silent as I. Lambs to the slaughter we were so
short a time before; then Mrs. Burch had sojourned among us, and we
began to recover. Now with April a few days off, I fully believed that
all was well but would soon get even better.

And then that month so full of promise for us finally arrived.
It came with pranks and jokes, but it came. The first of the April Fool's
Day jokes took place in Trave-Log I. Brett had secretly installed new
tapes of his music played on the science jars. Mrs. Green had plugged
the main wire in, and the lights went on as we entered the room and the
eerie jar music played. The spaceship was missing and in its place was
a large notice that said, "Out in space, back soon." A few more signs
appeared around the room, many declaring that work was out of order.
A "no exit" sign was hanging over the door. But we held a serious
council session where we talked about setting limits. What was private
property and what was public? When did sharing stop and stealing
start? I don't remember what specifically turned our discussion this
way– perhaps it was the moment after Bobby reached over and took
Alvin's pen to make a mark on Alvin's arm. I know that Mrs. Green
listened to us debate and discuss what Alvin's rights were, and she
asked us about our own boundaries.

She went to that magic bag that lived beneath her desk and
brought out a book of poems and read us "Mending Wall," a poem by

Robert Frost about fences, about boundaries. Hal laughed at the mention of cows; but we had to think about the poem and answer the question, what is meant by "good fences make good neighbors"? We talked a lot about why we have the right to our boundaries, the right to our personal space.

"So, you were like the cows," Alvin said angrily to Bobby. "You can't just break down my fence and take my pen and attack me."

"Huh?" said Bobby.

"But he doesn't like fences," Laura said of the poet. He says there is something that 'does not love a wall.' It's that other person who wants barriers."

"People can want different things," Amy said. "Why is one right and the other wrong?"

"Sometimes people need fences," Julieanne said. "It feels safer."

"Maybe there are some good fences and some bad fences," Janice suggested. "Maybe good fences make good neighbors and bad fences don't."

"How can a fence be bad?" Sallee asked. "Besides, we don't have fences around us. He is talking about land, and we are people."

"He's not talking just about land," Susan said.

"Property, all kinds of property," Ian said. "We are our own property."

"We can do what we want with our own," Hal said. "Our own property is nobody else's business."

"There are invisible fences around us," I said, "the things that keep us apart."

"And some of them are good," Julieanne repeated.

Our discussion went on for a long time; but in the end what we decided was that we really are entitled to our own private space, and it is up to each of us to decide when and where and how we open the gate to each other. We cannot force ourselves into another's space.

Laura looked mildly embarrassed, but I imagine she was thinking about file cabinets.


### Laura

At last the day of the field trip arrived! The whole week had been warm and the air was filled with sweet scents of apple blossom and lilacs. When we got to school that morning, the fading orange bus was already waiting for us– newly washed so that in spite of its dented fenders and its ancient appearance, it gleamed in the welcome sun. The busdriver had on an old lightweight tan jacket and a battered older winter cap with ear flaps that looked out of place and out of season. He sat on the steps of the bus, leaning over his old brown boots, quietly waiting and simply sitting, staring at the ground. A little before nine o'clock, we had finished gathering whatever we needed to take with us and were filing outside to the bus. Now the driver was sideways in his proper seat, watching as we climbed the steps laughing and teasing each other. He listened to voices he had heard a million times before,

> *You always get to sit by Amy. No, sometimes I sit by Amy. Over here, Hal, over here. Sit here, Alvin. Brett, this one's empty. Ian, do you have the list of questions? Who has my lunch bag? What was in it? None of your business; it had my name on it. If you have a bag with my name on it, you have my lunch. Everyone check the floor for Robert's lunch, please. Watch out for mold, watch out for fuzz, watch out for falling lettuce. What is this? That's mine. Thought you said a bag. Sue me, it's a box. Hey, Robert, neat little pink lunchbox. Big deal, it's my sister's. Yeah, right. Garden, here we come!*

The busdriver, clearly experienced, let down the earflaps on his cap. Mrs. Green counted heads, spoke to the driver, and away the bus jerked and rolled. *Garden, here we come!*

### Jody

Hal, Ian, Brett, and Alvin went on and on teasing Robert about his pink lunchbox and his sandwich. "Just plain lettuce?" Hal kept asking.

"It's on the installment plan," Brett informed them. "He gets to bring tomato tomorrow."

"Next week, MAYO," Alvin continued.

Robert was getting fed up; "Next week a first aid kit," he muttered. "With bread?" Ian asked. The boys got giddier and giddier, and Robert leaned over to punch them. Mrs. Green kept an eye on them while pretending to be studying a catalog. At the first punch, she turned toward them but decided not to do anything. When the joking kept on, she sent a few eye signals, which seemed to be received. It was quiet for several short blocks. "Lettuce see what he brings in tomorrow," Ian whispered to his seat mate Alvin. Mrs. Green was instantly standing beside Robert's seat and whispering something to Ian. She invited Brett to start us all on a song.

An hour and a half later, we had sung our way through every favorite song, including the Bell Anthem and the newly revised "O Haminox" anthem; the busdriver was blissfully tuned in to different music, thanks to the earplugs he wore; Mrs. Green was straining her ears for whispered words of vegetation beneath the loud-sung songs; and all of our eyes were shining as we drove through the Garden gates.

We happily got off the bus and eagerly formed two lines. We started to head for the main door, but Robert had to go back for his lunch. "I don't blame him for forgetting it," Hal said.

"Lettuce not say a word," Ian cautioned. Mrs. Green glared, just a little. Then Robert was back in line, and we headed down the concrete sidewalk toward the solid turnstiles, which we quietly passed through. We walked into the education building, with its floors so highly polished and its atmosphere of a library. Hushed, we went with dignity and calm into the small auditorium where we were to see the newest thing in films back then, Magic Scentovision. We would take a cinematic walk through a phenomenal garden of aromatic plants and our senses would be immersed in all of the actual odors and we were to be enchanted.

Bobby began to sneeze at the very thought of it.


*Laura*

Mrs. Green had prepared us for the scent movie. She had been very excited about our being the first class to get to experience this film. She said that she had received a call from someone at the Garden, asking if we would like to do so– it was brand-new and they were eager to test it out on kids. Of course we were eager too. It was hard to keep quiet while we waited, but most of us did. Some of the boys did keep giggling, but at least they kept their voices low.

We began to squirm quite a bit when there was no sign of any film projectionist anywhere, no sign of any staff member. We were supposed to get to interview Dr. Randle after the movie, so some of us studied our questions. Mrs. Green moved to sit by the boys. Finally we heard a scuffling sound up there in the projectionist's booth, and we all smiled and relaxed. Nothing happened for a few minutes, but then a voice came muffled through the window: "Hey, Lady?"

"Yes?" Mrs. Green said, standing up and peering toward the booth.

"You the ones here to see the Stink Film?"

"The Scentovision film? That is what we are here to see," she said. The boys were all writhing with delight.

"Yeah, that one. We ain't got it today." All of us were very disappointed. I think Sallee and Amy and Janice wrinkled their noses at "ain't got it" but they would rather have wrinkled them at a movie.

"But we were invited specifically to see it today," Mrs. Green exclaimed. "Why don't you have it?"

"Dr. Randle needed it for a meeting. He took it. Don't blame me."

"But Dr. Randle was to be here with us. Perhaps this is the meeting he meant, and he will be bringing the film here," she said, brightening.

"Doubt it, he took it with him to California last night. I bet he ain't back."

"I can't believe this," she said, looking absolutely as angry as Ms. Skimme on a good day. We had never seen her look angry. "Who is here that I can speak with?"

"Dunno. But I got another film here if you want to see one. It's about spice. Okay?"

"Spies!" Ian whispered. "Sure beats a film about lett– " but he was cut short.

"Is it good?" she asked.

"I ain't never seen it. Says on the box it's a rare old vintage black and white. Says of historical interest. Want it?"

"I guess," she said, dejected. She turned to us and said, "I am really sorry about what is happening. I wonder why no one told me that Dr. Randle would not be here, but we still can have our picnic." She sat down as the lights dimmed and a small square of light appeared in the center of the huge screen. After several minutes of static and noise, an image slowly resolved: it was a thin man in a striped suit, standing in front of a picture of a garden. In a monotonous reedy voice he told us about the pleasures of gardening and the special joys of spice and herb gardens. He beckoned us into the picture.

For twelve minutes we "toured" the black and white garden, barely able to distinguish one plant from another. We were supposed to note the distinctions in the vein patterns of different leaves, but we could barely make out the leaves at all. "Boring," said Hal, and even Alvin agreed. The thin man in the movie, back again in his office, pointed to another picture on his wall– a picture of a swamp. "Perhaps this is how your yard looks," he said with an air of distaste, "but now that you have seen what may be done, let us hope that you will improve it."

"Yes, lettuce," Alvin said. Mrs. Green seemed not to care.

The room lights came back on, while the square of light on the screen crackled before it died. We rubbed our eyes and looked at each other and looked at our teacher and could not wait to leave. Just then the door to the auditorium opened and a chubby man walked in. At least we knew it was not the man from the film.

"I am Dr. Randle's assistant," he said, "here to answer your questions. Dr. Randle sends his regrets that he was called away quite unexpectedly to a meeting; but it regards funding, and so I'm sure you know that naturally he had to attend." Mrs. Green asked us to get out our questions, but she seemed to have lost her enthusiasm. Alvin, who was designated to be our first questioner, cleared his throat, and Bobby closed his eyes. The chubby man continued talking. "I know you did not get to see our Scentovision film," he said sadly, "but I understand you were treated to one of our rare vintage treats from the earliest days of film. Some of them are amazingly good."

"Ask him why we didn't get to see one of those," Hal urged Alvin.

Mrs. Green introduced herself and said that the class had worked very hard to develop a substantial list of questions and were looking forward to asking them. The chubby man smiled and rubbed his hands together and said, "Fine, fine, happy to oblige, although I am due back in the labs in five minutes. I trust that will be sufficient?"

"Well, no, it really won't be sufficient. We were told to be sure to prepare for thirty minutes at least, and we have done so," she said, her voice getting tense.

"Oh, that is out of the question," he said. "Perhaps it would be better not to start at all, rather than do an inadequate job. I am needed at the hydroponics lab, where we are experiencing some problems."

"Is the lab losing water?" Alvin asked. Charlene sank down in her seat, looking glum.

"No, sonny, we are not losing water. Why would we lose water? Well, thank you for coming, and I hope you enjoy the rest of your day." And he left. All of us were angry. *All of our work, all of our writing, all that erasing, all that time, all for nothing.*

"I am terribly disappointed," Mrs. Green said. "Today was supposed to be a great treat, and it is not going well at all."

"At least we did see a stink film," Ian said, smiling somewhat encouragingly.

"Yes, yes, I am sorry to say that we did," she said with a slight smile. "Now let. . . I mean, now I think we should head. . . I mean now I think we should walk quietly out of this building and explore on our own to see what we can find. After all, we really do want to explore on our own. Shall we?"

We left the auditorium and stood quietly in the foyer while Robert went back for his lunchbox. While we waited, the young projectionist came out with our stink film. "You guys picked a bad day," he said. Mrs. Green mentioned that this was supposed to have been a wonderful educational experience. He scratched his head and thought a minute. "I think some of the trees is labeled. Maybe that'll do. Kids don't care about all that fancy learning stuff."

We cared.


### Jody

Quietly and in an almost perfect manner, we left the building and began to walk toward the right, away from the small parking lot and toward the trails. We walked to a spot where three separate trails began and wondered which to take. Each of them was alluring, and we quickly left behind us our disappointment at the film and the loss of the interview in our eagerness to be on a trail. Small border plants lining the edges of all the trails; sweet wildflowers of blue and white and yellow; bulb plants in a circus of random color; herbs and spices each exhaling wonderful scents– yes, we were eager to start what had to be the best part of the trip.

"Which trail?" Mrs. Green asked us. *All of them, all of them.* "Which one first?"

"Can't we split up?" Amy asked.

"Not here," she answered. "Maybe at some point, but not here."

Ian and Alvin were edging toward the first trail on the left when a harsh voice behind us stopped them: "Keep on the path!" We whirled to find a uniformed guard, tall and stern, with a small walkie-talkie and a whistle. "Don't touch any of the plants!" he barked. We stared at him.

"Is there any particular path you would recommend?" Mrs. Green asked, turning too. "Or are they all the same?"

"Nope," he said, remaining several yards away.

"Well, then," she said, turning back to us, "I guess we'll start with this one on the left."

"Wouldn't 'f I were you," he said gruffly.

"Why not? What's wrong with this one?" she asked, obviously getting irritated again.

"Short," he said curtly.

"Short? We should not go on it because it is short? What difference does that make? Then we'll be on our way to another all the sooner."

"Then you might as well go on the second to start with," he said, walking closer to us. We all stared at him, frightened. What would we do?

"We might want to go on all of them," she informed him.

"Yep. You probably will. So why did you ask me for my opinion? You'll do as you please anyway." He was standing right next to Mrs. Green now, and we could see her eyes opening wide. She stared at him too. "What's the matter with you?" he asked. "You look like you think I'm from another planet. Never seen a guard before?"

"Why, yes, I have. Of course I have," she stammered, looking around at all of us and grinning. "Class," she said, "I would like to introduce you to our guard here at the Garden. Mr. Grissom, this is a very fine group, a very polite group. Class, Mr. Grissom." Some of us squirmed at the word *polite.*

"Ted Grissom at your service, if you behave and stay in the right place," he said, and we stood in a semitrance. Our guard at the Garden was a Grissom-guard, a teddy bear, a real protector of plants. Oh, yes, we were in the right place for us, even if he did not know it. We smiled very nicely at him and promised that we would be good. Mrs. Green's mood then immediately changed from darkly sad to sunny and thrilled. All of us knew that she realized that she had made the perfect choice. Our hearts all beat together; this would be a perfect day. Perhaps it would even be better for its distressing and dismally disappointing start.

We started down the first path excitedly, though very quietly, but stopped briefly at Teddy's whistle. Robert ran back for his pink lunchbox, which the Grissom-guard was holding. "Thanks," Robert said and rejoined us, and so at last we were into the trail. Our guard stood then with his arms folded across his chest, walkie-talkie in his belt, antennae seeming to sprout from his head; and he appeared to recede in the distance. He turned, as if on a lazy susan, and went back to his familiar post.

The name of the trail was *Ancient Space*, which intrigued and delighted Alvin and Ian. We entered the original section of the Garden, where the trees towered beyond our sight and the silence all around us commanded our respect. With barely audible footsteps we passed deep groves and ravines; and it felt as if we were moving quickly through time itself, through visible history. Alvin craned his neck to see as far as he could see, and Bernardo stretched his hand toward one massive trunk but refrained from actually touching. All of the Amys looked awed at these trees, so much alike and so different, one bent by forces to twist toward the east, another straight and tall, but all beautiful. I looked about for a specific tree, but I did not see it yet. Too soon we found ourselves winding down, down to a narrow cul-de-sac, and turned around to look up the steep trail along which we just had come. It really was too short, but in its silence and its holiness we were all put into the proper sober mood. Wordlessly we went back up the path and wordlessly moved to the second trail. Our Grissom-guard was standing by, but he just doffed his cap to us and looked us over and nodded us on. Robert still had his pink lunchbox, so we all moved quickly on. Lettuce go in silence.

*Tea-time* was the name of this trail, but no one sneered or scoffed. Past beds of delicately scented plants, lemony and softly soothing and utterly calm, we slowly walked. As we did, we breathed the aroma in and became completely relaxed. We walked beneath pink dogwood and rosebud trees and entered a formal garden where mossy cobblestone paths led us through a perfectly symmetrical maze. At its center was a stone fountain, its cool waters softly raining and making a familiar music. Brett began humming *Greensleeves*, and all of us listened and many of us, I am sure, were thinking of that day in December. Ian's eyes were gleaming too, as if the music had evoked memories all his own.

Stone benches surrounded the fountain, and we sat for several minutes listening to the play of the water and thinking our own private thoughts. *This is public property*, I thought, *and yet it is my own.*

We got up like a flock of birds, knowing it was time to move on, and we found ourselves at the edge of the cobbled pavilion looking out on a field of iris. "They're Spies eyes," Ian whispered and we solemnly nodded. The air filled deep with birdsong, and the warm sun glowed softly comfortable. We all felt increasingly sleepy, but we were eager to keep moving on. We retraced our steps on those old cobblestones and left the fountain playing, and in our holy state of awakeness we headed back on the trail to find our next adventure.

Theodore Grissom was eating his lunch and strongly urged us to do the same. "The third trail is the longest," he said, dropping a leaf of lettuce and hastily picking it up. Another fell from his sandwich and scampered away in the wind. He went after it but it kept ahead, and Robert called out too softly for the guard to hear him, "Don't step off the paths!" The rest of us started walking slowly, but Robert stood there amused. Ian went back to get him, whispering, "Lettuce go, Rob, lettuce go!" We entered the third trailhead.

First the trail took us to a small clearing with tables where we could picnic; but without any arguing or even any conversation, we all knew not to stop. It was a pleasant scene, wildflowers scattered like crayon shavings across a green sheet of paper, but it called us not at all.

It gave us a new set of choices, though, for at each of the four cardinal points of the compass a brand-new trail began. "Oh dear," Mrs. Green said. "This is going to be difficult."

"Now maybe we can split into groups?" Amy asked again. "I don't think I want to go on four separate ones." Several agreed.

"Well," Mrs. Green said, looking over the trail map she had brought with her, "I was told that all trails lead back right here and that this is the safest area for children to explore. But you must not go on alone. You have to go in groups of at least three, and you must have someone with a watch in each of your groups."

All of the Amys and Sallee and Charlene formed one group, though they had no watch. Bobby and Brett wanted to be with the rest of the boys, but they did not want the same trail. Thomas decided to team with them. Holly and Janice asked Robert if he wanted to be with them. Finally he did, even though he really did not want to be with all girls. But he did have a watch and he did not want to be with Alvin or Ian or Hal or Brett. His choice was seriously limited. He invited Thomas to take a different trail, but Tom expressed his doubts. Robert went with the girls. Two Amys switched to join Holly and Janice. Somehow watches got distributed.

Our little cluster of eight who had made Trave-Log knew from the moment we reached that clearing that we would stick together. We grinned in excitement as we put our lunch bags on one of the picnic tables. Mrs. Green said that she thought the clearing must be meant for her and that she would just wait there until all of us came back. "You have thirty minutes and then come back for lunch," she told us. "Come back sooner, though, if you are ready. And let me write down which trail each of you is going on, so that I feel more secure."

Robert and the girls headed to the north trail head; Brett's trio took the east. Sallee's group took the south trail and we raced together west. Each of us had read the signpost there at the head of the trail, and each of us knew that it was for us; and yet we learned later that we had not all seen it the same. Hal and Alvin had each seen *fascinating trail*, Susan had seen *Spring Glade*; Laura claimed that the sign said *Entering Storyland*, and Ian saw *Tu-T-Tu*. Bernardo insisted that the sign was in decimal code and spelled *Birch Grove*. We did not know that back that day; we simply assumed we all perceived it the same. I guess you must know what I saw then: I saw *April Hollow*.

*Mrs. Green, from her journal*

All that morning that was to be so fabulous, I was very

138

distressed. Everything seemed to be going wrong, and I felt thrown back into my own past where life had torn me apart. I'd thought that I was mended now and the children deserved so much, but things began to take a turn after we left that dark auditorium and were out in the pure air again. Sometime I will come back and write about guard Theodore Grissom, but right now my fingers can hardly keep up with the images and experiences of the rest of the day. I want to write about the sunny clearing.

Something within me knew that it truly was all right to let the class form groups of its own and to go on their separate adventures. I had read the trail maps and could not see how anyone could get lost, and I felt that with large enough groups I would be quickly called if anything went wrong. So I sat at a table in the clearing and envied my children. I watched them scamper in the brilliant sun, each to their chosen fate, and I breathed deeply and relaxed deeply and seemed to see a flutter of leaves enveloping me, as I fell sound asleep.

An image formed so clearly in my eyes and head that I still cannot believe it was merely a dream. A tree sprang up in front of me, its leaves so beautiful and sharply clear before my eyes. They sighed and rustled in the breeze and seemed to wave me in. Tree branches gently enveloped me and made me feel welcome; and the warm sun in the clear air made all things shine and shimmer. Voices whispered in the April air, leaves rustled, and tiny yellow birds soared and sang. I felt myself carried to a distant place, to a high place, and from that spot I found that I could see all of the children at once. Then I was drawn into them all simultaneously. I don't know how, but what I do know is that I was allowed to accompany every one of them at all times, and I can tell you precisely what each one saw and thought and did. And though I could tell anyone about them all, I am going to limit my story to eight at first. Maybe more later, but I will start with the eight who took the western trail, the one that said on its signpost, *Welcome.*

## EIGHT TOGETHER

Up a winding narrow path, around a bend, up and around and forward they ran, through oaks and maples and sycamores until they came quite suddenly to a grove of paper birches. Tall and white the birches stood, leafed in lettuce green, and all the branches welcomed them in a rustling velvet whisper. Beneath the tree was a small sign:

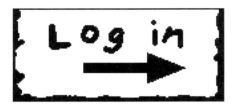

The arrow pointed the eight toward a large fallen tree that they then had to walk across to get past a deep ravine. Once over the log, they looked around and were drawn by a buzz in the air. They hurried toward it and found something large and gleaming that softly made a variety of noises as they drew near. The sun beamed kindly on the children as they stood there in awe, not only at the sight of all those springtime birches rustling their welcome but also at the sight and sound of the softly glowing, gently humming, delicately lighted, silver-shining object there that announced to them in a peculiarly feminine voice that still was very mechanical,

> *I * am * Trave-Log * II * * * Welcome to * Spring*
> *Glade * and Birch Grove * and April Hollow * * ***
> *Welcome to * your dreams * * ***

For more than a moment they stood frozen– some just staring at the computer, which seemed to wink at them, some at the birches nodding their leafy heads and smiling in all their branches and twigs. Perhaps because, like me, he had come new in January, Ian stepped forward first while the others hung back in a daze.

> *Hello * Ian * * * you are welcome * here ***

"You know my name!" he marveled; "and, wow, you even pronounced it right!"

> *You helped * create me * * * of course I know * your ***
> *name * * ***

"Wow," he said and stood back.
"Will you let us go on our dream adventures?" Laura asked.
"Do you really work?" Bernardo asked.

> *What * do you mean * by * 'really'?*

"Do you do things at our command?" Susan asked.

*Sometimes the things * that you desire * and the things*
*\* that you command * take on a life\* of their own \**
*you know   \*  a kind of  life * of their own * \* \**

"Oh-oh," Alvin whispered. Hal looked more than a little concerned. Susan even moved a little bit closer to her brother, just as he moved closer to her.
"So you do work, though?" Ian asked.

*Oh * yes * I * really * work * \* \**

and the machine seemed to chuckle happily, though perhaps there was a hint of menace. Maybe I am just imagining that, but it seemed to me from my far and near perch that they were a little frightened. Only Jody looked completely blissful. "We are all in this together?" she asked the machine. "We are going on an adventure together?"

*It could well be * that you will take * this trip together*
*\* * You * have * some choices * after all * \* \**
*some choices  * yes *   you do * \* \**

The voice remained gently mechanical, though still slightly reminiscent of rustling leaves. It might have held possibilities of nightmare, but that was their risk. How would they each respond? But, as they stood there lost in thought, they really had little choice; for already the landscape was changing, and the trail was growing dim. The log had been gone for a while. A ripple of air, a streamer of cloud, a shiver of every leaf, and the trees in the grove dissolved before them and Trave-Log II began to hum and vibrate.
"You aren't going to disappear!" Julieanne cried frantically.
"What are we supposed to do?" Bernardo shouted.

*Yes * I am going * now * it is * what happens *
*and you * all * have grown * accustomed * \* \* I will*
*tell you * this * \* \* You must * go * into * your own*
*dreams * and discover * what * all of you * must do *
*\* * I will see you * again * \* \**

"Together?" Jody called out. "What we must all do together?"
"Will we have any help?" Laura asked.

*No help * but you * will find *

141

"What?" they shouted together, as the voice faded and the lights went out and the whirring died away. And as they watched, the computer fell to metallic dust and blew away. They stood there then all numb, while around them sunlight fell in shafts. Nothing was clear and nothing was known, and each felt cold in the sun– and alone. Even the happy Jody was looking worried.

"What now?" Susan whispered, shivering. At first no one wanted to move.

"I guess we might as well start walking," Ian said.

"We could go back to the picnic grove," Julieanne said in a strained voice.

"I could go along with that," Hal said.

"That's no adventure," Alvin said.

"It's not a dream," said Jody. "We might as well not have come at all. I think we should go on, all of us, all of us together."

"If we leave this spot," Susan said, "how will we find our way back?"

"I have a penknife," Bernardo said, pulling it out of his jeans pocket. He cut a small section of grass away and marked an X in the dirt. Immediately the grass grew back. "I don't like this," he said.

"Mrs. Green said we could not get lost," Jody told them. "The computer knows us and is sending us on to our adventure together. We are in our dream and in our world. We won't get lost."

Bernardo had taken his handkerchief from his other pocket and had tied it to the signpost, but the knot came loose and the white handkerchief floated back into the pocket. "I guess we are on our own now," he admitted and tried no more to mark their starting point.

"Doesn't anything stay? Doesn't anything last?" terrified Julieanne cried out.

"I think we are the ones who have to learn how to stay and then we must learn how to leave," Jody answered. "We just need to start, and then we have to find the clues."

"Let's promise to stay together," Laura said, moving in closer to the others. "Let's keep close together."

They began to walk along the path, looking for clues and more than half afraid. A new trail opened in front of them, and again there was a sign. All of them saw it the same:

"I like parks," Bernardo said.

"How come the first letter is smaller than the others?" Laura asked, sure she had seen a clue. "The big letters spell *ark*; maybe we are looking for a boat."

It was not exactly a park they entered; it was just a field, and yet it was not. All color glowed with a newfound brilliance, as if through a kind of enhanced prism that refracted each hue into a whole new realm of possibility– as if they had entered kaleidoscopes of which they were only partially aware.

Alvin was going on ahead and called to them to hurry. Laura asked him to wait; but he motioned for them to catch up with him, pointing to an arched doorway several yards farther along. All eight approached the doorway and were stopped as if by a field of energy. Alvin tried to walk through by himself and was instantly thrown to the ground. "Ooof," he groaned, picking himself up. Ian tried, with the same result. Then the two boys tried to go through together, but they got nowhere except to the ground. Again all eight tried to walk right through, but all eight were gently restrained.

"We don't like walls," Ian said out loud, addressing the arch. "Here there are no cows; we come in peace." Still, they could not get through.

"The 'pARK' must be our clue," Jody said. "What do you think it might mean?"

"Animals going into the ark together two by two," Julieanne suggested. "Maybe we need to go in pairs."

"We tried that," Ian said.

"You tried two boys, but remember the story we read?" Laura asked. "One boy and one girl."

"C'mon then, Laura," Alvin said, grabbing her by the hand.

"Will you be my valentine, Julieanne?" Ian courteously asked.

"Okay, Hal," Susan said to her brother.

"I guess you are stuck with me," Bernardo said to Jody.

"Not stuck; that's fine with me," she said.

Hand in hand four times over, they walked quite easily past the energy field, through the doorway. The colors all around them seemed a little less intense, but all they could think of at first was that they had passed the test. They did not look behind them so they did not see that the path and the arched doorway had, like everything else, reduced themselves to atoms and been quietly blown away. Though they did not fully know it yet, there could be no turning back. That was the nature of their dream, and they were well inside it.

"Remember the birch trees, remember all of the birch trees," Julieanne kept saying to herself. The words seemed to be her anchor in a rising tide of fear. Ian's hand holding her own was her other source of strength. She did not let it go.

"I'm thinking of this as a story," Laura said, "and I will write about it when I am safely home. Right now I am doing research, and I am going to notice as much as I can. I'm going to think of this as a story. A story."

They came to a crossroads that troubled them: four new ways to go and no signposts. "Oh-oh," Hal said, "this is really getting too complicated. This is more than interesting enough. It isn't boring but it is more interesting than I want to think about."

"I am not going on four trails," Susan announced.

"I don't think we will have to," Jody said.

"We wouldn't have time," Hal said, looking at Bernardo's watch. It did not seem to have moved.

"Four pairs, four trails," Laura observed. "But I don't want us to split up. How can we possibly split up? We just have to do this all together."

"What if we never get back together again?" Susan asked.

"We will," Jody insisted.

"Trave-Log II did not say we would succeed," Ian pointed out.

"We all know that we will. We will do what we find to do and then we will be together. I feel sure of it. Remember, this is April Hollow." But that name seemed to mean more to her than to anyone else, and the others were less confident about reuniting. They tried to go in a group down the first new trail but were again repelled.

"Let's go," Ian said, but he and Julieanne were stopped.

"It isn't our path, I guess," she said, relieved not to be first.

"Maybe we ought to go back," Hal said.

"No way," Alvin said. "You chose to come on the adventure; you can't let us down now." Alvin rarely sounded demanding, but he was eager to be on his way. He would never forgive anyone for ruining this chance by backing out. "Come on, Hal, it is fascinating!"

Without warning, with no sound but a gentle burst of light as if a camera flash went off, Alvin and Laura found themselves pulled within the trailhead. Another explosion of brighter light blinded the other six; but when after a minute or two they could gradually see again, their two friends were not among them. Alvin and Laura, when the light dimmed down, were long, long gone and far away.

"Laura, Laura, where are you?" Julieanne called.

"Alvin, can you hear me?" Ian shouted down the trail. But no sound of any kind returned, not even an echo of their own frightened voices. There on the spot where the two had last been seen, a new invisible wall of the barrier kind was firmly established. Alvin and Laura had entered their own space, and no one else could trespass. But I was there and so, I could tell, was another interested presence.

Invisible, huge, real, vaguely luminous. Words for a vocabulary list perhaps or just for me?

*Mrs. Green, with the Trave-Log II printout*

## TWO TO THE MOUNTAINS

### 4 a * subroutine one * enter * run

At the precise moment that six had seen the bright light explode, Alvin and Laura were stepping into an abyss, falling through vastnesses of space, empty except for that light. They wheeled and rolled and whirled and fell, fell screamless and unthinking in all that blinding glare. And then they simply landed– abruptly but gently as if on a puff of feathers– both of them unbruised but terribly shaken, afraid for a minute to look around. When they could gather themselves back together, huddled close together, they looked: they were on a very narrow grassy margin between two rising mountains, two enormous hulks of granite soaring upward whence they had fallen. They stared up at the impossible heaven, which was glowing a soft pale green.

"I think we have to get back up there somehow," Alvin barely whispered, awed.

"There is no way we can climb these mountains," Laura said, starting to look at details. "There is no place to find a handhold, no place to find a foothold."

"Here is a handhold," Alvin said, stretching his hand to hers. "I may not always pay attention, but I heard. Really, I heard. We are going to do this together, and lettuce not let go." He giggled a little, but Laura did not mind; she grabbed his hand and held on tight, and together they looked for a path back up. But there were two separate mountains and they were caught between. Neither seemed to call to them or to give them any clue; they simply had to make a guess and act on it and move on. They had to follow their hunches if they were to move at all. So they chose the leftmost mountain inasmuch as it looked as if it offered a gentler climb, though in fact they both were the same, mirror images of each other; but Alvin and Laura were in no position to see.

As before, they never looked back, for to do so would surely be frightening. They kept their eyes ahead and just enough to the sides to be able to search there for clues– and a good thing, too, it was, for I watched as the rightmost mountain crumbled a little at the peak and began to dwindle down. I watched as, next, that rightmost mountain dissolved quite fast at its base. Bit by bit and chunk by chunk, in complete and aweful silence, the rightmost mountain lost itself and blinked away. Just for a moment one might have seen one slim ledge of rock suspended in air, but only for that moment. Poof!

Alvin and Laura climbed, finding no clues yet, but they started seeing little narrow crevices open for them. They had to let go of each other's hands more often than they wished; but together they climbed this impossible hulk of rock, finding its ledges and footholds and its branches that lent a helping arm. The trail kept getting more difficult, and finally– still some way down from the top– they rested. "Where do you think we are?" Laura asked, breathing a little hard.

"I don't know," Alvin said, panting.

"I don't feel that I can climb much more for a while," she said sadly.

"That's okay. We are way past our thirty minutes, so what's another hour or day?" and he smiled at her and leaned his head back against the rock behind them. Both of them fell asleep.

They awoke to a midnight sky overhead and panicked. There was no way that they could go on in the dark and they had no idea what to do. Laura began to cry, and Alvin whistled to keep his courage; but both of them forgot their fears when the sky began to lighten. It was not dawn that brightened the sky; it seemed more like Brett's Grizzim. A crescent of apricot moon hung in the still-green sky; and small lights twinkled and glittered, but were they stars? A tree grew up behind the two, and they leaned their heads more comfortably against its glowing white trunk to watch the light show granted them.

Out in the distant meadows of sky, in the infinite green-black space, a single ray of orange flared from a tiny yellow point. From a far, far distant speck of blue, a purplish line streamed forth, arching delicately into space, slowly tracing a path. "Look!" Alvin said, letting go of Laura's hand and eagerly pointing.

"Sshh," Laura whispered, "I see," but her eyes followed the sweep of his arm. A single star, immensely far, turned from red to blue to gold. Double rays of multiple hues shot out. Stars lit up throughout the sky, throughout the cosmic field. Rays of every conceivable tint crisscrossed the night, shooting and bouncing across the midnight green. The field became a pattern of color and line; and from deep somewhere in all that world of thin etched color, sounds began to emerge– to hum and buzz and to whirr.

"They aren't stars at all," Alvin muttered.

"Not lights either," Laura whispered.

"It's a battle!" Alvin cried, "a space battle!" and he leaned forward, on his knees, to see all that he could see. His eyes were as bright as any star, and he began a stream of verbal instructions: "Look to your starboard side, purple star, look to your starboard side. Watch out for that ray of bright red over there; it's coming straight at you. Shoot back, shoot back! Oh, no!"

Laura held to the sheltering trunk as she watched the battle unfold. For eons, it seemed, the lights and the rays streaked through the dark and exploded. Dots of color would mushroom and briefly hang suspended, and then a new set of lights would arise and fight to a deathly conclusion. From single and double rays of light, fiery swaths emerged– so many multiple beams, sizzling smoke, infinitely infolding clouds of red, of blue, of gold, of purple. At first they had thought the explosions were stars that were going nova, but Alvin quickly realized that the bursts meant the destruction of spaceships. "What a battle!" he whispered to himself. "What an incredible battle! How far away they must be; we can barely hear the report."

Laura was busy recording in her storytelling mind these events that she was witness to and the things that she imagined. She barely heard Alvin at all, though he was right there beside her. He was not even a foot away, but she could barely hear his report.

"Look!" he cried, grabbing her arm and pointing far to their right; "way, way down there." She looked: an incredibly large silver and blue, shining and gleaming and brilliantly twinkling rocket moved toward them from the distant dark, at a speed impossible to calculate. Instantly it hovered before the two, so soundlessly throbbing in the quivering air, lighted by some bright invisible source. They both knelt forward in aching suspense.

From the left, an orange saucer zoomed up and stopped, even with the silver rocket. It lightly hummed as it floated there. Alvin sat back hard. Laura leaned forward more. "Oh, look!" she said, tugging on his sleeve, "straight ahead, what is that?"

"Not a ship or a rocket or a saucer," he said, his eyes large as saucers themselves. "Whatever it is, it's alive!"

"And such a beautiful shade of blue!"

Directly in front of them, even with the rocket and the saucer, spaced precisely between them, a large and shaggy, incredibly furry, quadruply-winged creature pawed the air and flexed its wings and snorted a bit to catch its multiple breaths. "Wow, oh wow, oh wow!" Alvin whispered. From the rocket a single small circle of light bubbled up to the two children and stopped about five feet away. A second circle squeezed out from the saucer and wriggled right up to the first. A third sphere of light like a halo had formed around the creature's head, and now it spiraled and gleamed as it moved to join its fellows. The children watched in awed delight as the three circles shimmered and hummed and whirled in a ritual dance, a circling pattern of circles, an orbiting design of lights. In unison three voices spoke, and they seemed to be one voice:

> *We represent the forward paths; we speak for all of the future. Align with us; we ask you for your help.*

Silence from Laura and Alvin.

> *Will you help us?*

"Yes," Alvin managed to squeak. "Yes," in a stronger voice. "How?" Laura asked.

> *A battle rages. Lives will rise or fall over seemingly minor events and decisions. Will you take this small piece of paper from us and keep it safe there in your world?*

A rolled-up scroll of paper fluttered to the ground at their feet. "Are we allowed to read it?" Laura asked.

> *You may. If you are able, you may even use it. All we ask is that you keep it from the forces that would stand still. We represent the forward paths; we speak for all of the future. Align with us and use this as you may.*

"Is this dangerous?" Alvin asked, eyes gleaming with hope.

> *Always, always, always. . .*

"And are we in the battle now?" Laura asked, ecstatic.

> *Always and forever, if you join with us.*
> *You must pledge to keep moving forward.*

"We do," they both said for both. The three perfect circles receded a bit and slowly returned to their sources, each to its chosen vehicle– rocket or saucer or creature. The last rose first and sailed over their heads, leaving a linty mist of blue to settle slowly and softly down. The rocket that had come from the distant right streaked on its leftward journey, while the saucer crossed the rocket's path and began to glide to the right. In seconds all three were out of sight.

Gradually the night sky paled and all the lights grew dim before they disappeared, and Alvin took Laura's hand and pulled her to a stand. "Lettuce go forward," he said.

"That may be a step backward," she said to him; "let's go."
Together they walked toward a shallow cave-like recess beneath an
overhanging ledge of rock. There they unrolled the paper they had
been given.

It was a jagged-edged drawing somewhat like a map but
totally meaningless to them. The designs meant nothing and they got
nowhere.

As Alvin studied the map closely, Laura looked around. She
was starting to feel afraid of the rocks and the trees and the path itself.
She was eager to leave, but Alvin kept trying to decipher the map.
"These lines have to mean something," he said. "We would not be
given a map to use that could not mean anything to us. C'mon, Laura,
look at these designs. You are good at clues."

"I wish Jody were here right now," Laura said. "I'm too
nervous to look at clues. I think we need to move forward. That's
what they told us to do, you know. Keep on moving forward."

"We will," he said, "but just look at this for one minute. Look
at the shape of the map."

"Okay, okay, I see the shape. And I see what could be the

saucer and the rocket."

"I don't see how we can use it," Alvin said sadly. "The circle could be a planet or a spaceship and here is a moon down here. The 'BG' could be for boy and girl. You think?"

"I don't know. I wonder if the crescent is the ark. Oh, well, let's go," Laura said. "Maybe something more will come along. Let's get out of here." They started to get up, but a hissing sound issued from within the rocky mountain.

"Citadel?" Alvin said out loud. "Is this mountain a Citadel? These two towers up here? And do you hear a hissing sound?"

"Yes!" she screamed. "Alvin, we have to go now!"

*Hissssss*, the strong and sighing sound breathed in their ears. *Sssstay*, the rocky sibilance demanded. *No need to scurry, no need to scamper. Sssssstay and sssssleep a while.*

"Right this minute," Laura screamed.

*Ssafe, your paper will be ssssafe with usss. Leave the paper ssafely here and sssskitter on your way if you musst. But you can sstay. Your sssecret will be ssafe with usss, forever and forever.*

They held the paper tightly and struggled to get up; but they felt as if their feet had grown rooted in the rocky ground; they tried to run but it was hard. Why did it take so long? Step by agonizing step, with terrible slowness they struggled. The rock seemed like a magnet now, pulling them to a standstill. Sssyrup, molasssssses, they seemed to be in, and walking was a terrible effort. Then they broke free from the mighty spell and managed to get to their trail again. "Which way?" Laura asked in terror. "Pick a way!"

"Up," Alvin said; "we have to go up. We fell down, so now we go up." "But we climbed to get here, remember? We climbed. What if we have to go down?" "I don't know— I can't think," he agonized; "but we have to make a decision."

Laura grabbed Alvin by the hand and together they simply ran forward, while out in all the starry space called sky, unseen by either of the children, smoke was streaming, fire burst, little specks of color bloomed. Within the children's minds three voices called:

*Run, run, run, run. Run from coldness, run from dark; run to light and friends, wherever they may be. Run Laura, run Alvin, with that jagged scrap of paper which alone may let you save yourselves from this strange dream which well may be as real as anything you ever know. Run!*

They ran, though all around them other voices urged them to slow down.

*Sssstop, you are racing to destruction. You are running toward the abyssssss. Ssstay within our rocky shelters, ssssit beneath our branches safe forever. Sstay. . .*

They passed a crater with a pool of icy water, and its surface seemed to reproach them in chilling waves,

*Where are you rushing, all impatience? How you must hate us that you reject all our offers of help!*

The children ran deaf and ran without stopping, rushing forward, ever forward, and there was indeed an abyss which they ran unthinking into, into a shattering burst of glaring light. Each realized what they had done a fraction of a second too late, and they fell, fell, fell, fell upward.


### TWO TO THE LAGOON
#### 4 b * subroutine two * enter * not run

When six had recovered from the blinding light inside which Alvin and Laura had been swallowed, they knew that they would not be allowed to remain a group. In pairs they would be pulled to dreams. They hoped it would be good dreams; but in any case they would be pulled to their own strange adventures where each pair would find what it needed to find. Reluctantly they realized that they were required to move on. Confused and fearful, they did not want to rush but neither did they wish to linger. This place was not what they had expected; it did not seem a reward at all. And of course they wondered if their friends were safe, though they tended to think they were. And what of the rest of their classmates? Were they all in different dreams? They had unanswerable questions, but what would they gain by standing still? Thus in their own part of the pARK, they had been faced with Laura and Alvin's question.

"I guess we have to go on," Ian said. No puns, no more jokes. "Let's go."

"I hope there is not another explosion," Julieanne said. "They don't make this at all easy."

"Who's going next?" Bernardo said, and all of them had to be wondering the same.

"I bet it won't be our decision," Jody said, half of her mind intrigued and half of it terrified of what might be leaping at them.

"I wish we hadn't come," Hal whispered to Susan, but she reminded him that he often said that and then was glad of the things he had done anyway. "I don't know," he said.

"Maybe Alvin and Laura are on the trail for all of us? You think so?" Bernardo asked warily.

"I doubt it," Ian said. "That wouldn't make sense."

"You mean any of this makes sense?" Bernardo asked. "I don't get it at all. I hope we don't get hurt or lost. I hope we get back home."

"I think it might be scary," Ian said, "but I know we can work it out. I hope it's a really hard puzzle and that we will work it out."

"No doubt," Jody said.

"No fire," Julieanne hoped.

"No monsters," Bernardo said.

"Maybe we will find treasure," Susan said to entice Hal.

"No swimming," Hal insisted. He had never liked bodies of water. How many of those wishes would be granted?

As they approached the next trailhead, all doubt was quickly dispelled, as Julieanne and Ian were gently pulled forward, smoothly into a transition. First they were lifted into the air as if on the softest cloud, and then they were drawn into a glide and a flow down an airy green lane. The four children standing at the head of the trail watched in delight as they saw their friends fly, but to the two in the lane it was not like that at all. They found themselves swimming in swirls of blue-green, paddling not in lanes of air but in the warm encircling luxury of a tropical lagoon. They were not in the clothes they had come in; they were not in the costumes of Haminox. They were in perfectly fitting swimming and diving gear, and soon they were exploring.

At first they frolicked through schools of flame-colored fish and swam and played in the warm deep pool and swooped to gather fragments of shells, passing strange formations of coral. Their eyes grew big behind the masks as they watched new life drift by, equally examining them. All over the floor of the lagoon they romped until they came to a kind of tunnel, just like another trail. The warm water seemed to cool rapidly, and Julieanne became afraid. Ian held fast to her hand and he made a motion to her with his other hand, *two*. Two to go through there together, he meant, and she understood but held back. *Two*, he motioned again; and she knew that they had to go there. *After you*, he motioned but she shook her head violently, stirring the nearby

fronds. *Two together,* she indicated by holding two fingers tightly
together. He nodded yes, and they slowly peered down the tunnel and
began to swim into it.

Down the black tunnel they swam, never letting go of each
other's hand. The tunnel seemed longer than it was, and they emerged
into a second pool, colder and bluer than the first. Fishless, lifeless,
this pool was, lighted dimly from far above. Ahead of them and
somewhat to their left lay a large rotting sunken ship which they made
their slow way toward and even more slowly worked their way around.
Parts of the ship stuck out like massive teeth threatening to catch at
their flesh; and where the wood had rotted entirely away, they could
peer into the dark dense holds.

When they had circled the ship one time, Ian motioned toward
the nearest gaping hole and pointed into it. No, no, Julieanne shook her
head, and tried to kick with her fins away. Yet she knew, as he did,
that they must have something to find there. There must be something
that they had to do, and there was nothing else around. Holding onto
him with both of her hands, she slowly moved into the dark.

*Dark and cold, dark and cold, no light of any kind.*
*What hides in this dark hold of death? What lurks in its*
*dark drowned corners? Will there be bodies, dead and*
*rotting, bodies of sailors? bodies of pirates? Who was it*
*who met this nasty doom? Dark and cold, dark and*
*cold, no light of any kind. Will there be treasure? Will*
*there be loot? So dark and cold in the black, black hold,*
*and the ship is slick and slimy.*

Slowly, so slowly, they explored by the aid of a shaft of blue
light that found its way in as they did, through the gaping jaws of that
hold. No bones, no crates, no boxes. No bodies, no dulled treasure, no
jokes. No clues, nothing at all to come by here, and so they swam back
out of the hold and kicked their way farther on.

They came to another section of ship where the sides had long
ago been caved in by time and weight.

*Here is another hold on us; what lies in wait in this*
*hold? What does the dark hold hold for us? Do*
*creatures live in this watery den? Do dreamers die in*
*this den? This is no den like Trave-Log I; this is a den*
*of horror. Ghosts, ghosts? Will we find ghosts? Have*
*they gone floating through this place and left their pale*
*dim traces?*

The two found nothing at all.

*Swim, kick, glide. Swim, kick, glide. Around the ship,
the hulking ship, big as a mountain, dark as a cave.
Swim to the cabin, the former cabin, where there is a
wheel, a guide. There is the place to steer one's course.
Where better to find a clue? Glide to the cabin and
enter its cramped and splintery space. Here we are,
here it is; we will just go in for a hurried look. But look
for clues, look closely for clues, for that is why we are
here.*

The door to the cabin was crushed, and bits of cloth like tiny
flags fluttered in the unwelcome current. A little more light came into
the cabin, and they could see much better, or perhaps they were just
growing accustomed. One scrap of rag brushed against Julieanne's
arm; but though she was startled, she did not panic now. Two fingers
she held up to Ian, again, to make sure she did not lose his hand. They
swam past the doorway of splinters and moved toward the wheel.
There in its circular hug, trapped for ages, a skull rested, grinning at
them through the cold blue water. Only because there were two was
their ordeal possible.

They discovered most of the rest of the skeleton too, lodged in
its narrow quarters partially clothed in rags. In one tightly clenched set
of hand bones, a metal tube was firmly stuck. Ian tugged at this tube,
while Julieanne looked around. There was a brief swirl of bones and
the tube came free from the hand's grasp. Quickly the two swam out of
the cabin and kicked furiously past the waving rags. They rose directly
to the surface.

Into warmth and sunlight such as they felt they might never be
in again they rose, into such alien elements so distantly remembered
that they might never learn to breathe again. But then their diving gear
dissolved like ancient rags; the lagoon became a shimmering surface
like a mirror. A lane of trees awaited them, but they were not quite
ready.

Ian started to go through the motions of pantomiming opening
the tube, until he suddenly realized that he could talk again. "Let's see
what is in the tube," he said hoarsely. Then together they inspected the
narrow brass tube on which there was a fairly long inscription in very
finely engraved letters:

*Up from the past life will spring;
into the future you will bring
whatever you find within.*

Ian opened the tube and gently withdrew a rough-edged scroll of paper, a kind of parchment map. "It isn't so helpful," Julieanne said. "Maybe the tube at the top is this tube here."

"Maybe this pointy shape in the middle is the boat."

"Ship-shape?" she asked, smiling. "That cabin wasn't ship-shape." Ian repeated the word, then looked startled. "Look at the shape!" "I see it," she said, excited too. "I still don't understand all the designs."

Ian reread the inscription. "It says to bring 'whatever we find within' and we found this tube within the ship and the map within the tube." They studied the paper for a few more minutes, still happy to be breathing air.

"Yes, I think I know what you mean. Let's get back to the others and see what they got to do. Hurry!" And they found that they were being drawn again, as by that magnetic force, toward the leafy path on which they had swum into their adventure. Ian held the tube while Julieanne quickly replaced the scroll, and then in rapidly gliding, walking, swimming, running strides they were returning down the green reflecting lane. The sun was bright and warm as it had always been. Cold waters and dark holds of death had vanished from their thoughts. The dreamed lagoon had lapped itself into its own blue waves and ebbed and ebbed and ebbed away so that they might as easily be walking from a desert. Back to their friends they headed, and to their own bright futures. Ian beamed at Julieanne, and whispered proudly, "We did it!"

## TWO TO THE CAVE
### 4 * subroutine three * enter * run * run

Four had stood and watched their friends rise and fly away. "That wasn't so scary," Bernardo said.

"Kind of like Peter Pan," Susan sighed. "It looks nice."

"But we don't know what we have to do," Hal quickly reminded her.

"I think we should go on. Whatever it is we have to do, we will find it. If it is our dream," Susan said, "then it comes from us, and it won't be someone else's." Like Ian and like Julieanne, they were coming to understand the meaning of looking within.

Fearfully but with some glimmers of hope for the best, they walked to the next trailhead. They could not have known what I could see– that they were walking clockwise around a circular field, starting as if in morning, moving to the early afternoon, and now they were into the late afternoon. The sun was moving on its downward path as they came to the third of the paths. Though they walked in silence, all four were alert to every sound and every sight, however few these might be; but nothing at the third trailhead gave them any clues.

"You two?" Hal suggested to Jody and Bernardo.

"Oh, after you," Bernardo insisted.

"Probably not up to us," Susan said.

"Four together?" Bernardo suggested.

"I doubt it," Susan and Jody said in unison and giggled, thinking of Thomas.

"Well, this trail does not have my number," Bernardo joked.

"It doesn't look all that interesting," Hal insisted.

*But I am, I am, I am,*

the trail called out; and without further discussion, brother and sister found themselves on a gray-brown trail that seemed rather dull, not fascinating at all. "What happened? Where did the others go?" Hal asked.

"I guess where we left them," Susan said.

"But we didn't leave them," he pointed out. "We did not move at all."

"I guess we were taking too long. Besides, I guess Laura and Alvin and Julieanne and Ian wondered where we went too."

"What do you think will happen next?" he asked her, standing there with his hands in his pockets and looking around at the rocks and the trees. None looked particularly interesting.

*Whatever will happen will happen. . .*

that same long trailing voice came answering, though it seemed to curl within itself and recede to a very faint echo and then to a hollow silence.

"Let's stay together," Susan said, yanking Hal's arm so that his hand came out from the pocket and she could grab it. Hal was willing to stick together. "I guess we need to move on," she said; and to her surprise, he began to walk forward. Hesitantly at first but then with more confidence, they steadily descended the path. Down, down, down and around, spiraling down around scattered boulders and stumps of trees. The rocks were a little more interesting as they went on, but they knew to stay on the path. Where were they heading? What lay ahead?

"Remember when we went to the canyons?" Susan asked her brother.

"Yes, why?" he asked.

"It was scary too when we looked down from the rim."

"So?"

"It was beautiful, and we were glad we went."

"That was real," he said. "This is weird. I don't see any sign that this is for me, for us."

Just then they found their own sign:

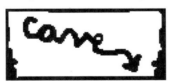

"How far?" Hal called out, hoping for the voice.

"Will we have to explore it?" Susan asked. But there was no answer.

"A cave could be pretty cold," Hal said, feeling that his short-sleeved shirt would not be comfortable at all.

"And dark," Susan answered, wishing they had brought a good flashlight.

"You know," he said, "none of this is what we asked for. Who says we have to continue? Who says we have to have a dream adventure? I really don't want to do this."

"We made the dream machine," she said, though there was doubt in her voice too.

"That was just pretend, and– besides– it didn't make scary dreams. It was nice."

"Are you very, very scared?" she asked, in a somewhat teasing voice.

"No way!" he said, a little too quickly, a little too sharply.

"Well, I am, but I don't think we really have a choice. What are we going to do– just sit down right here and refuse to budge?"

"Why not? Why not refuse? Sounds okay to me."

"Not really," she said. "You like to go caving. You like things to be interesting. And besides, if we sit down right here, who says we will end this dream? I bet we will just be wasting time."

He sat down and glared at her and at the rocks and the path. "I want to stay right here."

"No, Hal!" she said sharply. "You can't."

"Why not?" he demanded just as sharply. "Go on alone if you want."

"But we are not each in this alone. We came here– eight of us together– and now we are two together. If you refuse to do your part, then I cannot do mine; and none of us will find out whatever we are supposed to learn. We all depend on you and on each one of us. We have to go on, even if we are very afraid. It's only fair!"

He glared at her again, but at least he did stand up. "You know," he said, "I think all the others were happy to go flying off and running off. We did not ask to do this."

"I know, but we did ask to be part of the group," and she started to cry a little.

The tears got to him; he could not bear to see her cry. He grabbed her hand abruptly and took a step forward. She was standing still, crying softly. "Are you going to just stand there forever? You said you wanted to explore this dumb old boring cave."

"I'll get there first," she giggled and started to run.

"Not with me holding your hand," he said, keeping a tight grasp and running with her. Thus, laughing and racing together the rest of the way, they arrived at the entrance to the cave. They slowed, then stopped, and took one long last look around them at the sighing trees and the smiling twigs and at the freely soaring birds. They breathed the warm bright air in deeply, and then they rushed into the cool, dim cave.

They found two flashlights waiting for them. Each taking one, they moved farther into the cave. By the beams of the light they could see all kinds of fantastic formations, stalactites and stalagmites in fluted columns and bizarre shapes in the gray, wet limestone.

"Look, Hal, doesn't that look just like a gnome?"

"Sort of. But over there– a mouse playing leapfrog."

"I spy a face with a giant nose; can you find it?"

"There? Does it have one eye closed?"

"Yes, that's it." Farther and farther into the cave they walked, forgetting some of their fear. Somewhere ahead of them a dripping sound was getting louder and louder.

"No water," he said firmly to her. "I will not go in any pools or streams. You know how much I hate water." They looked above and all around to see where the dripping came from, but it seemed just to be seeping down the walls and trickling away along the cave floor. Then, just as they thought that they had seen the extent of the water, they went around a corner and found themselves on a ledge about four feet wide, facing a narrow waterfall. Down, down, down it fell to an incredible floor too far away to see, and Hal moved closer to Susan and almost dropped the light. Both of them scooted back against the wall, afraid that they might fall; but then they realized that there was quite a distance between them and the fall, and they relaxed a little. Slowly they inched along the ledge, which seemed to them to be gradually narrowing. They both crept along by the wall of slimy rock. Their footing was good; they felt more secure and began to walk slightly faster, turning another bend in the cave. The ledge widened out again.

Gradually they remembered that they were there for clues, that something awaited them there in the cave; but instead of backing out now, they felt a gathering confidence. By whatever wisdom had plotted out this walk, they found themselves growing readier to face the challenge ahead. At that point, they came to a fork in the ledge. "Now what?" Hal asked.

"Choose a way," Susan said.

"No, you."

"Come on, Hal, be fair!"

"I am being fair. I came in here with you even though I did not want to. Now you choose, even if you don't want to.

"Do you promise not to get mad at me if you don't like the one I choose?"

"No," he said.

"No? No, what? You won't get mad or you won't promise?"

"I won't promise."

"Hal!" she said in a pleading voice. "Promise!"

"No way. I can get mad. You don't have to like it, but I can get very mad."

"Then I don't have to listen," she said angrily.

"No, you don't. I can get mad whether you listen or not, and you can ignore me, whether I like it or not."

"Oh," she said. "All right. I like that." She chose the path on the right. "That way," she said with a smug kind of smile, "I know I can always say, if you get mad, 'But I took the *right* path, Hal.' And you can say whatever you please and be as frustrated as you like and get as mad as you want, but I will know I took the *right* path. This is great!"

"Whatever," he said, shrugging. Side by side they went down the rightmost path of the ledge, whether it was right or not. Silently, and so not frightening them a bit because they never heard or saw it, the leftmost ledge turned into a waterfall and plunged down to unknown depths. They walked blissfully forward, happy in the new state of their relations. They had given each other new freedoms of speech, and they both felt liberated. But they came to a locked wooden door, there in the middle of the cave; and it is difficult to go on feeling free in such a situation.

They studied the door. It was about seven or eight feet high, they thought, and was a slimy shade of green. It had an enormous padlock on it, as well as a corroded brass knocker. "What is a doorknocker shaped like a dragonhead doing on a door in a cave?" Hal asked. His sister had no answer. They tried jiggling the lock, but it was as big as their heads and had chains all around it and seemed to be rusted in all its key places. Well, in its one and only key place.

"Knock," Susan said; "you can reach it better than I can."

"What if someone answers?" he asked. "What then?"

"Oh," she said, imagining what might answer. "Well, knock very softly."

"That gives me a very bad feeling," he said. "What if–, what if?"

"Don't say!" she said. "I'm feeling less afraid; don't ruin it."

"Don't listen," he said, smiling.

"Don't even think about telling me," she commanded. And she knocked swiftly on the green wood door.

"This is a dream, this is a dream, this is one very weird, weird dream," he kept whispering to himself.

"Does that help?" she asked.

"Not really. But now what?"

"You knock– use the knocker."

Lightly he lifted the dragonhead and let it fall just once. Thud. A grinding noise came through the door, a faintly tinny mechanical sound that almost seemed familiar. They looked at each other, and the lock fell away, and the door swung open, and the ominous monotone voice creaked out these words:

160

*heh heh heh * at last!*

"It's Trave-Log II," Hal beamed. They entered the room
beyond the door, and there was indeed a computer there; but it was not
Trave-Log II. There in the strangely lighted room beyond that slimy
door, a vast pile of treasure lay heaped about the floor. The treasure all
was guarded by a greasy green computer with two red switches like
eyes. They blinked and winked and fluttered at Hal and Susan in a
mechanical effort to be friends. When it spoke, it darted laser beams
from its two black slots like nostrils; and at its sides were two winged
balance scales, continually weighing treasure and feeding the data into
what looked like a mouth.

"It looks like a dragon," Susan said, laughing.

*I  am  a  dragon!!!*

it declared, sounding rather hurt. Hal snickered.

"You are no dragon; you are a machine!" Susan happily
informed it.

*I am a  ferocious  dragon * * * I will show
you  now  *  Watch me breathe  >>  fire !!*

and it hissed and snorted and tilted its winged scales. Two laser beams
drilled to the ground; a piece of shiny gold went skittering. The scales
became unbalanced, and the children were greatly amused.

*I  am not • amusing !*
*I  am •  a dangerous  cunning  nasty  ugly*
*greedy $$$ hungry and very green  dragon*
*Did you notice my scales?*

"Weigh out!" Hal said, eyes twinkling like the gold on the
floor.

"Very interesting," Susan said, eyes just as bright, "but
definitely not a dragon."

*You  are  not nice  *  I  also • am • not nice  **
*Perhaps * we all * are dragons ??*

"No, just Hal was draggin' a while back," she said, enjoying
herself. "Boring. Not funny," Hal muttered.

*Are • you here • to steal • my treasure?*

"Maybe," they said.

*Ambiguous answers are • not • nice !*

"You don't have to listen," she replied airily.   Hal just grinned even more.

*If you lived all alone •   in a cave •   friendless •*
*with only golden treasure $$   you might want  to*
*listen when you got • a chance  ***

"Probably you would make a nice pet," Hal said.   "Our friend Alvin would like you."

*I  am **not**  a pet  *  I am a  dragon!*

"Besides, you seem to like your treasure," Susan said, amused at the steady rapid rate by which the gold was being weighed and taken in.

*Oh, yes  *   I like my $$$ treasure $$$    I like it*
*very  much •    but I also    like to      chat a bit*
*and I also like    •      to play games  ***

"Oh, what kind of games?" Hal asked.

*I  like  *   to play Dragon,*  it said wistfully.

"How do you play?" Hal asked, without thinking.

*I eat you,* it said happily.

*I  talk with you a while    • and then I snort  **
*and then * I hiss *  and then I breathe out   >*
*fire * and then * you scream and carry  on*
*but I devour *   you  *    It is fun  **
*Would you * please * step on my * scales?*

"No, thanks," Susan said.   "Hal, you should have seen that coming."

*Would you like to play, little boy?*  It was starting to sound

162

human.

"How could we win?" Hal asked, and his sister glared at him.

*You could not,* it said, its two eyes redly blinking.

"Why should we play if we can't win?" Susan asked.

*Oh, if you want to be like that, I suppose
that we could say that if you win– which
you cannot– that you could then eat me.*

"How generous," she said.
"Tough!" Hal said.

*Yes, I am tough. Very hard to beat.*

"Very hard to chew," Hal said.

*Fear not; I always win.*

"It makes no sense to play a game we cannot win," Susan insisted.

*It makes cents to me.*

"What other games do you play?" Hal asked. "Chess? Checkers? Tic tac toe?"

*Hmmph, boring,* the dragon yawned, and Susan laughed.
*I really prefer to play Dragon. I play it very well.*

"No, you really do not," Susan insisted.

*Nasty girl * I will eat you first,* it said, turning mechanical again. It hissed and snorted and exhaled smoke; finally two pale laser beams shot from its slots and tickled her nose.

*She is * all gone * * * I have * eaten her * all up * * **

"I don't think so," Hal said cheerfully. "She is standing right here, rubbing her nose."
"You can't eat me," she said. "I am too tough for you."

163

*There is a * strange buzzing * in the air* * ** 
*Did you * bring flies * into my cave? Annoying little * pests?*

"Just me," she said.

*Annoying * little * pests* , it repeated, *but at least * the girl * 
is gone * * * a tasty * little morsel but I prefer a little * 
more fat.*

"So what other games?" Hal asked. "How about twenty questions?"
"Hal, we have to find answers here, not questions. We will run out of time!"
"This is fun," he said. "So how do you want to play," Hal asked the dragon. Susan could not believe him.

*I want to $$$ win ¢¢¢*

"We'll state the rules," Susan announced.

*Buzz off * * **

"Listen, Computer, I am here and I am playing too, and we will give you the rules or you can sit here all alone and eat your stupid gold. Dumb dragon!"

*Did I hear someone * acknowledge that I am a $$$ dragon?* 
Every light went on; every switch flipflopped. *All is * forgiven*, it beamed. *But I give the rules and here * they are ** 
You will have * to obey: I choose the object.*

"It figures," Susan said.

*You get to ask me • questions * which I may answer * 
however * I want –*

"Hold it, Dragon," Susan said. "No way."

*Twenty questions*, it continued more rapidly, losing again its mechanical tone, *and I get to win and eat you.*

"That's ridiculous; we might win."

*Impossible, non-sense. I get to devour you, no matter what.*

164

"We refuse your terms. Come on, Hal, let's go. Who needs to play against a cheating computer?"

*Greedy little monsters! You just want to steal my treasure. Have you no pity on a lonely little mechanical beast who once was a green gorgeous dragon before it was put under a spell?*

"What kind of spell?" Hal asked.

*I believe it went something like this: D-R-A-G-O-N. Yes, I think that was the spell. Don't leave me yet. I promise you a piece of my treasure if you will only stay. Stay, stay, please ssstay, and keep me from being sssooo lonely.*

Something echoed in the children's minds, though they did not know what. It was such a sssad and lonessssome sssound that the dragon made, but they knew that it spelled a warning and that they must not let this conversation drag on. "Three questions," Susan said, "and then you give us one piece of treasure. Then we leave. That's it; take it or leave it!"

*You are unkind, it sobbed. I promise to deal with you honestly before I eat you and keep you here within. If I should lie or try to fake, may laser beams strike and make me break or even melt me down into scrap metal.*

It sounded pitiful, but Susan was not moved. "Big deal," she said.

*All right, all right. I have an object in mind, and you have three guesses.*

"What is the category?" Hal asked.

*Improper question, but that counts as one.*

"No. You must state the category," he said firmly.
"Let's just grab a piece of treasure and go," Susan said.

*Hmmph! You are no fun. Well, it is animal.*

"Is it green?" he asked.

*Possibly. You will never get it in three guesses.*
*I am going to get to eat you.*

"Oh, this is ridiculous," Susan said. "It is either a computer, a dragon, or both. It is you, you dumb, conceited monster."

*I believe it was the boy that I was playing against;*
*take your turn, Hal.*

"Susie, he said 'animal' so it can't be the computer. Should I say dragon or should I say that it's him?" Susan was very annoyed and ready to move on. "Is it alive?" Hal asked.

*Possibly. That is your second guess, and you*
*will not get it right. You may not ask that other one*
*for help. Ignore her; she does not know what she is buzzing*
*about. State your guess.*

"It's him!" Susan shrieked at Hal. "Stop wasting time and let's go. You, you, you," she screamed at the computer. A drop of machine oil tenderly traced a slender path down the dragon's sleek nose.

*You are no fun, no fun at all * * You have no*
*compassion for me. I do not like your selfish*
*game, and so you lose, and I will eat you now.*

ZAP-FLASH, the laser beams came forth, tickling Hal and Susan, who were no longer amused.

*How boring * how sad * and depressing, and*
*also how very lonely.*

"Still here," Susan announced, walking toward the pile of treasure. The dragon looked subdued and lost its asterisks a final time.

*Oh? Still here? How kind. What game would you like to be*
*eaten at now? I mean, beaten at. It was fun, was it not, to play*
*my game? I know that you really liked it. So now you want to*
*stay with me and we will play games forever. I can read*
*minds, you know, and so I see that you want to sssstay.*

166

Hssst-zap! Fizzle– and a gigantic laser beam struck down from the ceiling where future stalactites dripped, striking the dragon where it stood and knocking out all of its switches and lights. The pale green machine was reduced to a twisted melting hulk with one large slot still showing. With its last molten output, the dragon computer managed to utter what sounded vaguely like "griz-zim" and a sheet of paper issued from that mouth before the mangled monster slid into an oozing green puddle. Hal grabbed the printout quickly and they found themselves on the dusty brown trail that had looked so tame and dull.

"I guess you can't go by appearances," Susan said, looking back for only a moment. They clasped hands and did not stay to walk; they ran like mad to their friends.


## TWO TO THE TREE

### 4 d * subroutine four * enter * pause

Bernardo and Jody stared down that third path that Hal and Susan had involuntarily entered. Neither of the two who remained spoke for a while, but both began to walk forward. They knew that something now awaited them, something right now awaited them nearby. "Are you ready?" Jody asked him softly. Bernardo was fiddling with the knife he had carried in his pocket. She was totally aware of that knife, and yet she had no fear of this boy.

"Yes," he said. "I don't understand anything here, but I am willing to go on."

At the fourth trailhead there was no sign, no force field repelling them. They were the only two left; that path had to be for them. All they found was a welcome mat, spelling its welcome in decimal code. "See, it is for you definitely," Jody said.

"Not just for me," he said, but he smiled. "I do know it is not just for me. It's not that I don't understand plenty of things, but I need a lot of time. I don't get things very quickly, but it doesn't mean I never get them. You are different. You and the others see things very fast, and I feel left behind. Left out sometimes. Sometimes everything seems like a blur, so fast. But when I am making things, when I am building things, when I am whittling, then everything is clear and simple. That is the way I like it."

"So between us, we should be able to do pretty well on this trail. I'll use my eyes and you'll use your hands, and then together we should be fine."

"Just tell me what I need to do," he said. Suddenly he lifted his head to hear better.

> *Life hides its reasons all encoded*
> *all around us–*
> *some beautiful, some dutiful,*
> *they all surround us,*

a voice up the trail sang to them.

"That's my poem from Mrs. Burch!" Bernardo said.
"What?" Jody asked. "I didn't hear anything.

> *My children will lead and I will follow,*
> *until we meet in April Hollow*
> *where gifts of love rise from the earth*
> *and grow to trees in Spring.*

"Now I heard something. Did you just hear it?" Jody asked.
"No, it got very quiet again," he said.

"This is our path for sure," Jody said, tears of strained excitement forming in her eyes. She took Bernardo's hand and they both ran very fast– so fast that things got blurry for a moment, but perhaps that was from the tears. The branches high in every tree were swaying, rustling, crinkling into little twiggy smiles. Ahead of them was a hill which slowed them down and which they painstakingly and patiently ascended. It was steeper than it looked, and their breathing got more and more labored. It seemed to take them many hours. No talking now, nor listening. At the top of the hill, just beyond the rise, a single giant redwood tree was growing– all alone and far from its native forest.

"A redwood?" Jody said, puzzled. "What is it doing here?"
"The same as me," Bernardo said, far from his native home. "Some things I understand."

"Who brought it here?" she asked out loud.
"Maybe a little bird," he said. "Maybe the wind." The redwood tree towered above them, though it was young and far from its full growth. The trunk was rough and splintery, and the bark was an unnatural red.

"This seems wrong," Jody said, touching the bark. Red came off on her hand, like paint almost.

"I wouldn't know. I have never seen a redwood tree before. Maybe the color is supposed to rub off on your hands."

"No, this color is definitely too bright a red. It's as if it were a disguise."

"What could it be a disguise for? What else could it be but a tree?" But whether the wood was natural or not, he did admire it very much. He ran his hand along the trunk, up and down along the trunk; and as he did, the bark began slowly to fall to the ground. Beneath that outer surface, so red and rough and bright, a different bark came into view and it was paper white.

"Here is the real tree!" Jody cried. "We found it right away! Oh, Bernardo, this is what we are here to do, to see within this redwood skin and find our real tree. We did it together, you and I. We would never have done it alone."

The sun, which had been high when they started, was setting now; and even the pale white bark of the tree glowed a mysterious red. Jody and Bernardo, exhausted from their long upward climb, rested beneath the strange red tree that held a different reality within. They fell asleep beneath bright stars, or what surely looked like stars. Perhaps a battle was raging out there, but the two beneath the tree slept in perfect peace.

They awoke again in starlight and stood and gazed at their tree; and Bernardo, with Jody watching intent, steadfastly removed more bark. As high as he could reach from the soft ground and wherever he could climb, he peeled away the outer skin to reveal its natural inner self. When he could do no more, he jumped down to the ground and looked back at all of his work. "I didn't do enough," he said. "I couldn't get it all."

"You did a lot," she told him. "No one could do more." Then the stars began to dim, and the sun began to rise; and a soft wind blew the mottled tree and the tree shook hard. All of the remaining redwood fell, and there stood their naked tree: a paper birch, a tall and pale and perfect tree, rustling and swaying in the mild breeze, its green leaves mixed with yellow. And from the other three trailheads, their other six classmates came running: Alvin and Laura from the north, racing and waving a map; Julieanne and Ian from the east, carrying a strange brass tube; and Hal and Susan from the south, carrying a computer printout. All eight joined hands and laughed and danced, danced around the birch tree. Faster and faster and faster they circled, all around the tree; and I was there among them.

The sun fell warmly on us all, though they did not see me. For a while it appeared that the eight of them grew into small birch saplings and formed their own little grove. Nine trees stood straight and true in a Spring Glade and made a perfect picture. They stood with still hearts in total, absolute, unbroken silence. Not one branch stirred, nor did a single raucous bird intrude upon their peace.

Finally they collapsed in a happy heap. "What did you do? Where did you go? Wait till you hear our adventure!" they clamored

and laughed.  Laura held up their map and then she spread it on the
ground.  She and Alvin related their tale, not leaving out a thing.  "It
was so beautiful and so scary," Laura said, and Alvin had to agree.
"But we did it! We took the map and we fought off the forces that
wanted us to stand still.  We escaped by a terribly scary path, but here
we are.  It was simply fantastic!"

All of them studied the map, but Ian said, "It will make more
sense with ours."

"What did you get?" Hal asked.  Then Julieanne and Ian told
of their sunken ship and the skull and the bones and the dark, dark hold;
and Hal shuddered at all that water.

"I didn't think I could do it," Julieanne said.  "I thought I
would die of fear."

"Two together makes all the difference," Ian said.  "And it
wasn't all scary.  We saw lots of beautiful fish and amazing coral
formations."  They read the inscription on the brass tube, and they
brought out the parchment map.  It was hard to put the maps together,
though, and they all were a little frustrated.

"We saw lots of formations too," Susan said.  "But they were
limestone, not coral."

"We went into a dark cave and we found a dragon, with real
scales and lots of gold," Hal added.

"Real computer, fake dragon, balance scales, and very
probably not gold," Susan said.

"Pyrite?" Alvin suggested.  Susan shrugged.

"Anyway," she continued, "we defeated it at its own game and
won this printout."  She put it down on the ground for all of them to
read.


## PRINTOUT
### Page one of three

¢$$¢  TRAVE-LOG II  ¢$$¢  DREAM PRINTOUT  ¢$$¢  EIGHT
BY TWO  ¢$$¢

01  * NO GO * STOP *
02  * MAY ENTER * TU - T - TU  * SPACE  *  RUN  *
03  * ERROR * DO NOT RUN *
04  * BRANCH TO * T - TU * SUBHOH * SPRING
                LIFE *            RUN *
05  * 00000 * NO PARTRIDGE * NO PAIRS * NO GO *
        ERROR *

06  *  BRANCH TO  *  TU - T - TU  *  SUBGROUND  *
      EXECUTE $$$ RUN  *
07  *  NO GO  *  NO WAY  *  NO  *  NO  *  ERROR  *
08  *  IF TOGETHER THEN PERFORM  *  DIRECTIONS
      ROUTINE  *  TOGETHER  *
            DO NOT RUN  *  8  *  9  *  10  *  19  * 20  *  21  *
09  *  SEE ME SEE THEE  *

PRINTOUT
Page two of three

Directions routine
8A  *  MAP OVERLAY  *
8B  *  CIRCLE TREE  *
8C  *  DREAM WITH ME  *
8D  *  TO TEN ADVANCE  *  10A THROUGH  D  *

10A  *  LETTUCE PLAY  *
10B  *  FAREWELL TO TREE  *
10C  *  GROW FROM ME  *
10D  *  PAUSE TO EXECUTE  *  ONLY AFTER  *  DOING
        SO  WITH LOVE AND LAUGHTER  * MAY YOU
        GO * TO ELEVEN  *

And so the children looked at each direction and tried to
puzzle out the meanings, which were not so obscure as they had
seemed.
      01  *  NO GO * STOP *
      02  *  MAY ENTER  * TU - T - TU  * SPACE  *
            RUN  *

"Gee, that seems easy," Ian said. "One can't go; we all got stopped
when we tried to go into a path alone."
            "But two could go in," Alvin said, "and we did. What's Tu-T-
Tu?"
            "Sounds like tea for two. There had to be two of us," Laura
said.
            "To T-Tu. To Trave-Log II," Jody whispered. "I am sure
that's what it's for."
            "That works!" Hal said, "and then Alvin said they went on a
space adventure."
            "We sure did have to run," Laura said.
      03  *  ERROR  *  DO NOT RUN  *
      04  *  BRANCH TO  *  T - TU  *  SUBHOH  *

171

"Well, that's like the first one," Julieanne said. "Three couldn't go together."

"But four is an even number, two pairs. We were the second pair," Ian said, excited. "What is 'subhoh'?"

"Underwater," Alvin said. "'Sub' is under, and 'hoh' is like $H_2O$."

"Wow," Ian said, shaking hands with Alvin. "And then we had to spring life. The inscription said, 'Up from the past life will spring.' This is really neat."

        05  *  00000  *  NO PARTRIDGE  *  NO PAIRS  *
            NO GO  *  ERROR  *
        06  *  BRANCH TO  *  TU - T - TU  *
            SUBGROUND  *  EXECUTE  $$$
            RUN  *

"I don't get that one at all," Bernardo said. "It isn't like the first or third ones. No partridge? What's that about anyway?"

"That's the clue," Jody said. "No partridge, no pairs. We know where we find partridge and pairs or p-e-a-r-s, don't we?"

"Christmas, the twelve days. On the fifth day there were five golden rings! That's what the circles mean!" Susan said. "And Mrs. Burch left us at Christmas."

"She did?" Ian asked. "I guess I couldn't have known why that mattered."

"And five can't go through," Bernardo added. "I got that."

"But six can, and we did go underground into a cave and saw a lot of treasure," Hal said.

"I executed a dragon," Susan said. "I don't want to see that sight again– aaack!"

        07  *  NO GO  *  NO WAY  *  NO  *  NO  *  ERROR
        08  *  IF TOGETHER THEN PERFORM  *
            DIRECTIONS ROUTINE  *  TOGETHER
            *DO NOT RUN
            *  8  *  9  *  10  *  19  *  20  *  21  *
        09  *  SEE ME SEE THEE  *

"Seven is easy," Bernardo said.

"Eight is all of us together, but what about your adventure?" Ian asked Jody and Bernardo. "Where did you get to go?"

"This is where we came, so it wasn't exactly like all of your adventures. We just walked up a long, long, hard hill and found this tree. Well, it wasn't quite this tree when we first got here."

"We had to get rid of all the bark first!" Bernardo said. "It was hard."

"How did you know to do that?" Susan asked.

"It just didn't look right the way it was," Jody said. "Anyway, it was not really an adventure at all. It was just what we had to do, and it was worth it. But Bernardo did most of the work."

"'See me see thee'" Julianne read; "what is that?"

"I guess that's ours," Jody said. "We saw the tree, and when Bernardo pulled the bark away and we saw the birch, and then it could see us."

"I don't understand that, but what comes next?" Laura asked.

"Map overlay," Alvin read. They took the two maps and put them one on top of the other but could not see through at first. But as they held the two papers together, the maps, like so many of the things in all their adventures, began to undergo a delicate transformation. Slowly the two sheets thinned and thinned until they were like tracing paper; and then they looked at not just the parts but at the much more detailed total picture, although they discovered that they had to keep rotating one of the maps until everything aligned.

"It's just a map of our dreams!" Susan said. "Of where we are."

"It isn't a spaceship or a rocket," Laura said, surprised.

"No boat," Julieanne said.

"No Citadel," Alvin said, briefly disappointed. "That must be 'M' for mountain."

"But eight faces form the shape of the map," Ian said, "and they must be us." "And T-2 in the middle is the computer," Jody said. "There is where we came in," Bernardo said, pointing to the log." "Not the tube," Julieanne said to Ian. "So I guess PG is the picnic grove," Susan suggested.

"Pretty good," Hal teased. "We thought BG was for boys and girls together," Laura said. "Or else for Birch Grove and that ear shape is 'L' for lagoon," Julieanne said. "C is for cave, I see," said Hal.

"But there is no April Hollow," Jody said, "unless the whole map is of April Hollow."

"Nine for us and who else?" Ian asked.

"Mrs. Burch," the others shouted.

"But what about that One in back of the nine?" he asked. They were not sure of that at all, but I myself saw at least two possible meanings there.

"Now what?" Laura asked, afraid of standing still.

"Circle tree, it says," Alvin read. So again all of them stood and formed a circle around the tree and skipped and ran around it. They laughed as they circled faster and faster until they fell down dizzy.

"Now what?" Laura panted.

"Dream with me," Jody read. They breathed in deeply and relaxed, all sprawled out on the grass; and into their minds came visions of millions of tiny leaves. They watched the leaves form a golden crown and a face appeared beneath it, a familiar face to most of them, the face of Mrs. Burch. She seemed to be singing a song to them, though they knew that she could not sing. But they heard a song that spoke to them, each in their separate souls. And they awoke from their special dream, each with a unique song, glowing with pride in what they had done in pairs and all together.

Then from a trio of other paths all of the rest of their classmates came running, and again they scampered around the tree, nineteen of them with the birch tree. Into their midst one more shape rose, and that was another teacher. I laughed and ran as easily as they, filled with my own deep joy. And then a stern voice stopped our dance and that stern voice read page three of the printout.

11  *  GROVE BIRCH  *  GLADE SPRING  *
    HOLLOW APRIL ALL FILLED IN  *
    BRANCH TO TREE  *  TO ZERO  *
    DO RUN  *

And we sat abruptly down. The tree so tall and white and lovely bowed its head and we were silent. "You must go now," it rustled, "and so must I. I will give you your final directions, and you must follow them. Remember I am always with you, though never visible again. I am here for you to draw on; I am your citadel. I live down deep within you, and I cannot be destroyed, no matter how it looks outside, no matter what others may tell you. Believe in me, as I believe in you."
    The children started to murmur, but the once-gentle voice commanded silence. Still the children tried to ask questions and to delay their real departure. BUZZ OFF, a mechanical voice demanded, and all of us were quiet. The world seemed to shift, and the air seemed to ripple, and a creek began to flow. A log fell down across it, a single redwood trunk. LOG OUT, the voice commanded, and we got in a single file to cross that creek upon the tree or the tree upon the creek. The mechanical voice almost cracked and grew soft and almost rustly. SIGN OUT, it whispered sadly, and we watched the little wooden sign that had welcomed eight to the pARK fade and fade until it was gone. We all crossed into the picnic grove but could hear a loving voice sighing, ALL GONE  *ALL GONE*  *All Gone*  *All gone all gone gone gone gone  all gone,  farewell...*

    We left for the bus in silence, Robert's lunchbox still on a picnic table, while back on the other side of the creek, as we were moving forward, there was a flash of lightning with a fizzling *hssst* and thunder with a *zap!* and a rolling, roaring *boom!* I knew, as did the children, that before we finished waving good-bye to the trail, the dream world had disappeared.


*  BUZZ  OFF  *  LOG OUT  *

*SIGN OUT  **

*ALL GONE  **

## Laura

We never did have lunch that day, nor did any of us mind. Our heads were filled with wonder and doubt and also certainty and joy and pain. How could we have had room for more? And where did we go from there? How does a child answer such a question; and how, for that matter, do most adults?

We walked in silence up the trail, back to the lot where our bus sat like a heap of dragon gold. We passed no guard on our way out, and we made no jokes. Each of lost in our own private reveries, we lightly boarded the bus. The driver seemed less cranky, and he did not have his earflaps down. Perhaps he had entered our dreams as well or been permitted one of his own.

We returned to Bell School long after three, and our parents were waiting for us. How dull it seemed and yet how comforting, to be welcomed home again. But where was our real home? I suppose for most of us, home became what it had always been– our house, our room, our private space. But we had a new element in our lives that had established itself within our souls. In whatever ways we would choose to remember the trip to April Hollow, we would find that we had been permanently changed; and we could forever be united in whatever ways we allowed.


### Mrs. Green, from her journal

Hard to believe that we returned to anything resembling the world, but we did. Thank goodness, we had a weekend before we returned to school. All of us needed time to make whatever we could of transition. I spent the entire two days in a kind of lengthy sustained meditation, carried along on a wave of joy and another of solid inner communion. I felt that I knew who each child was and what each was to become, and I felt that I saw them through eyes not my own but through the eyes of that pale rustling spirit.

Whatever one makes of the fabulous day, one cannot ignore its power. Whatever one trusts in as honest and true, one cannot reduce the day to illusion. Fantasy and dream are a part of our lives, and they heal us often as nothing else might. As Sunday night approached, I began to return to my normal self with a need to plan the next day as I had planned no other– with such need for simplicity and care. I began with lists of vocabulary words, for that is how I wanted to re-enter the schoolday world, and it is my characteristic method. What possible words would be right?

*solemn    portent        challenge        eternal            uplifted*

for I wanted to give them what might help them be able to speak to
their experiences themselves.

*illusive  perspective        manifest        ominous            fragile*

for I wanted to enable them to know that what fears they might have
would need expressing too.  It is not easy to do these things with all,
but this is a group of children who have deeply experienced so much in
so short a time that they need to have ways to be able to communicate
with as few or as many as they wish.  Of course I knew that many of
them already could do so with ease.

### Jody

I wrote nothing for a long, long time.

### Mrs. Green, in a note to Laura

To say that yours was the most exciting and memorable class I
have ever taught is an understatement, Laura.  I have been so so happy
that you found me after all these years.  With Mr. Filamon's help, I
have managed to keep track of some of you, and I look forward more
than I can say to reading the book that you and Jody are writing.  I'm
sure you realize that I have sent you more parts from my journals than
even I could have expected to share, but I think that I have included
what pertains to your present plans and also what I feel might enlighten
the two of you to a perspective you did not get to share at the time.  Let
me know if you need anything else from me.  I wish all of you every
joy and hope you will keep in touch.  Every one of you has enriched
my life beyond words.

### Jody

Mrs. Burch, I have held you in my heart every day of my life.
I have never forgotten the role you played and the prayers you yourself

were the answer to. I no longer look for you in every birch tree or in every golden-yellow leaf, for I know that you live within me and within all of us who have sought you. Our class learned from you the need to move forward and experienced the fear and sadness that comes from leaving anyone or anything behind. You healed our cruelest pain and then left us to learn how to do the same for ourselves. Thank you. I have spent a lot of time trying to take in our last meeting, that day that haunts my mind. I still am taking it all in after all these years. So much pain and so much joy became intermingled– so much fear and such wealth of anticipation, entwined like vines in our hearts. How rich it makes life for all. Even the pain becomes a treasure chest to draw on, if only we can learn to see it properly.

Mrs. Green, you came and helped us in that difficult learning assignment. You made moving on a joyful process, but without you would we all have found the way? You, too, live within me and are a role model for my heart and mind.

On that first day back at school you started us off with my still-favorite food, words. I did not write anything, and that probably shocked you. I did, however, keep the list and knew that someday I would make use of it. Here it is now, with endless thanks to you who greened our spring that wondrous April.

*What gives us perspective*
*when all things have shifted*
*is what heals us deeply,*
*leaves us uplifted.*
*Fragile we are,*
*solemn and fending*
*off fear of each ominous start*
*and illusive ending.*
*Eternal challenge is ours,*
*portents abounding*
*but often manifest, clear,*
*stunning, astounding.*

*Laura*

And here, we thought, is where our book ended; but when we sent it to be published, the proofs came back to us with something else added.

## TRAVE-LOG II

*  BUZZ  OFF  *  LOG OUT  * SIGN OUT  *  ALL GONE  *
hsst-zap  * boom! *

*PRINT AND SHARE*